S

# UNKNOWN
# MISSION

# UNKNOWN MISSION

## John Creasey

David McKay Company, Inc.
Ives Washburn, Inc.
New York

UNKNOWN MISSION

LIBRARY OF CONGRESS CATALOG CARD NUMBER: 73-81179

MANUFACTURED IN THE UNITED STATES OF AMERICA

## Author's Note

When this book was written there did seem a real chance
that many of the neutral nations could be kept out of the
Second World War. Because the balance was so delicately poised, the smallest trifle could conceivably do
harm. For this reason I used fictitious names for people
as well as countries. 'Scovia' however does not represent
any one nation; but rather an ideal among nations which
may, one happy day, be realised.

J.C.

# 1

# The Honeymoon Expert

'Now on honeymoons,' said the red-faced and jovial man leaning against the bar, 'I'm something of an expert.' He lifted a glass of beer to his thick lips, drained it, winked prodigiously to the barman, then turned to a tall, fair-haired man who was drinking a whisky-and-soda. 'That's if you call three plenty of experience, Mr Morely. *And* free to have another if Miss Right came along!'

'Indeed,' said the man who called himself Morely.

'Believe me,' said the red-faced man earnestly, 'when I say expert I mean expert. Fill the glasses up, George, fill Mr Morely's as well as mine. First night at Canterbury, on to Dover, Paris, a few nights in the old gay city and then maybe a trip to Lucerne. That was my first honeymoon. Next, I had a cruise—and was it a cruise! Ever been to the Canary Islands, Mr Morely?'

'No nearer than Lisbon,' admitted Mr Morely.

'Lisbon? Where's that—oh, I know, Spain, isn't it? But the Canary Islands, you really should go there. I—ah, the drinks. Your honeymoon far behind, Mr Morely?'

Morely lifted his drink and said 'Here's luck', considered the honeymoon expert with lazy grey eyes and a contemplative smile.

'Far enough,' he admitted, 'although I can't claim your experience.'

'Well,' said the jovial man, his lips pursed and his small bloodshot eyes looking at Morely owlishly, 'it takes all kinds to make a world. Some people like honeymoons, some don't.'

'Shouldn't married life be all one long honeymoon?' inquired Morely gently.

'One long—well, maybe you're right.' The speaker seemed to be recovering from a shock, but quickly plunged into the itineraries of his second and third honeymoons, during which monologue Morely bought him a beer which disappeared promptly. Morely appeared to be paying full attention but, at the first break in the narrative, glanced at his watch and whistled.

'Half-past seven! And I've to dress for dinner. My wife won't be in the mood to be reminded of honeymoons if I'm late. You'll excuse me, Mr . . .'

'Smith,' supplied the red-faced man promptly.

'Smith,' repeated Morely as he moved towards the door. 'Shall I see you again?'

'Never sure in my game,' said Mr Smith. 'And since the war . . .'

He said many other things, but the fair-haired man was mercifully out of earshot, for when the doors of the White Swan Inn were closed few sounds went beyond them. There had been a time when the White Swan had been a draught-ridden hostelry with creaking boards and heavy plush curtains, when the charm of its appearance had merged with the perfection of its setting, for it was between Lyndhurst and Bournemouth, one of the loveliest parts of the New Forest.

In those days the inn had been small, while the demand for its hospitality had increased, and the balance of its profit had grown so substantial that even the owners were impressed.

The fair man who called himself Morely had known the inn during its earlier and—he thought—happier days, but only for a snack while driving from London to the

Dorset cottage which always lent him quiet and peaceful-
ness and relief from the strain and the hustle of working
for Sir Robert Holt, who directed British Secret Intelligence. Entering it on the previous evening he had scowled
at the tall, square-set, red-brick edifice which had been
~~~~~~~~~~~~~~~~~~~~~~~~~~~~~riod building, and
"unthrubfully..."  ittering chromium
[9]  d panelling which
~~~~~~~~~~~~~~~~~~~~~~~~lred years.
Untruthfully, he had signed the visitors' book as
Benjamin Morely; with equal mendacity he had signed
also that the lady with him was his wife. Unblushingly he
had filled in the forms that in time of war were calculated
to increase the risks of assuming false names, gone to his
first-floor bedroom, kissed 'Mrs Morely' and told her she
was a wicked woman, and then discovered that the staff
at the White Swan had changed as completely as the
building itself. But the beer and the cooking—now
*cuisine*—left little to be desired.
Out of his suitcase had fallen three small pieces of
coloured paper, which had moved the chambermaid to
smile and tell the rest of the staff that a honeymoon
couple was in Number 5, and you could tell it the way
they looked at each other.
He did not know that the red-faced toper in the bar
had overheard the gossip, but when he left the bar and
walked quickly up the stairs to his room, he was debating
with himself the truth of the other's claim to the ubiqui-
tous name of Smith. How many Smiths could boast of
three honeymoons?
He did not tap on the door of Number 5, but opened
it an inch, and waited until from within a pleasant voice
called:
'All right, darling.'
'Mr Morely' went in.
Half-sitting, half-lying on the twin bed nearer the bay
window which was blacked-out with heavy curtains, a

9

woman looked up at him with a smile which gave her an expression of serenity suggesting the wisdom of the ages; the smile of a woman who loved and was loved. She looked tiny, for her slim pyjama-clad legs were drawn up, with her knees near her square chin. Her dark hair more unruly than untidy made her face seem small yet set it in a framework that often made the man hold his breath as he looked at her. Her cheeks had a natural glow, her eyes were a vivid blue-grey fringed by long, dark lashes.

'Who was she?' she asked.

The fair man chuckled, stepped to the bed and sat down, running his right hand through her hair.

'If there'd been a beautiful siren, sweet, I don't doubt she would have sirened me.' He stopped smiling and his eyes were serious as he looked at her. 'If you allow me out of your sight what else can you expect?'

'That is not funny,' said Mary Dell, and eased herself further up on her pillows. 'Developments?'

'I'm not sure,' said 'Mr Morely'. 'A large and stout one who calls himself Smith has been spreading himself on the subject of honeymoons. I wonder how many ships go to the Canary Islands without calling at Lisbon? And how many men who can afford to take three continental honeymoons don't know that Lisbon is in Portugal?'

'Did these honeymoons run concurrently or consecutively?'

'A point,' admitted Bruce Murdoch, by which name he was better known, and to which he had full right. He kissed her lightly, and stepped to the wardrobe. 'We're dressing for dinner, if you don't hurry you'll be late. Mary, could any man with a veiny face, bloodshot eyes, a wart on the side of his mouth and a habit of breathing beer fumes right into your face have three romances?'

'Is he rich?' asked Mary.

'I can't vouch for hi. bank balance, but his suit would have been dear at a fiver. He doesn't clean his nails, either. One way and the other,' went on Murdoch thoughtfully, 'we can take it as read that the gentleman calling himself Smith was very anxious to confirm that we were honeymooners. Now was that simple curiosity, or does he need to know? And if he needs to know, why?'

Mary slipped off the bed, tall and graceful.

'Could you be serious?'

'I could be. But I don't know whether to take Smith seriously.' Murdoch unhooked the hanger holding his dinner-suit from the wardrobe, went to his own bed and sat on the edge, not looking at Mary as he talked in a low voice. 'I'm so tired of waiting for something to turn up that I'm examining all possibilities with abandon. The Pink 'Un sends us here to watch over a Mr and Mrs Devereux who have not arrived and have not booked a reservation, and all we can get is a honeymoon expert or a liar. Possibly both.'

'A man with three honeymoons would have to be a liar,' said Mary. 'And a convincing one.'

'Yes. Therefore Mr Smith must be a liar one way or the other. I . . .'

He broke off, for the telephone standing on the table between the beds rang twice. He stretched out a hand for it, falling backwards on the bed, and Mary watched him as she slipped into a silk slip.

'Hallo . . . Yes, Morely speaking . . . Yes. I'll hold on.' He put a hand over the mouthpiece and glanced over his head at Mary. 'A London call, it's probably Holt to say he gave us the wrong address.'

From London, in a large room of a small house in Sloane Square, came the voice of Sir Robert Holt, whom many called the Pink 'Un. A not unpleasant voice although uncertain in its cadence and apt to squeak when its owner grew excited—or appeared to grow excited.

'And about time, these confounded long-distance calls are getting worse, the whole country's going to pot—

11

understand, to pot. And—and . . .' spluttered Sir Robert suggesting that he was getting close to apoplexy, '*you* have to do some damn fool thing like getting married, leaving me in the lurch at the very time I need you most, it—but it's the last time I'll trust you. Morely, are you going to see Dee, or aren't you?'

'I couldn't say,' said Murdoch amiably.

'Hmm.' At the other end of the wire the Pink 'Un was digesting the fact that the Devereux family had not yet arrived at the White Swan. 'Well, find out as soon as you can. Dammit, you're near enough to Bournemouth to pop in for an hour, aren't you?'

'If I could be sure he was in Bourne . . .'

'Of course you're sure, I told you, didn't I? Be a good fellow and slip in tonight, never mind about driving in the blackout, your nerve ought to be strong enough for that. I must have a report of your talk with him by midnight.'

'I understand,' said Murdoch.

The voice changed abruptly, unexpectedly.

'You do. I knew you wouldn't let me down! Midnight, most important. A wire will do. Goodbye.' Sir Robert rang off.

Murdoch replaced the telephone on its platform thoughtfully, and straightened up. Mary was now dressed in a black evening gown that clung to her figure, and Bruce eyed her with one eyebrow raised above the other.

'If we can judge by that, the Pink 'Un's getting worried, and he's expecting the Devereux couple here in time for a report to reach him by midnight. I wish he'd been more explicit about the whole affair.'

'He told us he doesn't know enough,' said Mary, 'and if you're going to dress for dinner, hurry, darling. Did he say anything else?'

Murdoch chuckled.

'Several things, mostly for the benefit of the operator downstairs. He also accused me of honeymooning! If

12

you're ready, go down and let Mr Smith try to pump you, but be sure to keep a yard between you, sweet. I'll be ten minutes.'

Mary Dell went out, Murdoch dressed quickly and tied his bow untidily while contemplating the affair of the Devereuxs.

Like so many others, it appeared to start from nowhere and threatened to end in the same place. Espionage, in the opinion of Bruce Murdoch, lost most of its attractions during a period of hostilities, chiefly because everyone concerned was far more careful than in the days of peace, even the armed peace that had finally broken over Danzig and led to the ravage of Poland.

Since that fateful day in September, nearly six months past, the Murdoch-Dell team of Holt's agents had started a dozen minor investigations, had helped to put three pro-Nazis and a Muscovite into an internment camp. Small jobs, even trivial ones, but necessary. Nothing that had happened affected Murdoch's belief that Sir Robert Holt was a genius, and that his control of Secret Intelligence was little short of miraculous.

All Holt had told him and Mary—who had worked together for nearly a year—was that the Devereuxs had been reported as 'acting suspiciously'. There were as many ways of acting suspiciously as there were new byelaws under the Emergency Decrees, and that meant next to nothing. Information, Holt had said, had reached him that the Devereuxs—referred to in their conversation as the Dees—were planning to visit the White Swan one day that week.

Could Mr Smith be connected with the Devereuxs?

Bruce shrugged, chuckled at the thought of Mary's probable detestation of Smith, then scowled as he saw her pyjamas flung carelessly on the bed. The Service demanded the nearly impossible from its agents. In his contract, and Mary's, there was a clause forbidding either of them marriage—and the contract had two years to run.

13

The ten months in which they had been completely in love with each other had seemed like ten years, and the demands of the service that they should work as a team, often presuming marriage, presented its difficulties.

Not that he could with honesty object to that. In what little spare time was theirs they were happy in a small, renovated cottage near Lulworth Cove—doing what the world called living together, and what Murdoch's man called 'acting the blurry fool', for they used separate rooms. Percival Briggs, the man, was glad despite his apparent disapproval.

Murdoch pushed the thoughts aside, and turned to the door. It opened before he reached it, and Mary came in. She closed the door before she spoke.

'They've arrived! I—Bruce, won't you *ever* learn to tie a bow?' She straightened his as she continued talking. 'The man's a poor specimen, darling, Poona-Poona but undersized. The woman's a beauty.'

'Hmm,' said Murdoch thoughtfully. 'Age?'

'She's no more than thirty-five, but he's well past sixty.'

'For the tie, many thanks. Had they arrived when you went down?'

'I saw them in the hall, signing the register. Room 3, next but one to this. Smith—judging from your description it was Smith—was in the hall too. He went up to his room, so it wasn't worth my waiting. Are you going to 'phone Holt yet?'

'Better send him a wire,' said Bruce. 'Just say I'm seeing Dee tonight. Are they in their room yet?'

'No, they're having a drink.'

'I'll drink with them,' smiled Murdoch. 'Don't be long, my sweet, I may fall quickly for the beauty.'

Mary laughed as he went outside, but there was no smile on Murdoch's face as he hurried downstairs. Holt would not have telephoned unless he had some reason to believe the Devereuxs were important contacts.

14

# 2

# Lucille

'No, my dear, no, I don't think I will. The first whets the appetite, the second damps it.'

Mr Devereux uttered a sound suspiciously like 'tee-hee' as he finished his joke, replaced his cocktail glass on the polished bar, and rested his blue-veined hand on Mrs Devereux's forearm. Her forearm was comfortably covered in a tweed coat-sleeve, and the little man's expression gave Bruce Murdoch the impression that he was sorry about the sleeve. To Bruce, he did not seem likeable, and he had one thing in common with Smith—his eyes were bloodshot. They were light-blue and prominent, however, where Smith's were brown and porcine, and they eyed the woman anxiously after he had finished laughing. 'Shall we go upstairs, my dear? The inner man calls, we must change; you know I never enjoy a dinner unless I'm changed.'

'I'm not changing, Charles.'

Murdoch had been prepared for the beauty of the woman, a beauty emphasised by a silver-fox cape draped over the dark-grey tweed costume. Since entering the room in time to hear Devereux's rejection of a second cocktail, he had been surprised by the sight of a silver-fox over tweed, for normally they would not have been worn together—and Mrs Devereux created the impression that she had been bred to be fashionable. She was fully three inches taller than Devereux; she was dark, exquisitely-featured and delicately made up. The lipstick glistened, velvety violet eyes turned towards Murdoch and did not look away. Her expression was bold.

Her voice surprised him.

It was attractive, in no way disappointing: but it was not that of an Englishwoman. French, Bruce fancied, with the second syllable of 'changing' going upwards, and the 'Char-les' made virtually into a two-syllable word.

Her advantage in height over Devereux did not make her tall, for the man was some five feet three inches. A thick Ulster could not detract from his thin, weedy figure. His face was dry-skinned and liberally wrinkled—wizened, in fact.

Devereux's lips parted a little, and his eyes showed disappointment. His grip on her forearm tightened.

'But Lucille, my dear, you know I prefer to change.'

'You may do what you like, Charles, I am not changing.'

She turned from the bar and stepped towards the door, passing Murdoch on the way. If her glance was not one of invitation, Murdoch had never known one. She walked easily, an absurd contrast with Devereux, who trotted in her wake. He contrived to get ahead in time to open the door, and Lucille walked gracefully into the passage. Devereux let the door bang as he hurried after her, and the barman winked at Murdoch but went on wiping glasses.

Three couples, all middle-aged, were huddled round a blazing log fire, on the other side of the room. It was bitterly cold; March was nearly out but winter retained its grip, and the people by the fire clung with English stubbornness to the illusion that a fire provided sufficient warmth.

Murdoch responded to the wink with a smile, thus confirming the barman's impression that the tall gent who looked as though he was Scottish was a gent indeed.

16

'You do find 'em, don't you, sir?' The barman spoke *sotto voce.* 'Care for anything, sir?'

'Not just now,' said Murdoch amiably. 'I'm waiting for my wife. Do you get many unexpected visitors these days?'

'Well . . .' The barman wrinkled his forehead, and rubbed a finger across his lopsided nose. 'Not what you'd call many, sir, but then you wouldn't even in peace-time, not with weather like this, enough to perish you. The gent was saying he'd run short of petrol, what with these ration cards you don't know what to do, and he under-estimated.' The sniff which accompanied that statement suggested that the barman could well believe Mr Devereux starting a journey without making sure that he had enough petrol to finish it. 'Most of our clients is local,' went on the barman, 'except for two what've come down out've London. Blimey, who'd leave London if they could stay, that's what I want to know.'

'Not scared of bombs?' smiled Murdoch.

'Me, scared? Spent four years out in perishing Flanders in the last war, sir; if your name ain't writ on a bomb you're okay; if it is it'll git you wherever you are.'

'A cheerful way of looking at it,' said Murdoch. 'But you should be glad of business, George.'

'Sam, sir. Yes, sir, business is business, but the way some people goes on you'd never think there was a war. Gimme this, do that, complain about the food—but I didn't ought to be talking, sir.'

'It'll do you good to get it out of your system,' said Murdoch amiably. 'Well, we'll be a small crowd in the dining-room again, I suppose.'

'More'n usual, sir; there's the two just come, two others arrived half-an-hour ago, but they said they was coming—Mr Cole's a reg'lar, *and* a gentleman, sir. You can always tell it, can't you? The minute I set eyes on you, I thought there's a gent if ever I see one, begging your pardon for the familiarity, sir. Got it written all over

17

you, just like Mr Cole. And then there's 'Is Nibs.'

Murdoch looked puzzled.

'His Nibs?'

Sam grinned crookedly.

'A French gentleman, sir, he come this afternoon. 'Im and his man, sir, both French or I don't know the langwidge.'

'Four years ought to have given you a smattering,' said Murdoch, lighting a cigarette. 'I—ah, here she is. I'll be back for a nightcap, Sam, meanwhile have a drink yourself.' He slipped a shilling over the bar and stepped towards Mary who had just come in. He nodded slightly to answer the question in her eyes, and went with her to the empty dining-room. A waiter brought the menu. Bruce ordered clear soup with grilled turbot to follow, and as the man went off Mary said:

'So you saw them?'

'And Mr Devereux is like Smith—a liar one way or the other. He said he'd run out of petrol, but the Pink 'Un knew he was due here; which proves he wants it to be thought that his coming was unpremeditated. Reason for doubting the sincerity of Poona-Poona. A good description, darling.'

'Thank you, kind sir. It's odd, Bruce.'

'Yes. There are three other fresh ones today, we should see them all in here. A Mr Cole and lady, Mr Cole being a real gent like me according to Sam the barman, and a Frenchman called His Nibs. Lucille's French, too.'

'*Who?*'

Bruce chuckled.

'Mrs Dee has the roving eye. I wouldn't trust myself with the lady. She dislikes Poona-Poona, and she isn't going to change for dinner, which might mean that she's hungry, but could mean she wants to get down quickly. She seems to wear the trousers.'

Mary smiled thoughtfully.

'And he called her Lucille.'

18

'The Dees have come to meet someone, presumably someone already here,' Murdoch said. 'The three couples in the bar are the stodgy middle-aged type, and have been here some days—we may be able to rule them out. Which narrows it down to Cole and His Nibs—Cole being the other gentleman. And here's the waiter—look into my eyes as if you adore me, darling, it will strengthen the honeymoon illusion.'

'Dee could have come to see Smith.'

'Yes. But Smith is definitely of the lower orders, nothing Poona-Poona about him.'

He stopped as the waiter placed soup in front of him, and then in a mirror by his side—he had chosen the table because of the mirror which enabled him to see the whole of the dining-room—he saw the door open, and the Devereuxs come in. Devereux was in rough Harris tweeds, and looked ill-at-ease. His wife had taken off her coat, and was wearing a white silk blouse fastened high at the neck. Her hair was jet black, possessing a bluish tinge beneath the subdued wall lights. Her eyes met Murdoch's, and he fancied he saw a smile in them.

Or challenge?

It was possible that the Devereuxs were aware that they were being watched, and yet he found it hard to believe. They made no effort to get a secluded table, but sat in the middle of the dining-room, Lucille sideways to Bruce. Mary's lips were twitching.

'A conquest, darling!'

'She's probably feeling the need of a change from Poona-Poona,' said Bruce absently. 'Eat your soup, and concentrate on the problem. Ah, another contingent.'

Two couples of the stodgy brigade entered, and a little man followed. Bruce saw him clearly in the mirror. He was no taller than Devereux, but carried himself with an air that immediately identified him as 'His Nibs'. His sallow face, dark hair receding from his forehead, his thin, compressed lips and the backwards tilt of his head

19

probably calculated to make a weak chin seem more prominent, had invited Sam's nickname. Narrowed and dark eyes glanced swiftly round the room as the Frenchman stepped to a table in one corner, facing Bruce. The waiter hurried to pull a chair out, the Frenchman fastidiously raised his trousers to adjust their fall as he sat down. The shoulders of his blue serge coat were a trifle too square, the waist a shade too shapely.

'He looked at us all,' said Mary, 'but not for long.'

'No. Of course he may not know who he's going to meet, if he's going to meet anyone. The only other possibles, sweetheart, are the Coles.'

'And Smith,' Mary insisted.

'Smith seems to have attracted you,' flashed Bruce.

'I don't think he impressed you enough,' said Mary. 'He's so obviously a bad type.'

'I don't trust the obvious. I . . .'

'Pray silence for the turbot,' said Mary as the waiter approached.

Bruce continued to watch the mirror. He was irritated when he saw the door open at a moment when the waiter leaned over him, preventing him from seeing the newcomers, but managed to see that they passed the Devereuxs with no more than a casual glance. There was a thick-set, square-shouldered man in a dinner jacket, and a slim, red-haired woman whose green gown made her look demure.

Bruce's interest centred on the man.

If it were possible to have a typical English squire, Cole fitted the bill. Red-faced without being florid, he carried himself with an air of assured self-satisfaction. His hair had been dark but except for a single patch by his right temple it was now grey, groomed in a manner that added to the distinction of a face and head that were impressive, for his forehead was broad: grey eyebrows, thick and bushy, shaded wide-set, clear grey eyes. His nose was arched but narrow, the upper lip long and

20

deeply grooved, the lower pushed forward slightly, heightening the impression of a square, cleft chin. He was obviously familiar with the dining-room of the White Swan, nodded at the waiter, and then leaned forward to address his companion.

Her demureness, the green gown, the red hair waved but not dressed to any startling fashion, were apt to detract from her face, in which her green eyes were easily the best feature. Seeing her eyes, it was difficult to worry about her lips, her chin or her cheeks. They were brimming over with good humour, and her hand rested for a moment on Cole's fingers.

'Distinguished gentleman with leonine head,' murmured Mary; 'what peculiar ideas you have, Bruce. I still prefer Smith for my suspect.'

'Seriously?' asked Bruce.

Mary shrugged.

'No, not really. I haven't altogether lost the holiday spirit, darling. I can't believe that anything really serious is brewing here, and yet—well, His Nibs *is* a character.'

'I'd say a caricature,' mused Bruce. 'Smith would fit in nicely as a bodyguard for the Dees, the Coles, or H.N. They're a queer assortment, and Holt would not have telephoned unless to make sure we took the situation seriously. I wish I'd brought Percy.'

'Why?'

'To look after Smith, who isn't yet at dinner.'

Nor did Smith come down to dinner. A low hum of conversation, with each couple keeping their voices at a decorous level so that only an occasional word was heard, the chink of glasses, of knives and forks, the rustle of damask napery, the flickering glow from the fire strong enough to throw shadows despite the shaded wall lighting, the luxuriously appointed room with the light polished oak surrounds and furniture simple and on modern lines, merged with the near silence.

'And what,' asked Mary as they waited for their coffee,

21

'do we do now? Shadow the suspects from room to room?'

Murdoch's brows met, and he spoke deliberately.

'Don't you feel the atmosphere, Mary? His Nibs looking up from his plate, a furtive beggar if ever there was one, the Devereuxs' not saying boo, Poona-poona subdued, the Squire giving his full attention to his lady who doesn't wear a wedding ring . . .'

'He could be a bachelor, or even widowed,' said Mary. 'It's all so peaceful, Bruce.'

'Yes. Well, we're going upstairs and we're leaving our door ajar to hear all the comings and goings. An advantage of Room 5 is that practically all our hopefuls have to pass it—Smith has Number 1, though, that's a snag.'

'Supposing they all stay in the lounge?'

'No one as frigid as these folk will unbend and start getting talkative in public,' said Bruce. 'If anything happens it'll be upstairs, but stand guard over the lounge if you want to.'

'No, darling, I'll come up with you.'

Next moment they heard Cole's voice clearly for the first time. It was mellow and resonant, that of a man used to command.

'Serve our coffee in the lounge, will you?'

'Very good, sir.'

'I'll stay down,' whispered Mary.

'Right,' said Bruce, 'it's probably wise and I'd rather deal with Lucille on my own!'

They sauntered into the adjoining lounge. Mary picked up a magazine while Bruce walked slowly and thoughtfully upstairs, wondering which of the guests were most likely to interest the British Secret Intelligence.

He was a step from his bedroom door when he stopped, making no sound on the thick pile of the carpet. The door was unlatched, and open a fraction of an inch. He remembered closing it and pushing against it before he had left.

22

A chambermaid, or . . . ?

Murdoch put his fingers about the handle, and opened it wider, listening intently. He heard a rustling from within and the sound of heavy breathing. He pushed the door sharply open and stepped inside; and he saw the back of Mr Smith, who was on his knees and lifting the contents from the bottom drawer of the dressing-table.

## 3

# Apology from Smith

The man had not heard Murdoch approach.

He was intent on his task and apparently not happy about it, for beneath his breath he swore. The first thought that passed through Murdoch's mind was that no man fully experienced in searching a room would have been surprised so easily. His second was to wonder if the visitor was searching for evidence that he was connected with Sir Robert Holt. His third was to wonder whether this was the only room so far visited.

Silently, he lifted a book from a bookcase by the door, and then said gently:

'Busy, Mr Smith?'

The man by the dressing-table stiffened, but did not immediately look round. Bruce saw the back of his neck turning red, heard his breathing quieten, and then saw his slow movement towards his pocket. Bruce snapped:

'Keep your hands in sight!'

Smith's hand stopped, and he stood up, turning as he moved. His lips looked thicker as they turned back over yellow teeth, his little porcine eyes were narrowed and ugly.

'I . . .' he began.

'Don't talk out of turn,' said Murdoch sharply. 'Turn round and hurry about it.' He took two steps towards the man, wondering if Smith would go for the gun which was probably in a handy pocket. The man's right hand moved an inch, then stopped; and he obeyed, his back to Murdoch again. Murdoch moved swiftly, gripped the other's right wrist and forced it behind him in a hammer-lock that made Smith gasp, and at the same time dipped his hand into the right pocket. His fingers touched the cold steel of an automatic, and he drew it out. He stepped back, levelling the gun towards Smith.

'So you travel armed while you burgle bedrooms.'

Smith's lips pressed together, and he looked past Murdoch.

'I—I didn't mean, I—Mr Morely, don't give me away, give me a chance.'

'I'll give you a chance to explain. What do you want?'

'I'm flat broke, haven't got enough to pay my bill, I've had to stay a couple of days more than I meant to. I was desperate I tell you!' Smith moistened his lips, stared at Murdoch as in appeal and held his hands, square, stubby and calloused, out beseechingly. 'You're on your honeymoon, I knew you'd have some loose cash about. If the dicks—I mean the police—get on to me I'm done. Give me a break, I won't do this kind of thing again.'

'It won't do. No man of blameless reputation talks of the police as dicks. You haven't shown me any reason why I shouldn't hand you over to the manager, and I don't feel disposed to compound a felony. I don't like you well enough.'

'I ...'

There was nothing more likely to keep a man in a state of jitters than constant interruptions, and Murdoch knew that well. He spoke sharply across the word, and moved the gun.

'What's more I can't afford to lose money, and I don't know whether you've visited other rooms or not. I don't believe your story, and if you haven't found a better one

25

in two or three minutes, it's the manager and the police. What are you doing here?'

The threat steadied rather than made Smith more perturbed.

'Okay, okay, it was a lie. I'm doing a job for a friend of mine, looking for something, see? You haven't got it. I've finished here, It must be one of the others. Would fifty quid be any use to you?'

Murdoch stared.

*'What?'*

Smith put his hand to his breast pocket swiftly. Murdoch cocked the gun, half-prepared to find the man carried another in a shoulder holster, but Smith drew out a wallet—and the wallet was tightly crammed with five-pound notes. The stubby fingers trembled.

'I mean it, fifty quid's fifty quid and I'm not doing you no harm.' The little eyes watched Murdoch narrowly, and Murdoch knew that the man had been acting, saw him to be dangerous, for the cunning expression in his eyes held somthing else—the hard, sideways glint of the hardened gunman. 'Be reasonable, Mr Morely, and you won't come to no harm. I'm offering you . . .' Smith grew loquacious, became the man he had seen in the bar and even recaptured his affability, as though he believed 'Morely' would be reasonable when close to fifty pounds. 'I'm offering you a nice little lump of cash, we can all do with it these days, and I'm telling you I won't snitch—take a thing that don't belong to me, see? Or to my Boss, and that's the same thing. I . . .'

'Who is your Boss?'

'You never mind about that, you wouldn't be glad if you knew him.' Smith laughed—genuinely, but with a brutal note that gave Murdoch a tingling feeling down his spine. 'Certainly you wouldn't be glad, it don't do to cross him. Be reasonable, Mr Morely. Look . . .' He counted ten five-pound notes, and added half-a-dozen singles. 'There's a bit extra, I'm not mean.'

26

Murdoch sat, slowly, on the foot of the bed.

'I might,' he said reflectively, 'let you go if I knew just what you wanted and could be sure you weren't just putting your hands on all the loose cash you can find.'

'Aw, cheese it, what do I need with loose cash? There's three hundred in this, buddy, three hundred of the best. I'm looking for something that was lifted from my Boss see. This is on the up-and-up.'

'Or the take-and-take,' said Murdoch. Absurdly, he felt like laughing, for Smith talked with the assurance of a successful salesman, and he would have looked at home auctioning wares at an East End market. 'What was stolen?'

'A letter, see, just a letter and a coupla photygraphs. They don't mean a thing to you, they ain't . . .' Smith's voice and expression became suddenly virtuous, and he smacked the wad of notes against the palm of his left hand. 'They ain't worth a thing to anyone but the Boss, and they're his, mister. You ain't compounding no felony, you're doing me a good turn and making a bit on the side, see? Come on, 'ave a heart, I can see you're inclined that way right now. You won't ever regret it.'

Murdoch frowned.

'You're lying good and hard, Smith, but I don't particularly want to be mixed up with the police.'

The change in Smith's expression was a transformation. The desperation disappeared, and he grinned, the glitter turned to a gleam that was almost friendly.

'*Don't* you, then? Mister, I'm no chicken; the way you took my gun was good, I'll say that, it was good. Maybe you've good reason to keep away from the dicks, eh? Don't mind me calling them dicks, do you? You picked on that pretty smart.'

'Don't jump to conclusions,' warned Murdoch. 'I don't want it known I'm down here, that's all it amounts to, and if it weren't for that you could go to the devil. As it is—put the money on the dressing-table.'

27

Smith grinned, and dropped it behind him, where it littered Mary's brushes and creams. He smacked his hands together and stepped forward, a picture of good humour.

'Okay, that's a deal! Now hand me the sneezer back, and we won't say no more about it—*Mister* Morely. I'm all for ro-*mance*, no one ever said Jem Dace was a spoil-sport.' He uttered the name without realising it, Murdoch believed, and Murdoch's heart thumped: that was a piece of gratuitous information he might find useful.

He wanted to kick 'Mr Smith'.

But he had succeeded in finding a way of letting Smith go without making the man wonder why; and Smith had to go. Most of his story had been fictitious, but that there was a 'Boss' was an obvious fact.

'That's good,' Murdoch said. 'But I'm holding the gun, Smith. I'm not letting you run around armed.'

'Okay, okay, plenty more where that come from, and I don't blame you being careful. No ill-feeling?'

Before Murdoch could stop him he had gripped his right hand, gun and all, and pumped it vigorously. Murdoch clenched his left for a short swing, believing that the man meant to fight, but Smith dropped his hand and moved towards the door. As he opened it he touched his forehead insolently, and then disappeared. The door banged.

Murdoch stood up slowly.

'So he was very scared of the police, our Mr Jem Dace,' he said softly. 'Pinky was right, but who has the things Dace wanted so badly?' He slipped the gun into his pocket, feeling more confident with it, and stepped to the door. He opened it an inch, listened, and heard only the dull echoing of footsteps somewhere on the floor below. Then he sat in an easy chair where he could just see into the passage, with a magazine on his knees, and he thought deeply of the mysterious Smith, *alias* Jem Dace.

28

Footsteps, muffled by the carpet, reached his ears. He saw Cole and the red-haired woman pass, followed in less than a minute by the Devereuxs, and he pushed thought of the intruder to the back of his mind. Cole had not lingered over his coffee, and . . .

Sharply, abruptly, a woman screamed!

It was a short cry, as if stifled before it had gained full utterance, and it came from the direction the Coles and the Devereuxs had taken. Murdoch stepped swiftly into the passage, to see the Coles standing by their open door, Lucille Devereux moving sharply towards them, and her husband standing with his hands upraised as if in alarm.

'What is it, what is it?' Lucille's voice was sharp, and her words told Murdoch that Cole's companion had screamed. Cole put a hand over her shoulder, brushed the palm of his free hand over his mane of hair.

'Don't be alarmed, please, we have had visitors.' Cole may have been startled at the first moment, but he had recovered something of his poise quickly. 'Try to stop trembling, Anne, there was nothing in the room of value.'

The woman in green was trembling from head to foot, her hand shook as she clutched at Cole's arm. Lucille reached her and put an arm about her waist.

'You poor little one, come with me. I have some smelling salts. The men can look after this.'

Masterfully she eased the other away from Cole, who seemed to have forgotten his companion and advanced slowly into the room. Devereux moved uncertainly, reaching the door just ahead of Bruce. He stopped on the threshold but Bruce went through, to see the room in chaotic disorder, a far worse state than his own had been.

Cole was staring about him, tight-lipped. Devereux gasped when he saw the mess. Lucille seemed interested only in the trembling Anne, who had received a shock,

29

thought Murdoch, greater than the circumstances seemed to warrant.

'Whoever it was made a thorough job,' Bruce said quietly. 'Is there anything missing, do you think?'

'Eh?' Cole stared at him blankly. 'Oh, a few pounds at the most, there was nothing here of importance. I—I wonder if you will go for the manager, sir? And perhaps you will see if my wife is all right.' He glanced from Murdoch to Devereux, who hurried away. Bruce hesitated for a fraction of a second, for there was a telephone within a yard of Cole.

Had he forgotten that, or did he want to be alone in the ransacked room?

Bruce turned to the door.

'Of course. And we'd better make sure that none of the other rooms has been touched.'

'Why should they be?' snapped Cole.

Murdoch stared.

'Well, why should this? A thief wouldn't stop at one.'

Cole made a patent effort to get himself under control: it was easy to see that he had been shocked and startled; Murdoch even thought frightened.

'Of course, I didn't realise that. If you don't mind . . .'

Murdoch went out, closing the door loudly behind him. He did not move along the passage, but opened the door again, silently this time. He could see Cole bending over a suitcase which had been opened, with the contents flung about the floor, and he saw the man's fingers run along the edge. He heard a slight *click!* and knew that the case had a false bottom. Straining forward, he saw Cole take something from it, look through what seemed to be three or four papers, and then heard the man's sigh of relief.

Bruce closed the door again, and hurried downstairs. To reach the manager's office he had to pass through the lounge, where Mary was sitting away from the fire,

30

opposite His Nibs. He nodded, and she joined him quickly.

'Burglars in plenty,' he said, 'and much funny stuff. Slip upstairs and get into the Devereuxs' room, will you?'

Mary lost no time.

Murdoch found the manager, a short, square-shouldered, military-looking man with an aloof manner more becoming a London hotel than the White Swan, at the door of his office.

'Can I help you, Mr Morely?'

'No,' said Bruce, who disliked the man's manner and the cold appraisal in his light-blue eyes. 'You can help Mr Cole, whose room has been burgled.'

'*What?*'

Murdoch repressed a chuckle, for the manager shouted the word. Coldly, he repeated the statement, and the manager pushed past him abruptly, hurrying for the stairs. In his eyes as the news had been forced home there had been an expression akin to that of Cole's—alarm, shock, and perhaps fear.

Alarm and shock were in keeping with his responsibility as the White Swan's manager: fear was not. The manager too might be worthy of investigation, while he, Bruce Murdoch, had yet to learn whether the other rooms had been visited by the industrious Jem Dace.

# 4

## Cash and Carry

The Devereuxs' room had not been touched, but while the manager was with Cole, His Nibs walked hurriedly along the passage at the moment Murdoch reached the head of the stairs. Murdoch could not easily be seen, and he paused. The swarthy, thin-featured face was set unpleasantly, and his head was raised a little as though he had a stiff neck. He walked with short, mincing steps, making no sound; a man practised in furtive approach.

His Nibs stopped by Cole's open door, then stepped straight in, looking at the manager.

'M'sieu Garsting, attention please! My room has been disgracefully entered, money has been stolen! Come, please, at once, the thief must be found.'

His voice was smooth, and the accent removed any lingering doubt of his nationality: he was French, like Lucille. Murdoch reached the door in time to see the manager staring white-faced at the Frenchman, and he saw that the manager's hands were unsteady.

But he spoke rationally enough.

'I'm extremely sorry, M'sieu Arnould, but the hotel has been burgled while we were at dinner, practically every room has been entered.'

The Frenchman lifted his hands, but for a fraction of a second he seemed relieved.

'It is bad, M'sieu, deplorable! The police, are they near?'

'I am about to send for them,' said Garsting. 'It has only just been discovered. Mr Morely, was your room all right?'

'I've seen nothing the matter,' lied Bruce.

'That's something, then. If you will excuse me, gentlemen, I will inspect the other rooms and then send for the police.'

'Shouldn't the police come first?' asked Bruce gently.

'That is my . . .' Garsting scowled, and then changed his attitude. 'Perhaps you're right. I'll telephone them from this room, Mr Cole.' He picked up the telephone, while Cole started to collect several small oddments from the chaos on the floor. Bruce offered cigarettes to Cole and Arnould, and said apologetically:

'I seem to be interfering a lot, Mr Cole, but the police might prefer to have nothing disturbed. They shouldn't be long in coming.'

'Eh? Oh, yes, I hadn't thought.' Cole spoke absently, smoothing his thick hair. 'It's an infernal nuisance, this. I suppose someone slipped in during the blackout, it's so damned easy these days.'

'Yes. Of course, it may have been a guest,' said Bruce.

'Such matters are for the police to discuss, is that not so?' Arnould looked intently at Murdoch and Cole, his dark brown eyes narrowed, one corner of his thin lips curled as if contemptuously. 'If you will please inform M'sieu Garsting I am in my room, I will be glad.' He bowed stiffly and went off, and for the first time Cole unbent.

'Queer-mannered little beggar, but a thing like this puts us all off our balance, I suppose. Not that you've lost yours.' He looked at Bruce keenly, while Bruce reflected that Cole had been heartily relieved to find the papers safe in the false bottom. They were probably in his pocket at that moment.

33

'Well, I wasn't robbed. I wonder how the ladies are getting on?'

'Good Lord! I'd quite forgotten Anne!' Cole laughed, and led the way towards the Devereuxs' room. It was worthy of notice, thought Bruce, that Devereux had not been out since Cole had asked him to make sure that the ladies were all right, which suggested that the little man lacked courage.

Mrs Cole had recovered sufficiently to laugh at herself. But there was anxiety in her eyes as she looked at Cole. Murdoch saw him nod, almost imperceptibly, and heard the soft, sharp intake of breath from the woman in green. Almost immediately she was vivacious and apologetic, thanking Lucille and Mary warmly, ridiculing her own fears.

The police had arrived and were questioning Garsting before Bruce and Mary were able to get to their own room. Bruce closed the door with his heel and leaned against it.

'Well, sweetheart, how did they behave?'

'You could say quite naturally,' Mary replied. She looked puzzled, however. 'I had a feeling that Mrs Cole expected something of the kind. And Lucille was almost too matter-of-fact.'

'Meaning she acted too naturally,' said Bruce. 'I had the same impression, and we're probably right. But we haven't yet learned who came to see the Devereuxs, and we don't know who Jem Dace was really wanting to rob. He . . .'

'Jem who?'

'Dace. Likewise Smith. I caught the gentleman red-handed but let him go. He was absent during dinner, the police will jump to that pretty quickly.'

'Why on earth didn't you keep him?'

'Too valuable,' said Bruce. 'He's better free, for the time being. He was searching for something he didn't find, and as we've heard no shouts of distress from the stodgies, it's safe to assume that he thought the Coles, the Devereuxs, ourselves and His Nibs most likely to have had what he wanted. Equally safe to assume that he knew that one of us certainly had it. Reasonable, my sweet, to assume that Cole was his quarry, but Cole has a false-bottom in his suitcase.'

'Come and sit down and tell me all of it,' said Mary, 'and don't forget the details. I knew I was right about Smith . . .'

'He is acting for a Boss whom he would not mention by name, and he seems to hold the Boss in considerable awe. I'd say it's an even bet that we won't see Smith again tonight, but listen . . .'

Bruce talked for ten minutes, Mary rarely interrupting, and when he had finished she frowned, wrinkling her nose.

'So the next thing is to look at Cole's mysterious documents?'

'It seems like it, and I fancy he'll carry them in his pockets. However, he can't sleep in his coat. At least, he's not likely to, and . . .'

'Mr Morely, please.' A deep voice called and a heavy hand knocked on the door. Bruce opened it, to admit a plain-clothes sergeant from the Christchurch Station; he assured that earnest young man that he was entirely at the disposal of the police.

'We're pretty sure of our man, sir,' said the sergeant. 'You may be able to help us—you knew Mr Smith?'

'Smith? Oh, the red-faced man. You can hardly say I knew him, but we'd had a drink together.'

'He was seen coming out of Mr Cole's room, sir, and he's missing now. I wonder if you will give me a description of him?'

'Delighted. An inch or two shorter than I, say five-feet eleven. Broad, but with sloping shoulders, dressed in plum-coloured plus-fours, stout—particularly at the waist—red-faced, veiny nosed, eyes inclined to bloodshot, blunt features, very thick lips—almost negroid, sergeant—and a wart on the right side of his nose. He walked with a swagger, moving his shoulders forward with each step.'

'First-rate, sir!' The sergeant did not hide both admiration and appreciation. 'Far better than the others, and we'll be able to get to work on it at once.'

'Bit difficult, finding a man in a blackout,' said Murdoch.

'It's troublesome, sir, but not impossible. You weren't visited?'

'No, luckily. Any serious loss, do you know?'

'Very little, sir, only one gentleman appeared to keep money in his bedroom, and that was just a matter of twenty pounds. Will you be here for a day or two, sir, in case you can give us other information?'

'Afraid not,' said Murdoch. 'At least it can't be guaranteed. Is it necessary?'

'No, if you'll give me an address where to find you . . .'

Bruce gave him the Cliff Cottage address, and the sergeant went out. Bruce rubbed his chin thoughtfully, eyeing Mary.

'Odder and odder, my sweet. Why should the guests at a hotel subjected to a minor robbery be asked to stay put? Particularly a guest who hasn't been robbed. Probability—someone with influence with the local police has suggested it. But—someone resident here? Manager Garsting, for instance? Or could it be Cole?'

'Aren't you jumping to conclusions?' asked Mary.

'I am, and I'm going to,' smiled Bruce. 'With so many odds and ends, we've got to find the important one to follow.'

'The essentials are straightforward enough,' Mary said.

'Let's have them as they occur to you,' suggested Bruce.

Mary talked quietly and with precision. She had

worked for Sir Robert Holt for two years before Bruce
had joined the service, and was as capable an agent as
he, with a far wider experience. The particular value of
their work to Holt, however, was their ability as a team,
for what one missed the other would see, and between
them they were truly formidable. If Mary's voice held a
faintly husky note, and thus made listening easier, Bruce
nevertheless was more concerned with her résumé of her
situation. She was leaning against the dressing-table,
where Smith—or Dace—had been, while Bruce sprawled
back on the bed, hands clasped behind his head.

'Before we arrived,' Mary said, 'we knew the Devereuxs were expected and were likely to meet someone
here. They might or might not be spies. Before the
Devereuxs arrived, Smith tried to pump you. Because
they arrived today, coinciding with the Dees, we considered the Coles and His Nibs ...'

'By name, Arnould.'

'Also suspect. Suspected,' added Mary wrinkling her
nose, 'but only of coming to meet the Devereuxs.'

'Dees, it's simpler.'

'Don't interrupt. Since dinner, we've learned that
three rooms have been searched, all belonging to the
suspects ...'

'Sorry, but it's four. Ours, remember.'

'All right, Smith presumably knew that someone coming here yesterday or today possessed something he or his
employer wanted. He wasn't sure which, so he tried each
room. Since that Lucille Devereux has seemed to take
the robbery too much for granted, her husband has
shown himself to be scared and jumpy, the Coles acted
queerly, His Nibs—Arnould—made more fuss than anyone, and—didn't you say Garsting looked badly
startled?'

'Very badly.'

'Well, that's all. Except that Cole took something

37

from his case which might have been the thing Smith was looking for.'

Bruce hitched himself forward, sitting cross-kneed on the bed.

'Nicely put, darling. So let's consider the possibilities. The Dees came here tonight either to give something to another party, or to receive it. Smith knew of the something and looked for it. Cole, to our knowledge, had a something. The probability is that Cole was going to hand it or sell it, we don't know—to the Devereuxs. Another reasonable fact: a third party wanted it, via Smith.'

'Not necessarily. If the Dees were going to buy it, they might have made an effort to get it without the cash.'

Bruce widened his eyes.

'I'd missed that. The Dees might be Smith's employers. It would ring truer if Poona-Poona wasn't quite such a swipe. Smith found his Boss impressive.'

'It could be the woman.'

'Yes. And it could be that Smith and the Dees work for the same Panjandrum.'

Mary laughed lightly.

'Bruce, we're doing wonders! Possibles, possibles everywhere, but nary a one to work on. Except getting, or seeing, what Cole was so scared about.'

'Which deed we do by dead o' night. Mary . . .' Bruce's face grew serious, a groove developed between his brows. 'We've been on light duty for too long, we're too frolicsome about this. Smith had a Luger, Arnould looks like a Paris *apache* who's done well for himself We're in deep waters, and everything considered I think we'll have Percy here in the morning.'

'Ring him now,' approved Mary.

Bruce lifted the telephone and called Cliff Cottage, in the lounge of which, sunk deeply into Bruce's favourite chair, Percival Briggs was absorbed in a paper-backed novel. Percy, short and stocky and blunt-featured, with

38

a pair of blue eyes that twinkled easily, and a caustic Cockney wit, had observed the proprieties by putting a newspaper on the other chair, on which rested his sizeable feet. A fire was blazing, and at Percy's right hand was a tin of toffees, for he had a sweet tooth.

From this comfort, the telephone disturbed him.

'Well, would yer believe it?' Percy demanded of the room at large. 'Wait until 'arf past blinkin' nine before 'e rings. I mighta been in me barf.' He stretched for the 'phone, shifted a mass of toffee from his right cheek to his left, and said stiffly:

' 'Ouse of Mr Murdoch, speaking.'

'I want you,' said Murdoch, speaking guardedly in order to make sure that the operator at the hotel could not hear anything worth reporting, 'to go to Mr Morely first thing in the morning, Briggs.'

Percy sighed.

'Okay, I never thought me 'oliday would last. What time?'

'Start before dawn,' said Murdoch. 'And Briggs . . .'

'Yessir?'

'Get out of my chair,' said Murdoch gently, and he rang off, imagining the ludicrous expression on the face of Percival Briggs. Between him and Percy there was camaraderie and friendship; if Percy appeared at times to be too quick with his retorts, they were not meant with disrespect.

Mary was smiling.

'I wonder he stands you, darling. Well, are we making an early night? What time do you start prowling?'

'One or two, I think, so we'd better get to bed. Tuck in while I go down for a nightcap with the rest of the gathering, their second thoughts might be worth observing.'

He was surprised to find the whole party assembled, with the exception of His Nibs. More surprised to find the Devereuxs talking animatedly to the Coles, with

Lucille gesticulating with hands that were very slim and white. Anne Cole had completely recovered and her wonderful green eyes seemed to be causing Devereux some embarrassment; in ten minutes he had twice rested his hand on her shoulder, the skin of which had the creamy flawlessness so often found in red-haired women. If Cole observed it he paid no heed, but concentrated on Lucille, who was more animated than she had been all the evening.

Murdoch detected nothing forced about their satisfaction; they were in genuine high spirits. Devereux's 'tee-hee' was much in evidence, Cole had a deep, baying laugh, Lucille's was throaty and attractive, Anne Cole's much lighter, more musical. There was no reason why two couples whose rooms had been burgled should feel like that.

The stodgies were gathered at a table, playing bridge. Sam polished glasses with deliberate efficiency.

After twenty minutes, Bruce went upstairs. Mary was in bed, one arm over the coverlet, supporting a magazine.

'Beautiful,' said Bruce, staring down at her. 'Sweet, you were born to be married to me. I won't forget this honeymoon in a hurry. Something has happened downstairs. I imagine the papers or whatnot have changed hands. Poona-Poona and the Squire are like old school pals, all four are on top of the world. It wouldn't surprise me if the Dees now have the goods. I'll make their room my first visit.'

'Oh, well,' said Mary, sounding forlorn, 'I suppose I must expect it. Lucille's very beautiful.'

To which Bruce responded ungallantly, and switched off the light despite a cry of protest that she wanted to read. He was in bed within five minutes, very conscious of his self-restraint; almost too conscious.

At half-past one he woke.

The bedside lamp showed Mary, sleeping with one arm curled about her head. He slipped a dressing-gown

40

about his pyjamas, and from a case took an automatic, putting it into his pocket. He added to it a skeleton key, with which he was competent if not expert, and, first making sure that the passage was deserted and dimly lighted, stepped out and made for the Devereuxs' room.

He had a shock.

The door was ajar, although the room was in darkness.

He widened the door, letting the passage light filter through, and what he saw gave him another shock, although this time he was partially prepared for it. The twin beds were empty, and showed no signs of having been slept in.

But from a cigarette tray a tiny spiral of smoke rose from a cigarette half-smoked and not put out.

It was the only sign of occupation in the room, for the Devereuxs had flown in the night, taking their luggage with them. He cursed himself for having failed to see the possibility, and hurried back to Number 5. Mary stirred as he reached her and rested a hand on her arm.

'Get up, darling, and dress.'

Her eyes widened, she blinked sleepily.

'Eh?'

'Sorry, but we've a journey ahead,' said Bruce. 'I'll be back in five minutes.'

He knew she would need no more telling, and went along to the Coles' room. It was shut, but not bolted, and the key turned easily after a little gentle manipulation of the lock. He stepped through, seeing enough from the passage light. The Coles had neglected one twin bed, and were sleeping face to face. Cole was snoring faintly.

Bruce looked for and found the case Cole had opened. He lifted the contents out quickly, ran his finger along the edge, and found the slight protuberance that operated the concealed hiding place. The *click!* seemed loud enough to awaken the sleepers, and he glanced round, but there was no alarm.

He inserted his fingers in the cavity.

41

He felt a thrill as he touched papers, but a moment later his heart grew heavy. The papers were thick, and bunched together. He drew them out, and a quick glance sufficed to show him that he was holding a wad of one-pound notes, a wad as thick as that which Smith had shown.

Bruce took one and left the others in the case but not the cavity, for the Coles deserved a shock. He closed the door behind him, and his own room found Mary dressed in a tailor-made suit, and one of the cases half-packed.

'What's it all about?' she demanded.

'Cole's exchanged his papers for hard cash, and the Dees have gone,' said Bruce, flinging his clothes on. 'They've a quarter of an hour's start, and we might catch them up.'

'Which direction?'

'We'll take a chance and make for London.'

Bruce drove faster than was safe in the restricted glow of their only head-lamp, cursing the blackout. They passed no car for fifteen miles, and the other side of Winchester resigned themselves to the fact that the Devereuxs were either too far ahead, or had taken the other direction.

'I'll pull up at a 'phone box,' Bruce said, and he sounded disgruntled. 'Percy had better come to London, and I ought to call Pinky, but telling him I've fallen down on the job after dragging him from his bed isn't so good.'

'He'll bear it,' said Mary, 'but it's mortifying, Bruce.'

'Mortifying! I'd call it . . .'

'Not just now, thank you.'

He grinned. 'Sorry. And that looks like a kiosk.' He pulled into the side and stepped towards the telephone booth. He was pulling the door open when he heard the sound of a car engine coming from the direction they had taken, and he hesitated. Mary looked through the rear-window, to see the wing-lamps and the shaded headlight of another car approaching quickly, and both of them felt a sudden increase of tension.

Bruce's heart jumped as the car slowed down; but not so much as it did when he saw Arnould jump from the car and approach him. For in the Frenchman's right hand there was a gun.

# 5

# Sir Robert is Irate

Mary did not recognise the Frenchman until he had stepped into the faint light from his car, and as recognition came she also saw the gun. She stiffened, but did not immediately move, for the other door of Arnould's car opened, and the driver joined his employer. She heard Bruce speak, and realising for the moment she was being ignored, she opened her bag and took out a small automatic. Silently and slowly she moved towards the open door through which Bruce had gone, while Bruce said sharply:

'What the devil are you doing?'

'I mean no harm, *M'sieu*.' Arnould's suave voice held mockery, perhaps a hint of threat, and in the dim light his face seemed sinister. 'You have something I wish to possess, it is quite simple. For it, I will pay much.'

'I've got nothing you could possibly want. Put that gun away.'

'You misunderstand me,' Arnould sneered. His English was word perfect, but spoken so slowly and carefully that he seemed to speak for a long time. 'I am not joking, *M'sieu*. Raise your hands above your head.'

'I'm damned if I will!'

In that second Bruce learned just how important the papers were to Arnould, knew that his first estimate of the Frenchman was right. Through the semi-darkness came a foot-long stab of flame, followed by a sharp hiss. For a fraction of a second Bruce was afraid; seemed to feel the bullet bite into his chest. Actually it plucked at his shoulder, thudded into the concrete of the telephone kiosk, then dropped to the pavement. Each sound seemed loud and vivid.

'Your hands,' said Arnould, without a change of tone.

Murdoch gulped, and raised his hands. He *was* afraid of another bullet, believed that this man would kill. But most important was the need to create the impression of being scared; hence the gulp.

'Look here, if you . . .'

'Victor, examine the gentleman's pockets.' Arnould did not look away from Murdoch as the man stepped forward. A tall, thin, sallow-faced Frenchman, as far as Murdoch could see in that dim light, wearing a chauffeur's cap and a heavy, dark coat. It was not the first time he had frisked a man, for his hands dipped in and out of Murdoch's pockets expertly, until nothing was left, not even small change. Stepping aside to make sure that Murdoch made no attempt to act because he hid the gun, Victor handed his haul to Arnould, who took it with his left hand.

'Watch him, Victor.'

The chauffeur had uttered no word, and he uttered none then. He stepped back a yard, took an automatic from his pocket, and not until then did Arnould lower his. For thirty seconds there was silence broken only by Murdoch's heavy breathing, while in the car Mary sat with her gun trained on the trio, wondering at what moment she could best interrupt.

'*Sacre diable!*' For the first time Arnould's voice lost its suaveness, thin lips turned back as he stepped towards Bruce, a hand upraised. 'Where is it?'

'I haven't the faintest idea what you mean,' said Murdoch with a greater show of courage. 'This is a lot

45

of tomfoolery. I—Good God, it's the fellow from the Swan!'

Arnould licked his lips.

'So insignificant, *M'sieu*, you did not immediately recognise me? Victor, slit the linings of his coat immediately.'

Victor, still without a word, dipped his hand to his pocket, to exchange the gun for a knife. It was the moment when no gun was trained on Bruce, the best moment for Mary to interrupt, and she took her chance. Quiet but imperative, her voice came:

'Drop the gun and put your hands up!'

She slipped from the car, so that they could see her hand. Both men started and looked towards her, and Bruce moved. His right hand stretched out for Arnould's gun, wrested it away before the Frenchman realised what was happening. Victor was breathing hard, and hesitated, but did not hold on to his automatic.

'Nicely timed, Mary! Bless you! I can't understand why the efficient Arnould forgot about you.'

Arnould's tongue darted out, but he said nothing. Bruce's voice hardened.

'What papers were you after, Arnould?'

The Frenchman looked at him defiantly. He showed no fear, and his voice held a menace even greater than his words.

'You will be advised to do nothing more, Morely. Because I am at a disadvantage that does not mean I cannot act most dangerously for you. Moreover, you know as much about the papers as I.'

'Just why?' Bruce said.

'Because you stole them from Cole.'

'Never in my life have I stolen anything from Cole or anyone,' said Bruce. 'You've made yet another mistake. Nor do you worry me; a man who can forget that I wasn't alone is just a damned fool.'

'Be careful, Morely!' Absurd though it was,

Arnould's voice and manner did sound threatening. 'I—but *M'sieu* . . .' The suaveness was back, Arnould lifted his hands. 'Why are we about to quarrel? If it is true and you have not the papers, we are both in the same position —we look for them. If you have them, you will find that I am not mean. Already you have received fifty pounds for a little assistance to me. For the papers—ten times fifty, *M'sieu*, and I shall not hesitate to pay you.'

Mary started. Bruce's smile was one of genuine enjoyment.

'So you used Smith, did you?'

'Smith works for me, yes. He also . . .' The menace crept into the soft voice again, Arnould's ability to create that aura was uncanny. 'He also advised me, *M'sieu*, that you had some reason for wishing not to send him to the police. A guilty conscience, that is the only thing. And also, you have already aided him. How unfortunate if the police should know he entered your room, but bought your silence with a trifling fifty pounds—*M'sieu*, I make myself quite clear?'

'Quite clear,' said Bruce.

In a matter of seconds he had to decide on his course of action. To take Arnould and Victor, question them at his town flat, or even at Sir Robert Holt's room, and thus try to force what they know from them. Or to let them go . . .

In ninety-nine cases in a hundred, he would have taken them.

But he placed little faith in his own or Holt's ability to make these men talk. The saturnine Victor, the sinister Arnould, looked and probably were capable of resisting third-degree refined to a far greater degree than Bruce knew how. He doubted whether it would be possible to get information from them; on the other hand if they were held for a time, they would be forced into inaction, he could concentrate on the search for the Devereuxs.

*If* he knew where the Devereuxs were likely to be.

47

Still he hesitated, and Mary stepped forward, to whisper in his ear while keeping her gun trained on them.

'*Try coming to terms. Force his price up. Tell him you'll go all out for the papers.*'

'It's an idea,' he said slowly, and he scowled at Arnould.

'If it weren't for that fifty I'd turn you over right now, but we might come to some arrangement.'

'So! You have the papers!'

'Quite wrong,' said Bruce, 'but I know who has them, and I might get my hands on them. If I do, five hundred is no use.'

'It is a good sum.'

'A round thousand, and we can talk business.'

'A thousand pounds for what you *might* do?'

Bruce grinned.

'I won't ask you to trust me that far. A thousand in return for the papers.'

'And where shall I be able to get them from you, if you are successful?'

'Anywhere in London you care to name.'

'It could happen that way,' said Arnould softly. 'If I can trust you, *M'sieu* Morely. In London, then, at the Regal Hotel, the foyer. On what day do you expect to have the papers?'

'If I'm going to get them at all, it won't be for a couple of days. Say the day after tomorrow, midday, at the Regal.'

'Oh, no, *M'sieu*! After dark, any time after dark—in days of no lighting, it is then so difficult to follow others.' For the first time Arnould smiled, but he did not look amused. 'I shall be there. You will come alone, you understand.'

'We shall both be there.'

'You two shall be treated as one,' conceded Arnould. 'And *M'sieu*, do not make the mistake of giving me the wrong papers, of trying to sell to two places. It will be

48

fatal for you to make mistakes, do you understand?'

'I'll leave them all to you,' flashed Bruce.

'*Msieu* imagines himself clever.' Arnould shrugged. 'Victor, start the car, we are leaving. *M'sieu,* the guns.'

'Oh no,' said Bruce, genially now, 'they can join Smith's for the time being. I may have a better use for them than you. And I'm afraid you're too optimistic. I don't trust you—*M'sieu.* Let the air out of their tyres, Mary.'

Mary covered a laugh, and went forward to obey. Arnould glared, and Victor moved forward angrily, but Bruce had them both covered.

'I'll be fifteen miles ahead of you before you can get the air in those wheels, and I'll admit I'll feel happier,' Bruce said. 'I wouldn't put it past you to follow me and try to get the papers for nothing. That wouldn't do at all.'

The hiss of escaping air punctuated his words, and Mary straightened up from the last tyre. Neither of the Frenchmen spoke as Bruce climbed into his own car, and took the wheel. Mary kept the others covered until the car began to move, and then she slammed the door.

Bruce chuckled.

'Nice work from start to finish! I wondered how long you'd be.'

'Just long enough, I thought,' said Mary. 'Bruce, they were *all* involved. It doesn't ring true.'

'It's true enough,' said Bruce. 'Those papers, I imagine, will have much interest for Pinky.'

'If he ever sees them.'

'You're tired,' said Bruce. 'Get in the back and have a sleep. It's the first time I've known you pessimistic.'

'I'll try to doze off here,' said Mary, and then her voice grew harder. 'I've never met Arnould before. I didn't like him at all.'

'It wouldn't surprise me,' said Bruce more lightly than he felt, 'if the dislike's not mutual. Which is one

49

of the things we'll discover later. I wonder if he'll turn up at the Regal?'

'If he doesn't, Pinky will rant.'

'Let him rant,' said Murdoch grandiloquently: but he wondered whether he had been wise to let Arnould go free.

.        .        .        .        .

It might be said that to Sir Robert Holt the outbreak of war had been a bigger blow than to any man in England. Unquestionably it had been a severe one. For years he had seen the prospect of war, and fought, talked, organised, prepared and even bluffed against it. An ungenerous Cabinet was once compelled to admit that Holt had once contrived to postpone it for three months, whereas Holt declared—and declared with vehemence and a sizzling choice of language—that if the Cabinet had seized the opportunity he had offered them, it could have been avoided for years, if not forever. Sir Robert, in short, had not seen eye-to-eye with the Cabinet before hostilities, and he did not do so afterwards.

The duty of most permanent officials at Whitehall is to do their job under varying Ministers, endeavour to do it successfully but—and primarily—please the Minister who might be in office for five and even ten years. Many may hold elected politicians in considerable contempt, but few say so.

Sir Robert was one of the few. True, he was a privileged person, answerable to three different Ministers—Glennister, the Foreign Secretary, Kershing at the Admiralty, and Marridew at the War Office—but that merely enabled him to spread his disfavours.

He was even further privileged, for hosts of young, middle-aged and old men as well as a sprinkling of women would and could do for the Pink 'Un what they could do for no other man on earth. He was a pink caricature of a man, and he raved and swore at them

50

and called them fools, and laughed if they called him one. He had his finger on the pulse of international espionage before the war and saw no reason for removing it afterwards. Nevertheless when the War Cabinet had been constructed and he heard the appointments, he immediately called for an audience with the Prime Minister, and, shortly and tersely, offered his resignation.

He had the pleasure of seeing the Prime Minister look taken aback and of having his resignation refused. That had strengthened his hand considerably. Ahead of him he could see many differences of opinion with the P.M. and the Cabinet, and now he could say with equanimity that he had offered to get out when he had seen that he would be expected to take orders which he would consider—he chose a word cautiously—impracticable.

With a clear conscience and the anticipation of many a tussle with bureaucratic officialdom, he had started to clean England of what an imaginative Editor called in a headline the:

## GREAT SPY MENACE

It was not a task he expected to finish. He hoped to halve the number of enemy agents, but knew that many would be flourishing after the war—just as many of his would be flourishing in Berlin. But he hoped to frustrate the activities of the major German operators.

Thanks to Murdoch, Mary Dell, and a host of others, he had so far succeeded. Which did not mean that there was no leakage of secrets, and while Bruce and Mary had gone to bed that night, Holt had been at Number 10. The gentlemen of Number 10 had not been pleased with him. Marridew, who was new to the War Office and to Holt, had gone so far as to say:

'It will not do, Holt. Arrangements must be made to tighten the grip on enemy spies. The loss of the Allaway Papers is a matter of immense importance.'

'To whom?' snapped Holt.

51

Marridew stared as if he had not heard right.

'Good heavens, man, to all of us!'

'Then why the hell weren't they kept locked up?' howled Holt. 'Left loose on a desk in an empty room while some fiddling crack-headed nincompoop went out for his elevenses. Not missed for two days, because the crackhead didn't realise they'd gone, forgot he'd had the file out. Is that the way you treat vital secrets in the War Office? 'Pon my living say so, it's the most outrageous piece of asinine idiocy I've heard in this room, and I've heard some. Enemy agents did you say? Look in the wastepaper baskets, you might find them!'

Marridew lifted pale hands and stared scandalised through *pince nez* high on his thin nose.

'Holt! I ...'

'Don't Holt me!' roared Holt. 'You haven't been here long enough to know that when you get on a high horse it's only half as high as mine. Sheer, unadulteratel carelessness explains the loss of the Allaway Papers. Isn't that so?'

Marridew swallowed hard.

'A slight error of judgement, perhaps, but . . .'

'Pah!' squeaked Holt. 'If there's no other business for me I'm off.' He looked at the Prime Minister, who felt uncomfortable. Only Glennister and Kershing seemed in no way perturbed by Holt's outburst, for both liked the man, respected and even admired him. Holt rightly called an 'error of judgement' carelessness.

'There is nothing else, Sir Robert,' said the P.M.

'The Allaway Papers!' exclaimed Marridew.

'I've had men looking for the Allaway Papers for two days,' growled Holt, 'since their loss was first reported. I don't need a conference to tell me what to do, and I'm not going to start now. 'Night, all.'

And Sir Robert stumped out.

In the hall he surprised the butler by chuckling aloud, but on his journey to a small house near Sloane Square his mood changed again. He let himself in with a key and walked up narrow stairs to a long, low room on the first floor, a room furnished except for one corner as a room in any exclusive club might be. Sumptuously. In the one corner was a small desk and a large chair, the desk littered with a miscellany of papers. Holt plumped himself down in the chair, scowled, rang for his man, who entered immediately. Gordon was large, stout, impassive; a smooth, white-faced servant worth his weight —said Holt—in diamonds.

'Wouldn't do for Marridew to see what I leave on this desk, eh Gordon?' Holt grinned at the miscellany, and then chuckled. 'Made him jump, though, he'll think twice about telling me it's "got to stop" again. Of course it's got to stop.' He glared at Gordon and roared irascibly: 'What damned fool thinks I want important documents stolen? Who thinks I like Nazi agents prowling around Whitehall? Got to stop, got to stop. I said it had got to stop, didn't I?'

'So I understood, sir.'

'Don't be impertinent. I want some tea. Remind me to get you a course of lessons in making tea; the stuff you serve up is poison.' He grinned. 'Water bewitched, tea begrudged and sugar bewasted. Heard that one before?'

'No, sir.'

'Oh, get out. It's a hundred years old if it's a day, and I've recited it a thousand times to you. Anything from Mr. Murdoch?'

'A wire, sir. He is seeing Dee tonight, and writing.'

'He's . . .' Holt groped for a telegram form on his desk, peered at it, choked and roared: 'He's wiring. Wiring! He's—I mean writing! As if he can trust this to the post, as if it isn't urgent, he's started now! It's that woman, bless her, she's turning his head. Go—and—make —tea!'

Gordon bowed and withdrew. Holt rocked to and fro in his chair, a finger on one of his three double chins. He had a vast pink face which looked as though he did not need to shave, and his features were rarely properly appreciated because of the chins. But his nose was straight and thin, his mouth small and shapely, a feminine mouth. Keen blue eyes which rarely altered whether he was laughing or ranting could and often did make men want to get out of his sight. His forehead looked higher than it was since, but for a faint fringe of greying hair above his ears, he was completely bald; and his head was as pink as his face. It was typical of Sir Robert Holt that when he first learned that many of his agents called him the Pink 'Un—or Pinky—he used Pink 'Un as a password. It was the kind of word no one, overhearing, would dream to be secret.

He seized a pencil and began to scribble on a pad in front of him. He scribbled fast and used large letters, and as he filled a sheet he ripped it off, screwed it up and threw it into a wastepaper basket, and started again. He put his thoughts on paper, using a private indecipherable shorthand, because he had found that he could not think clearly enough without doing it.

Gordon came in, with China tea. Holt drank three cups, scribbled afresh, drank another and complained bitterly to the room that Gordon did not know how to make anything, and then rang for his man again.

'You rang, sir?'

'Don't ask unnecessary questions. I'm going to have a nap. Call me only if Mr Murdoch rings through—no, don't, tell him to come here at once, absolutely at once, drop everything and come here. Tell him it's important.'

'He will probably gather that, sir.'

'Yes, I suppose—Gordon! That's more impertinence! Gordon . . .' Holt stood up, a man of medium height who looked short because of his massive pink head; and his eyes were narrowed, Gordon knew that he was worried.

'Very important, Gordon. Important enough to let the war last another year.'

'Shouldn't I ring Mr Murdoch, sir?'

'Not until morning. He's working on the job now but doesn't know it, and nor did I. Wake me at seven with some of that excellent tea of yours.'

Gordon smiled benignly as the caricature of a man he loved went into his bedroom.

# 6

# Whys and Wherefores

Bruce Murdoch had a flat in a monster block of buildings off Park Lane. It was small, but ample for his requirements, being used little more than as a *pied-à-terre*. He let himself in with a key, just after four-thirty on the morning following dinner at the White Swan. Hearing nothing, he switched on the light, to reveal a lounge-hall bare of everything but furniture on low, well-sprung modern lines. He moved to the dining-room, the two bedrooms, and the bathroom, finding them all empty, before he returned to the hall.

'Enter, woman. We are alone.'

'You're a fool,' said Mary. 'Was that search necessary, Bruce?'

'I've had feelings about this job since meeting His Nibs, and you feel the same. However, there's no reason to believe he believes Morely is Murdoch, and if he succeeded in following me I deserve all I get. Feel like a drink?'

'I'll make some tea.'

'Always the true disciple,' smiled Murdoch. 'Pinky and you would make a good couple. Carry on, while I 'phone.'

He called Sloane Square, to receive Holt's message, and promised to be at the house by eight o'clock unless he was sent for earlier. Then he disturbed Percival Briggs from the midst of his slumbers, and told the outraged Percy to start for London at once. And :

'What did you say?' he demanded sharply.

'I said it was the perishing limit, an' I mean it's the perishing limit, an'—sorry sir, me tongue ran away with me. All okey-doke, sir, I'll be there.'

For half-an-hour Bruce and Mary sat in an easy chair going over all the events of the night, so that his report for Holt would be in good order. At half past five Bruce went to bed, setting an alarm clock for seven-fifteen. At five past seven Mary entered his room, with more tea, and he smiled sleepily up at her.

'Darling, I don't know what I did without you.'

'Percy made your tea,' said Mary, 'and if you take as much sugar as that you'll get fat.'

'You leave my tummy alone, and run a bath, there's an angel.' He smoked half a cigarette before getting up, bathed, dressed, ate bacon and eggs with relish. At ten to eight he went downstairs and took the car out of the garage. At one minute to eight he was knocking at the door of Holt's Sloane Square house, and Gordon admitted him. There was barely room for Murdoch to squeeze past the butler in the narrow hall-passage.

' 'Morning, Gordon. Is he up?'

'He's been up for an hour, sir.'

'On the rampage?'

'A little perturbed I believe, sir.'

'Stand by the window for the pieces,' said Murdoch with a grimace. 'I've a feeling I'm not going to please him.'

'I can think of no one more calculated to do so, sir.'

'Which leaves me speechless!'

Bruce went up the flight of narrow stairs, wondering not for the first time why Holt had chosen what was little more than a cottage for his headquarters, and knowing that the cottage, one of a terrace, was the last place anyone would expect to find the Head of British

Secret Intelligence. He tapped, and Holt roared:

'Come in! Don't waste time!'

' 'Morning, sir,' said Bruce, stepping through and closing the door behind him. 'A bit chilly, but . . .'

'*Mister* Murdoch,' said Holt slowly, 'do not come in here to exchange compliments or discuss the weather. What have you done wrong? You would never say "sir" unless you had a conscience as guilty as Goebbels'. You've messed everything up, I can see it from your expression. I'm surprised you haven't brought Mary, you could hide behind her skirts. Or perhaps you think you can push some blame on to her in her absence. Well? Say something. I'm waiting!'

Bruce selected a large armchair, and sat.

'The Devereuxs,' he said, 'came, got what they wanted, and went.'

'Where'd they go?'

'I don't know.'

Holt's tongue darted out, the tip as pink as his face.

'I knew it the moment you entered. Which other enemies of the King's Realm has it pleased Your Idiocy to allow to escape?'

'A Mr Smith, *alias* Jem Dace,' replied Bruce, and kept a straight face.

'I—see.' Holt fingered his middle chin. 'Mr and Mrs Devereux and Mr Smith. And the next?'

'A *M'sieu* Arnould and his man, Victor.'

'A *M'sieu* . . .' Holt jolted up in his chair, glared, and then subsided, a smile hovering about his lips. 'All right, Bruce, now stop playing jokes on an old man. You didn't know it and I didn't know it, but the job was more serious than any we've had since it started.' 'It', on Holt's lips, always meant the war.

'I was afraid so, and I'm not sure I've played the right hand,' Bruce admitted. 'Shall I go on?'

'Yes.'

Bruce's story took twenty minutes. He included every-

58

thing that he could vouch for as a fact, as well as his impressions of the men and women concerned. He spoke unhurriedly and was not once interrupted, although from time to time Holt leaned forward and scribbled on his writing-block. He was scribbling as Bruce finished; a stranger would have thought him oblivious of the last half-dozen sentences.

Then he looked up at Bruce.

'You were right, unquestionably right about Smith and Arnould. You've given them both the impression that you're not on good terms with the police. Arnould will want to see you again. But the Dees—I wish you'd kept your eye on them, one or the other of you. You must have had a reason. You and Mary don't miss the obvious for the sake of it.'

Bruce shrugged, not happily.

'We agreed that we didn't want to arouse any suspicion, that it would be best if we were in bed early . . .'

Holt's lips puckered. 'Honeymoon evidence—yes!'

'And, the major error, we assumed there would be no developments until morning. As the search had already been made it seemed a safe bet that they'd be in no hurry. They wouldn't expect Smith back again.'

'Reasonable enough, and logical. A pity, but there it is, and we'll have to make the best of a bad job. What about their journey? Why didn't you 'phone me right away, I could have had a watch kept on the roads.'

'In the blackout? And which road? It did occur to me that a police call might help,' Bruce claimed. 'I might have 'phoned you if I'd had any idea of the business in hand. You'd told me just to see them and watch them and try to find out what they were doing. And you were emphatic about not letting them know they were being watched. So it seemed certain you wouldn't want them stopped.'

'I wouldn't have,' admitted Holt. 'I didn't expect you'd run into anything like this, Bruce; the best I hoped

59

for was a direct contact between the Devereuxs and someone unknown. My fault. I should have 'phoned you again last night, after that blasted meeting.'

'Meeting?'

'Cabinet,' Holt grunted, and thrust his head forward. 'Of all the—oh, 'pon my living say so, what's the use? They're politicians and you know what I think of politicians. Never be swayed by prejudice. Bruce, they're doing their best, and I wouldn't like the opposition any better.' He sniffed. 'Now—for your ears and Mary's only. Understand?'

'Yes.'

'Concerning Sir Frederick Allaway. Know him?'

Bruce stirred and lit a cigarette.

'The diplomatic adviser. yes.'

'Diplomatic adviser's good. They didn't take a blind bit of notice of him before the war. Too pessimistic, they said, even Adolf must keep a promise sometime or other, and why shouldn't it be the latest one?' Holt snorted. 'Well, Allaway had an idea concerning neutrals.'

'Neutrals?'

'Neutrals. He made it in the form of a memorandum, several pages long. He wasn't good friends with them—I mean the Cabinet—he'd been proved right and that wasn't too good. But Allaway has a chip on his shoulder. Expected a post in the War Cabinet, but didn't get it. Instead of talking to the P.M. he put his ideas in the form of a formal proposal. The proposal became known as the Allaway Papers. It was being considered in turn by each member of the Cabinet; they did have the sense not to have a lot of typed copies. It reached Marridew, the addlepate, and he was going into it when the latest Russian coup sent everyone dithery. Left it on his desk, told a secretary to put it in a special file, and that was done. Secretary was afterwards asked to get the file out, did so, but left it with others on his desk while he went to get a cup of coffee.' Holt grinned. 'I called it elevenses, Marridew was *not* amused. Secretary was immediately afterwards required for a different job, called *his* secretary to file all the papers on his desk, and carried on.'

'Good God!' exclaimed Bruce.

'Yes, isn't it? But in extenuation, my boy, at the time the importance of the Allaway Papers wasn't fully appreciated. And that particular chit on its own wasn't vital, since Allaway had done no more than whet the appetites of the Cabinet. He'd sketched an idea—no more—concerning neutrals. Anyway, the Secretary's secretary filed all the papers he saw, and Marridew and the rest of the Cabinet put their heads together over the Russian business, because that's getting serious. What do you think of it, Bruce?'

Sir Robert, Bruce knew, was liable to chase off into a different channel at any moment, but never just for the sake of it, and his opinion on the latest Russian move in the Baltic was required. He gave it pithily.

'The mailed fist, of course. If Stalin were Lenin there'd be a different tale, but . . .'

'That's enough, I don't want your opinion on Lenin and his dynasty! The mailed fist, that's all right, quite all right. *Frightening* the neutrals. The neutrals are making a brave show, but they don't want war. They'll give away as little as they can, but they will give away to avoid fighting. After Poland was wiped out in three weeks, who can blame them? Those blasted politicians, guaranteeing—never mind, we won't go into that now. Bruce, Allaway's idea *might* show a way of getting the neutrals together in one large *bloc* strong enough to prevent the Russian eat-'em-up-bit-by-bit policy. This way: A's in the Baltic, B's in the Balkans. Russia shakes the fist at A, and while he's shaking B kicks him in the pants. You get a rough idea?'

Bruce chuckled; the Pink 'Un was at his irrepressible best.

61

'Yes, very rough! But will you ever persuade a Balkan country that anything a Baltic one does affects it? They can't see that far.'

'Some can and do, but the majorities won't. On the same basis as the people over here he asked why we should help Czechoslovakia, or Poland. But Allaway maintained, and he's a shrewd fellow, that there's a common denominator for all countries who are at present neutral. That's practically all he said in the memorandum. But he hinted that he knew what the common denominator was. He went further, and included the Americas in his idea, a *bloc* in fact which was to make sure that the war doesn't spread. *If* it worked, of course: but Allaway wouldn't put up a proposition that wasn't at least possible. Clear?'

Bruce stubbed his cigarette out, and nodded.

'Only too clearly. The Papers were stolen.'

'Yes, filched off the Secretary's desk while he was out. That was the only time they could have gone, the drawer was locked and electrically sealed afterwards, they do take some precautions. It wasn't for forty-eight hours that the P.M. was able to think about the scheme again, goaded by Allaway threatening to give his story to the Press. So his Papers were sent for—in vain. That was two days ago. I wasn't told officially, but Glennister gave me an inkling, and I'd been putting out feelers. Incidentally, a clerk at the War Office disappeared, and didn't turn up again voluntarily. I was forced to leave that investigation to the police, who had already told me that Devereux had been known to associate with two or three enemy aliens now interned. Just before I went to the Cabinet meeting last night, I was told Devereux had been in the restaurant where the clerk was eventually found—and at the same time. Now that might mean anything or nothing, and I think it means a lot, *but* I didn't know until after the meeting how important the Papers were. However, I did 'phone you, you did gather there was something suspicious about the Dees, and for the rest . . . What are you looking like that for, Bruce?'

Bruce said savagely: 'I was thinking that of all the damned fools in creation, I'm the worst. To let the Dees get away! Those papers were under my nose . . .'

Holt plucked at his chin.

'A pity, a great pity, but you were working in the dark and so was I. Far too much blacking out, and I don't mean just at night. No use reproaching ourselves, Bruce; man who never made a mistake never made anything.'

'I suppose you're right,' growled Bruce, but he looked as if he had received a hard knock.

'I *am* right,' said Holt more briskly. 'Now, the brighter side! All the Papers can give away is that Allaway has some such scheme. Useful for an enemy Power, but not on its own vital. On the other hand, directly those Powers know we've a scheme under way, they'll probably start shoving at the smaller neutrals with all their might, as well as think up a counter offer. If it is an offer. And Arnould thinks it's worth a thousand pounds.'

'He may think it's a more complete scheme than it is.'

'Probably does, and if he buys it he'll sell again at a higher figure to anyone prepared to buy blind—and belligerent countries to buy blind.'

'He could be a working agent for one of them.'

'Conceivably. In any case he's in this country, and he hasn't got the papers. Whoever has will have to get them out of the country somehow, and that's not as easy as it sounds these days. Thing is, we want them back. I— *what's* the matter?'

For Bruce, who rarely did, had exclaimed profanely.

'Good Lord, Pinky, it doesn't make sense! If Devereux bought the things from the clerk, he wouldn't want to buy them from Cole. Cole would buy them from him.'

63

Holt scowled ferociously, not because of the 'Pinky'.

'Yes, he would, and that suggests Devereux took something else from Cole, and that in turn suggests the papers you saw weren't necessarily the ones we're after, and there may not be any sense in it at all.'

'Arnould, Cole and Devereux wouldn't make all this fuss about nothing.'

'No. Well, what do you want to do next?'

'Find Devereux.'

'So you should, but we'll have to have him looked for by the police; we can't spend the time on it ourselves. Pull yourself together, me boy. If Mary were here she wouldn't have given that answer.'

'Thanks,' smiled Bruce. 'All right—watch Allaway.'

'That,' said Sir Robert genially, 'is precisely what I've brought you back for. I've been on the 'phone to Glennister this morning, woke the sluggard up. He's arranging for Mary to join Allaway's secretarial staff, and you . . .'

Sir Robert broke off, turned slowly and majestically in his chair, and glowered at the telephone which had broken across his words. He lifted the receiver—one of four on the desk—and with a comically gentle enunciation said: 'Hallo.'

'Bruce saw his expression change as he snapped:

'You're sure? . . . Twenty minutes . . . An hour and twenty minutes, why the devil don't you speak clearly? . . . Yes, yes, I'll get busy right away, got just the man for the job here now, young Murdoch . . . No, I won't go myself, and you can tell whoever you like that I won't . . . All right, old man, give them my apologies and tell them I can't come for reasons of State. 'Bye!' He replaced the telephone and turned to Murdoch, who had risen from his chair and was standing with both hands deep in his pockets.

The Pink 'Un for once spoke without mannerisms, his voice brisk and businesslike.

'Not so good, Bruce. Allaway has disappeared. He was seen in his study an hour and twenty minutes ago, but he's not there now, and there are signs of a struggle. Hurry over, will you? St John's Wood, 8 Norton Road. I'll 'phone Mary to join you.'

# 7

# Signs of a Struggle

Sir Frederick Allaway was a bachelor despite the large house he maintained at 8 Norton Road. His entertaining, which was not frugal, was handled by a sister who. rumour said, had refused many offers of marriage in order to forward her brother's political career. That career had been only partially successful. He had reached high places, but not the highest—and the reason was not hard to find. He was a man honest with himself and with his Party, and he quarrelled with Party leaders too often and too violently for their liking. No dictatorship is more dictatorial than a Party Whip's, and a man whom many believed the right leader of the country, in peace or war, had been the Diplomatic Adviser to a Government which had preferred to listen to other counsel. Vindicated by the events of March and September of 1939, he had anticipated, not without reason, a post in the War Cabinet. His fellow rebel, Kershing, had been rewarded : Allaway had received an obscure post which had embittered him more than any other setback in his career.

Now Allaway had disappeared.

Miss Henrietta Allaway, a woman frequently in the public as well as the social eye, was waiting for Murdoch in the vast drawing-room of 8 Norton Road. This room was furnished on semi-modern lines, yet did not scorn a few Victorian pieces, a relic or two of Chippendale and

Sheraton, and radiator-heating. Despite the heating and the chill of the morning, the windows were thrown wide open and the air was frosty as Murdoch was shown in by a butler. He approached Miss Allaway, who was at the far end of the long room. She seemed miles away, and massive even from the door. She sat as though in state, and Bruce had a fleeting impression that she should really have two chairs.

His feet were buried in the thick pile of the carpet, and seemed to make his feet drag. In fact, he was going slowly deliberately, to get a better impression of the arrogant-looking woman in front of him.

She was dressed in a long, flowing, loose-fitting gown, high at the neck and falling over her deep chest. It was of maroon-coloured velvet, held at neck and sleeves by pearl set clasps. Her hands were folded in front of her, and on one finger was a pearl ring—a tiny cluster of pearls. Her hair, once jet black and now streaked with grey, was drawn back from her forehead, but not tightly. To Bruce Murdoch, who had not seen her at close quarters before, her hair and the style in which it was dressed seemed familiar.

Brown, impatient eyes met his. Her nose was large and prominent, her upper lip long and making the lines of her thin lips seem longer than they were. Her chin was pointed; she would have made a striking-looking man, and was remarkably like her brother.

'Mr Morely?' The assumed name had been used for the occasion, and Murdoch bowed.

'Good morning, Miss Allaway.' She did not seem the type to need any kind of sympathetic inquiry. 'May I know first whether the police have been advised of Sir Frederick's disappearance?'

'They have not. Mr Glennister was advised; I left the matter in his hands.'

'Do the servants know?'

'Ridgeway reported it to me, and he has instructions

67

to tell no one else. He is quite reliable.'

'So that only you and Ridgeway know that Sir Frederick is away?'

'That is so.'

'Thank you. May I see the room?'

Something like a smile showed in the woman's eyes, and Bruce felt that he had made a good impression.

'I'll come with you, if . . .'

'Of course.' He smiled, and the smile of Bruce Murdoch could be charming. 'Are we likely to be overheard?'

'No.' She walked with easy grace towards a door which Bruce had not seen before, and he stepped forward to open it. 'What is it you wish to know?'

'Three things,' said Bruce. 'Did Sir Frederick know a Mr Charles Devereux and Mrs Lucille Devereux?'

'The name is not familiar.'

'A Mr Cole, and a Mrs Anne Cole?'

'The same answer, Mr Morely.'

'A Frenchman, Arnould?'

He was startled by her reception of Arnould's name, for she stopped in the middle of a step, turned abruptly, and gripped his arm. Her fingers were strong.

'What makes you ask that?'

'I've reason to believe Arnould might be connected in any attempt to force Sir Frederick's hand,' said Bruce. 'When was he here?'

The woman started to walk towards the stairs that loomed in front of them.

'The day before yesterday, and yesterday morning. A man I disliked intensely, he seemed no better than a French guttersnipe. I believe that he put some kind of proposition to my brother.'

'You don't know what kind?'

'No.' Murdoch fancied that there was a slight hesitation before she uttered the negative, but she went on quickly. 'That is unusual, for my brother usually discusses business with me, even important matters unless they are official secrets.'

'For some reason,' Bruce said gently, 'Arnould frightened you.. He scared me last night too.'

'Last night!'

'I interviewed the gentleman, but I don't know where he is at the moment. However, that's immaterial. Another question, Miss Allaway. Was Sir Frederick planning any kind of trip?'

'Not to my knowledge. Why?'

'It occurred to me that he might have started earlier than was expected,' said Bruce, and for the first time he saw impatience in Henrietta's brown eyes.

'Nonsense. He was taken from here by force.' She did not speak again until they had reached a door on the first landing. She turned the handle and flung the door open, for Bruce to step through and see the chaos beyond. Except for a massive mahogany desk by the window, and equally massive mahogany bookcases at two walls, not a stick of furniture remained upright. It seemed the scene of a free-for-all among a dozen men, not a hand-to-hand scuffle for two or three. A vase of hothouse roses was smashed and the water had soaked into the deep pile carpet, the roses were trodden to bits; but one bloom had escaped. A small table was overturned and a leg was broken off. Two chairs were against the wall, one also broken. Two leather easy chairs were upturned, their cushions flung in separate corners. A dozen smaller ornaments were broken on the floor.

Bruce's lips tightened.

'And this happened this morning, when the household was awake?'

'It did, Mr Morely. The study is specially constructed and is insulated against sound. I do not find it surprising that no one was disturbed.'

'Oh.' She had cut the ground from under his feet, and he knew that unless he were careful she would assume

69

an ascendancy over him, rob him of the initiative. 'Was the safe touched?'

'It is not open.'

'Who had the keys?'

'Sir Frederick always carried them.'

'And would be likely to have them now,' Murdoch mused. 'Has anything been stolen?'

'Nothing as far as I am aware.'

'I don't expect to find much, Miss Allaway, but I'm going to look for the sake of looking, and I would like that safe opened. A safe expert might be able to do it within an hour, but if there is a duplicate key anywhere it would be helpful.'

The fiery eyes seemed to smoulder, but if she had a question in her mind she kept it from him.

'He kept one at his bank, but I doubt whether the manager will surrender it.'

'It can be arranged,' said Bruce, and without asking permission lifted the telephone and called Holt. He told him that Arnould had been a visitor, and put the problem of the safe.

'All right, all right, I'll look after that,' said Holt briskly. 'Anything there?'

'Signs of a struggle,' said Bruce, and smiled grimly as he replaced the receiver.

Miss Allaway watched him with an air of faint contempt as he righted chairs, and looked over every inch of the room. It was not until he had finished the floor and he was going through the half-a-dozen pieces of paper that had remained on the desk when he saw that Allaway had been writing a letter, and had not found it easy. There were three starts, all written in the fine, sloping writing of the Diplomatic Adviser, and each began: 'Lucille.'

Murdoch was rigid for a moment as he saw them, then he relaxed and pushed the papers aside for a moment, as if they were of no account. But as he looked up at the woman, five words were humming through his mind:

*'Lucille, I must see you . . .'*

Could there be any other Lucille in this tangle than Lucille Devereux?

In ten minutes he learned that there was a narrow private staircase leading to the landing, which Allaway used occasionally when he did not want to disturb the household. It was fitted with a special lock, and as far as his sister knew only Allaway had the key. He inspected the staircase, saw that Allaway could have been taken out that way without being seen by servants, and could easily have been forced or lifted into a car waiting outside. In short, kidnapping had been made easy.

But no one had called at the front door.

'Which means,' Bruce said, 'that he had visitors by the side door, Miss Allaway, whose presence he was anxious to hide?'

'Are you suggesting that . . .'

'I'm stating facts,' said Bruce bluntly.

He broke off as a butler approached, with the news that a Miss Day had come to see Mr Morely. 'Day' was Mary's name when she was travelling *incognito*. There was little she could do, little more that he could: the police would have to come, although that depended on what attitude the Cabinet took of the affair. They could hardly ignore it; but they might feel it necessary to keep it completely hush-hush, even from the Yard.

Within twenty minutes of Mary's arrival, the manager of Allaway's bank and no less a person than the Rt. Hon. Vernon Glennister arrived simultaneously, and the safe was opened. Glennister pulled open the inner door, and Murdoch and Mary watched with a tension neither could properly explain.

And then Glennister gasped.

'It's empty. Completely empty!'

It was then, without warning and without a sound, that Henrietta Allaway collapsed.

.        .        .        .        .

'Yes, yes,' said the Pink 'Un testily. 'I know you're a secret agent and not a detective. You'd make a lousy detective anyway. But I wanted you to be there first, and you haven't made a bad job of it. Henrietta wouldn't have talked so freely to a policeman. I'm surprised she didn't insist on Glennie or someone like him going there first. If that thick head of yours holds any idea, let me have it.'

'It looks as if our man is after the common denominator, now that he's got the Papers,' Bruce replied. 'And he can only get it from Allaway.'

Holt breathed heavily through his nostrils.

'Oh, it looks like that, does it? It wouldn't tell a fifth-form schoolboy that someone is going to get Allaway and his Plan if he dies getting them? And,' he groaned, 'you've two years of a contract to run. Lord save me from fools.' He grinned, and plucked his chin. 'A bad business, Bruce. The one possible contact now is Arnould, unless the police pick up Devereux and his missus, which I somehow don't think is likely. They'll show a clean pair of heels. Anyhow, Lucille seems to have had a nice tight grip on Allaway, even if he has kept his love life very secret. Or so he thought.'

Bruce stared.

'Did you know?'

'Knew there was a lady, yes. Didn't know her name, every right to have his peccadilloes, particularly since he's a bachelor. He'd keep it quiet from Henrietta, though, she wouldn't be pleased, not a bit pleased. The woman had a flat in Bayswater, 21 Solway Street. You'd better get along there and do some more detecting.' His chins quivered. 'Keep him company, Mary, in case the

72

woman's there. I wouldn't trust him with a real beauty, and he was obviously impressed.'

'I'll look after him,' promised Mary.

'Good girl, good girl. And . . .' Holt stood up, frowned, looked at them sombrely. 'I needn't tell you it's bad, as bad as could be.'

Bruce nodded. Mary turned to the door. They hurried downstairs, walked to the Square, and took a cab to 21 Solway Street. They were not surprised to find the flat was locked and their knocking and ringing unanswered. The lock was beyond Bruce's skill with the skeleton key, and from a telephone kiosk nearby he 'phoned Holt.

'I'll arrange it, I'll arrange it,' said Holt. 'Rather you'd got in by yourself but the Yard'll send a good man. Only hope you don't find Allaway's body.'

'So do I,' said Bruce slowly.

But the thought had been in his mind, as well as Mary's, and they waited outside the flat soberly. In fifteen minutes a nondescript-looking man arrived, introduced himself with his warrant card as Detective Inspector Wilson, and in three minutes had the lock open.

'It's as well you're on the right side of the law,' smiled Bruce.

'Isn't it, sir? I had instructions for you to go in first. I'll wait here in case you need me.'

'Right,' said Bruce.

He stepped through, with Mary close behind him. He was prepared to find Allaway here, although it was more presentiment than probability. He found the lounge-hall empty, but three doors open and leading from it. In the second room he saw a pair of shoes sticking up at an odd angle from the floor behind the door.

He said: 'My God, we were right! A moment, Mary.'

He stepped through, prepared to find Allaway dead: his expectations were not realised, although the man lying on his back at the side of a single bed had been

73

killed by a bullet which had not treated the top of his head pleasantly.

But that did not prevent instant identification.

'Well,' Mary said softly.

'Lucille Devereux no longer has a husband,' said Bruce as softly.

# 8

# Did Henrietta Know

The grim determination of the Powers That Were to maintain absolute secrecy about the disappearance of Sir Frederick Allaway told Bruce and Mary how seriously the Allaway Papers were considered by the Government. But there were limits to what could be done by Bruce or Holt. A superintendent, large and stolid and with owlish, unwinking eyes, two sergeants who controlled the fingerprint and photographic work between them, and the discreet, nondescript-looking Detective Inspector Wilson were entrusted with the handling of the case, while the Chief Constable and the Assistant Commissioner for Crime were left in no doubt by the Home Secretary of the importance of finding Allaway *and* whoever had kidnapped him. The murder of Charles Devereux was considered important only in as far as it affected the Allaway case.

The wheel of the police began to turn.

The clerk who had been missing from the War Office and later seen in a Bournemouth restaurant at the same time as Devereux was held and questioned but the police were forced to admit that his story rang true—he had taken the Allaway Papers, he had posted them to a flat in Bournemouth, which was later proved to be a furnished one, and that was all he knew.

Sir Frederick Allaway had been meeting the tenant of

the Bayswater flat for some three months, and meeting her frequently. But only once had he been seen in public with her. The description available was sufficient to show that it had been Lucille, whose husband had been murdered at the flat where she had entertained Allaway.

Very discreet inquiries were made of the Coles, who—a little to Bruce's surprise—really were married, and lived in a pleasant Manor House near Romsey. It appeared that they had made a habit of dining at the White Swan before their marriage, and for sentimental reasons spent a few days there from time to time. As the sentiment had lasted for five years there was every reason to believe it genuine. Cole, in private life, was what he looked—a country squire of ample means, generous, well-liked, last of a family which had owned Frayle Manor for two hundred years. A man who had kept himself very much to himself, hunting, shooting, fishing, wining—but until Anne Cole had happened along, reputed to be a misogynist. Unimaginative, a firm Tory, a good landlord to his farmers—everything, in fact, that such a man should be.

That was the police report; and yet Cole had received several hundred pounds for papers which—Bruce believed—had been those stolen from the War Minister's Secretary's desk.

An effort to make Cole talk might have succeeded, but on the evidence of Bruce alone it would be difficult to frighten or indict him. Consequently a chunky young man named Fuller was sent to Frayle village, half-a-mile from the Manor, and given an object in life: watch the Coles. Mick Fuller was both an agent of Holt's and a friend of Bruce and Mary. Fuller, who had a rugged face and a quite unconventionally square and aggressive chin, declared bitterly that he would rusticate when he ought to be in the front line; and more cheerfully, that the Frayle Inn beer was drinkable.

Ted Angell, a tall, absurdly handsome man, who often

worked in concert with Fuller, was sent to the White Swan to watch Garsting, whose reputation was sound, according to the local police.

Of the Devereuxs, no trace could be found of their life prior to living at a furnished flat in Bournemouth, a more luxurious apartment than that to which the clerk had posted the Allaway Papers. They appeared to have sprung from nowhere into Bournemouth.

Nor was there any trace of Arnould or his man Victor.

Jem Dace was a more fruitful subject.

He had twice been 'inside', several times escaped a prison sentence by a technicality, was known to carry a gun, to have been employed as a driver to a smash-and-grab gang, to have spent three years in America until deported by an impatient Government, and to be generally undesirable. Three months prior to the outbreak of war Dace had disappeared from the Paddington Hotel where he had lived for some time: the next report of him had come from Bruce.

'All of which,' said Bruce to Sir Robert Holt, on the morning following his visit to Allaway's house, 'helps us not at all. Or can you see anything through the clouds?'

'I can't,' growled Holt. 'Why was Devereux killed?'

'Too unreliable for matters of importance. More pertinent, did Lucille get any trade secrets from Allaway?'

'Don't believe it likely, although she probably tried,' said Holt. 'The man might have been angered by this confounded Government, but he was *pro patria* all the way. Don't run off with the idea that Allaway's staged a disappearing trick. Now what is important, Bruce, is this—did Henrietta Allaway know about Lucille? Where did you find those letters?'

'On the desk, under a blotting-pad. She might have seen them, but they weren't visible just for the glancing.'

'What did you think of the woman?'

'I wouldn't like to cross her.'

Holt chuckled. 'She even withers me—sometimes! A

fanatic, Bruce, her one object in life to see Brother Freddie in the Cabinet. However, I can't do more than have her watched but there isn't likely to be any development there. Allaway's room *was* soundproof, and a car was seen standing outside the side door that morning, no number taken, no details available. Just a "big car". Have you presumed it was Arnould's?'

'It's likely.'

'That's right, keep careful all the time, you're in deep waters. Well now! Someone has the Papers—someone else has Allaway. Strip your mind of any other facts, they're the two that concern us. Allaway has the common denominator he believes will line-up neutral states against the aggressor nations. Our someone will try to make him talk about it. That's what we've got to stop.'

'I'd rather like to have the moon,' Bruce said slowly, and Holt scowled.

'Yes, I know, it's sticky all the way, but you and I fell down on a part of it, don't forget that. Could be *our* fault.' Holt plucked at his middle chin, stared owlishly at Bruce. 'Sorry to rub it in, but you've got to make amends. Somehow.'

'Yes,' said Bruce.

'First contact'—the Pink 'Un squared his shoulders—'is Arnould. You're seeing him tonight. Any ideas?'

'I can only stall him, and try to have him followed. That won't be easy in the blackout.'

'Try,' said Holt, and waved his hand in dismissal.

A blanket of gloom descended on Bruce Murdoch on the way back to his flat. The Pink 'Un had not hesitated to admit his personal part in the mistake that had been made, not to blame others for omitting to tell him of its seriousness. Nevertheless it had been a chapter of accidents the worse because Bruce and Mary had believed themselves to be doing well when they had in fact been doing badly.

Nor was Mary in high spirits.

78

Percy, who had arrived on the previous day prepared to be melancholy, had seen the signs of domestic distress and was abominably cheerful. His voice, which cracked on high notes, was too frequently heard—until Bruce snapped at him and Percy retired, much hurt, to prepare lunch. It was not, Bruce said to Mary, so much that there was no apparent likelihood of getting on Allaway's trail as the fact that the failure was partly their fault.

'*Must* you keep harping on that?' Mary asked sharply.

'Well, it's true, isn't it?'

'Oh, it's true all right. But going around like a starved cow won't help us.'

'Like a *what*?'

'A starved cow,' repeatel Mary defiantly.

'Good God,' said Bruce, 'and only two days ago I thought I was happy with you.'

'If we'd paid more attention to our job than ourselves we might have avoided this.'

'Thank you,' said Bruce, and there was a bleak expression in his eyes. 'We live and learn, and certainly we make mistakes.' He stood up from his chair, stepped to a cocktail cabinet, and poured himself a small finger of whisky, then drank it neat. He stood staring at Mary, who was eyeing him expressionlessly, then with a sudden venom he hurled the glass into the fireplace. It smashed into a hundred pieces, and a splinter struck Mary's hand.

She winced.

Bruce saw her lift her hand, then saw the blood welling up from the cut. She looked away from it and towards him, and he had never seen such an expression in her grey eyes. They seemed to hold all the hurt in the world.

'Oh, my God,' he said slowly. 'Mary, I . . .'

And quite suddenly he was kneeling with his arms about her, their lips were close, the tension had broken although the flood of self-reproach from Bruce was not easily stemmed. Percy came in very quietly, since he was on his dignity, stopped, widened his eyes, and retired with equal silence but no dignity. It was some ten minutes before Bruce entered the kitchen and demanded iodine, lint and sticking-plaster, half-an-hour before he called for lunch, by which time both he and Mary were feeling frolicsome, while Percy's injured feelings were fully healed. Over coffee, Bruce said reflectively:

'The general strain, sweet, has rather got me.'

'Yes,' said Mary. 'I know. I tried to jolt you out of it.'

Bruce stared. 'Mary, was "starved cow" meant *just* like that?'

'Of course, idiot! You were beginning to scare me. Bruce, you've worked for some time for Pinky, you've had a wonderful run of success, and something's gone seriously wrong for the first time. Things do go wrong in the game, they have to—while we've worked together we've been lucky in getting results. It could be that we won't hear another thing about Arnould or Lucille or Allaway, and if it turns out like that'—she shrugged—'there will soon be another job to handle.'

Bruce said: 'We're going to handle this one.'

'We can't *make* things happen.'

'We can have a damned good try!' Bruce stood up suddenly, thrust his hands in his pockets and paced the room. His chin was thrust forward, his square chin and large, humorous mouth set in a thin line. His eyes were frosty, but in his manner there was something that had been lacking for twenty-four hours, and Mary knew that she had succeeded in what she had been trying to do.

'Mary, why did Henrietta Allaway faint?'

'It was a pretty big shock, darling.'

'She'd had the shock. She isn't the fainting kind. There was something in the safe, and when she learned that it was empty she blacked out. The safe held a secret, perhaps the secret of it all, and—*she knew what it was.*'

80

Mary's eyes glistened.

'Bruce, you're assuming the Allaways were plotting something deliberately.'

'I'm not. I'm suggesting that they were up to some game which would make sure Allaway got his precious Ministerial post. And the proof of it was in the safe. Henrietta's the key, I'll stake a fortune on it. Henrietta, oh Henrietta, why haven't you told the truth? Get Pinky on the 'phone, Mary.'

As she did so he stepped up and down the room, staring at the carpet, digging his hands deep in his pockets. He grunted when he heard her call him, took the telephone, and said sharply:

'Pinky, how far can I go with this thing?'

'As far as you like.'

'*Carte blanche*?'

'How white?' demanded Holt with sudden caution.

'Third-degreeing Henrietta.'

There was a moment of silence at the other end of the 'phone, and then Holt chuckled.

'All right, all right, only you're doing this on your own. I can't answer for repercussions.'

'Damn repercussions. If I can make that woman crack I think we might have made a start. I'll report in due course, but if there's any unexpected move, may I have Mick and Ted at hand?'

'What kind of move?'

'Travelling probably.'

'Reason?'

'Allaway won't be kept in England any longer than the kidnappers can help.'

'I'll arrange for them to be at hand,' said the Pink 'Un, soberly for him. 'Cole and Garsting can be watched by others.'

Bruce turned from the 'phone to Mary, and there was a glint of laughter in his eyes, an enjoyment of the chase which had regained its savour, rehabilitation of himself which—as he realised subconsciously—was mostly Mary's doing.

'Darling, I'm positively bristling with ideas! We'll strike a hot line either through Henrietta or Arnould; be ready to go anywhere.'

'Can you be sure they're going to try to get Allaway out of the country?'

Bruce grinned. 'Reasonably. The only hope is that they take him to a neutral country and not a hostile one, but I've a strong impression that Arnould's at the back of this business, and Arnould is very much a man to work for himself. I'm going to have another talk with Henrietta. Meanwhile will you get packed, arrange two or three different passages out of England, look after the passports and visas and whatnot. Ditto for Ted, Mick and Percy. Especially Percy.'

He reached for his hat, as Mary said:

'Are you coming back before visiting the Regal?'

'Probably not, I'd like to see Arnould on my own. I'm taking the miniature camera, to get a likeness of him.' He gripped her hand, pressed tightly and hurt the cut although he did not know it and she said no word. 'The one essential is to get Allaway back, after all no one can blame us for letting *him* go. Everything else is an aside.'

'I know.'

'I know I love you,' said Bruce, and went out quickly.

.        .        .        ,        .

The blanket of depression which had followed the blanket of darkness following the first few days of the blackout in London had lifted considerably more than the A.R.P. restrictions themselves. London's night-life, in fact, was nearly normal. It was different, of course. The clubs and restaurants, theatres and bottle parties, had their sprinkling of khaki-clad revellers, the blue-grey of the R.A.F., the dark blue of the Navy. There was a greater gaiety, larger quantities of wine disppeared, hot numbers were in frequent demand, cabaret shows grew—slightly—more daring. By that time the first wounded had returned, the first batches of officers and men on leave were in England, and where there were bright lights it was considered the thing to make the fun fast and furious. The kill-joys claimed that morals were deteriorating, and Bruce Murdoch—who had strong views on many things—wondered just how far morals were important. There was no normalcy in life, except what appeared on the surface.

Out of the gloom of Piccadilly, through the revolving doors that made blacking-out easy, and into the brilliantly lighted Regal's foyer, he stepped just after half past six that evening. He would have to bluff and stall with Arnould, but he believed he could handle that.

He kept in the background. Too many people knew him as Bruce Murdoch, and he was essentially Mr Morely for the night. A stream of people passed him, time and time again the swing music from the band surged through from the restaurant-cum-dance-room as the doors opened. Three times couples entered and were ushered discreetly to the private dining-rooms upstairs.

Arnould was due at six-forty-five.

As the seconds ticked by, Bruce found himself growing impatient, and more than impatient. He felt tension, as if Arnould was standing in front of him with a gun in his hand, as he had on the lonely road. Murdoch recalled that moment of fright, and knew that Arnould was capable of creating it again. His forehead was cold and clammy.

'Jerk out of it,' he muttered, and his words were just audible, although no one was near enough to hear them. 'He's three minutes late. If he doesn't come . . .'

The swing doors opened again, and this time someone he knew had come through, although it was not Arnould.

Lucille Devereux entered, a vision in a black evening-gown, and looked about the foyer as though for her cavalier for the night.

*Lucille!*

She saw him, her lips parted and her smile dazzled. Hand outstretched she stepped towards him, and her throaty voice held a throbbing note.

'My darling, how good it is to see you. Am I *too* late?'

# 9

# And Again Lucille

Bruce took the proffered hand and found the pressure firm, bowed over it, and felt the upward movement, as if she expected him to carry it to his lips. He did so. As he straightened up, glowing violet eyes seemed at once to mock at him and yet plead for his interest. She whispered:

'Wonderfully well done, M'sieu Morely! I could almost imagine myself that you were glad to see me.'

Bruce forced himself to speak.

'How could I help but be?'

'So, you act even with me? But this is no place to talk, you are right. I am a messenger—so charming a messenger!—and what I have to say is important. I took the liberty of booking a private room for dinner, a *tête-à-tête*, does it attract you?'

'With such a messenger, of course.' Bruce felt his pulse racing, for she *was* beautiful. The bluish tinge in her black hair, set in a perfect coiffure free from ornaments, was more pronounced than he had noticed before. She had used mascara sparingly, enough only to lend added brilliance to her eyes.

'Wonderful! The room is seventeen.'

'Could there be a third party in Room Seventeen?' asked Bruce gently.

'My word on it, M'sieu, we shall be alone. I come

85

because it is not safe for Arnould to venture out, even by night.'

Bruce shrugged. 'I'll have to chance it!' He stepped towards an attendant, and gave him the number of the room. The man whisked them to the first floor, and opened the door of the room with a flourish.

'Dinner at once, sir?'

'No. We'd like a drink first.'

'A cabinet is in the room, sir, as requested.'

'Thank you. I'll ring when I need service.'

'Thank *you*, sir.' The man bowed like an automaton, and closed the door on them.

Bruce stood with his back to the door, while Lucille laughed into his eyes, and lifted a long, white arm so that her fingers brushed his cheek.

'So solemn, *chérie*?'

'Just a little sceptical,' said Bruce. He slipped past her to the second room of the small suite, opened the door, and made sure that it was empty. His eyes gleamed at the sight of two divan beds.

He had not heard her follow him, but her fingers were on his arm.

'It attracts, M'sieu?'

'It would delight me,' said Bruce, 'for a honeymoon.' His eyes sparkled at the sally, and Lucille laughed deep in her throat.

'M'sieu, at that place you were too serious for a newly-wed, both of you. Either you were long married, or you were anxious to pretend that you were. But does it worry me?' She did not answer her question, but frowned a little petulantly. 'Am I to take off my own cloak?'

'I'm sorry.'

He slipped it from her shoulders and as he did so she leaned back against him and looked at him with her head resting lightly on his chest. A subtle perfume added to her beauty, and he felt his heart beating fast. He pushed her gently away, and took out cigarettes. Shrugging, she

86

accepted one. Two streamers of smoke went upwards, and he mixed a sidecar, slowly and deliberately.

'You are hard-hearted, *chérie!*' she said.

'I'm soft-headed,' said Bruce. 'I'm taking the chance that the ingredients weren't doctored before I came. To success, Mrs Devereux.'

For a moment he saw naked hatred in her eyes, although whether for him or for the dead Devereux he did not know. She was as motionless as a marble statue, and the pallor of her arms and shoulders was of alabaster.

'Why do you remind me of that?'

'Remind you?' He looked puzzled.

'Of that creature who . . .' She broke off, and shrugged. 'It does not matter, but understand please that I am Lucille. And you, M'sieu, if the register at the Swan is to be believed, are Benjamin. It does not suit you. How much more attractive'—she cocked her head on one side, and smoke floated between her eyes and his—'some other name. A Scottish name, for you are from Scotland. Ian, shall it be? Or Robert? Or the great Bruce?'

'Why not plain Ben?' He laughed at her, finished his drink, and then motioned to a settee. 'Sit down, Lucille, I prefer you at a distance.'

'That is not . . .' Her expression had changed, but he waved impatiently.

'Not gallant, I know, but I haven't come here to be gallant. I hardly expected Arnould to try anything so banal as a seduction scene. This is strictly business. Is that clear?'

Slowly, she sat down. Her eyes were expressionless, but the only thing he could be sure about was that she was not amused.

'So—business. That is a Scottish habit, is it not? Pleasure always comes afterwards.'

'I choose my pleasures.'

'You are offensive!'

'And likely to be. Why did you reserve this room?

Any business we have to do can be handled in five minutes, and without such expense.'

'You can be too sure.'

He shrugged impatiently.

'All right, let's have it. Arnould was to have met me here, but he's too scared to come out even in the dark. Or is he scared of me?'

'He does not like you, and it is not wise to offend him.'

'It's not wise to hold me up with a gun,' retorted Bruce. 'He may have his precious gang of roughnecks, but nothing about him or his friends has worried me yet, which includes *you*. And before we talk about the Allaway Papers . . .'

She was so startled that she half-rose from the settee. Bruce forced back a smile of sheer elation, for he had confirmed beyond reasonable doubt that Arnould was interested in the Allaway Papers; it was a minor success which bolstered up his vanity. He scowled, and deliberately lit a second cigarette from the butt of his first. As he faced her he operated a small camera, the lens of which was visible but hardly visible in a waistcoat buttonhole. He felt the need of a likeness of Lucille for future reference.

'I'm not in this for fun, Lucille, and I know just what I'm after and what Arnould's after. I . . .'

'How did you know?'

'People talk,' he said. 'Talk gets overheard. You and Mr Devereux were not always as discreet at the flat as you hoped. You forgot that walls do sometimes have ears.'

Beneath her rouge she had gone quite pale. She stared without speaking for twenty seconds, and now he knew that the hatred in her eyes was for Devereux. He found it nauseating that she should feel like that towards a dead man; it seemed to strip her of her beauty, emphasised the bone formation of her face, gave him a momentary

88

illusion of a death's head. It was uncanny and disturbing, until she spoke.

'That—*imbecile*! He . . .'

'He was not alone in talking,' interrupted Bruce.

'He would always talk, he . . .' She drew a deep breath. 'Forget him! What else do you know?'

'That the Allaway Papers are worth much more than a thousand pounds.'

'And then?'

'I'm selling papers, not giving information,' he said.

'You cannot sell what you have not got,' flashed Lucille. 'Those papers are quite safe. Arnould sends me to discuss other things.'

'So he's got them, has he?' Bruce said softly.

'Of course he has. I gave them to him. Had he known I had taken them from Cole in the first place, he would not have worried to contact with you—contact, that is right?' She had forgotten the earlier seductiveness, and was talking quickly, her words running into each other. Bruce dared hardly breathe, for fear of breaking her chain of thought. 'That fool Smith was the trouble. He was nearby and told Arnould that you had left, but did not notice me when I started. Arnould came to me to say the papers were lost, but *I* had them. He has, now. I . . .'

She stopped, then smiled slowly, the gleam returning to her eyes.

'I am talking much, M'sieu, perhaps too much.'

'Of nothing that matters,' said Bruce sharply. 'I knew you had the papers and hoped to get them through him —and for a consideration. That's fallen through, and I'm not interested in you or Arnould. I've a living to make.'

'It is difficult.'

'I've known worse.'

'It can be much easier, M'sieu. Arnould, he is remarkably clever, and he is arranging a triumph that will make one thousand pounds a thing to laugh at. You can help him.'

Bruce stared at her for a moment, then said intently: 'Just how?'

'That can be discussed later.'

'Later means danger, and I mean to keep myself free of it.'

'Just what are you doing, M'sieu?' Lucille demanded.

'Feathering my own nest while the going's good. Doing the same as Arnould, in fact. The Allaway Papers job is very important, in a day or two there'll be a big hue-and-cry. It's not a thing I want to stay with long. No, I'm not interested in Arnould's proposition, whatever it is. A man who will attempt a hold-up on a main road lacks something, and that something is caution.'

'He is lacking nothing,' said Lucille quietly. 'The situation was desperate, that is all. He had to come to see that the Coles could supply the Papers, he was told "yes" for I told him so myself, and when they were stolen, when you went off hurriedly in the darkness of the night, he felt sure that you had got them. He knew, of course, that you were not just there for a holiday.'

'All this talk leads nowhere.'

'There is something you can do,' said Lucille gently, 'for which he will pay five thousand pounds. A simple task.'

'Five thousand for a simple task?' Bruce barked. 'No, it doesn't impress me. Arnould is getting his fingers burned over the Allaway Papers job, and he's looking for someone else to take the rub when it comes. I'm not so easy; each for himself is my motto.'

He saw that her anger was rising.

'So we understand you are just a fool! You would be useless to him!'

'Then we needn't keep talking. Are you going to eat, or save the time?'

'Does five thousand pounds mean nothing to you?' she demanded incredulously.

'It means five thousand pounds, and I'd like it, but I want to know what it's about before I make any kind of promises.'

'It is very simple,' she said, and something in her manner told him that she was not trying to trick him into any commitment. 'At the White Swan you gave an address to a policeman, of a cottage near the Dorset coast.'

Bruce stared, expressionless but with his heart thumping. She knew where he lived when off duty, that Mary lived there; he felt quite certain that by now she, or Arnould, would have made the necessary inquiries. It made her a thousand times more dangerous for it opened up the possibility that she knew what he was.

He answered flatly: 'That is my business.'

'I hope it will be ours. Understand, it is simple, M'sieu. The cottage is needed only for a day, just one day, while a friend of ours stays there. During the night a boat will take him from the mainland to a ship at sea. It is someone who wishes to leave this country without being seen. It is of the utmost importance. Arnould, I know, would pay half now, the other when the boat arrives. For one who is feathering—what you say?—his nest, is it not an easy opportunity?'

# 10

# Cliff Cottage

Bruce took his cigarette from his lips. For perhaps thirty seconds he stood like that, watching her, wondering just how much of the truth she had told him, seeing the vast possibilities in her proposition.

She could not know him as Holt's agent.

And—who else but *Allaway* could Arnould want to smuggle out of England?

Her admission about the Allaway Papers, Arnould's two visits to the Norton Road house, and the disappearance of the Diplomatic Adviser made it seem feasible. And if he were right—he had little doubt of that—she was asking him to help smuggle out of England the very man he had to find.

'Why are you so silent?' she asked, and the brittleness of her voice told him she was desperately anxious for his answer.

'I was just wondering,' said Murdoch slowly, 'how far I could trust you and Arnould.'

'Trust us! It is we who are trusting you!'

'Arnould couldn't wish someone on to me, someone the police are looking for, and let it be known he'll be at my cottage, could he?'

Lucille laughed, a deep contralto laugh which seemed to wrap itself about him. She leaned back so that the lines of her slender throat were emphasised, and he could see her tongue quivering against her teeth.

'What's funny about that?' he demanded.

'My—dear—M'sieu!' She tried to steady her voice, laughed again, then regained her control; but her eyes were brimming as she looked at him. 'It is all so funny! Here is Arnould so anxious for your help, I could even say desperate—and here are you imagining such a thing. You have the careful mind, too careful. It is why you are not a great success, like Arnould.'

'I do all right,' said Bruce coldly.

'You think in hundreds, he deals in thousands always. 'And'—she was completely serious again—'this would be one of many such tasks. For your co-operation it would be a great reward, and it would be so safe. You and your lady you are English, not suspect. Cliff Cottage is lonely, but nearby there is a little bay where the boat can be brought in. You see, we have seen it, and learned how well it would serve for our purpose. I ask you, M'sieu, to think again.'

'I'll have to talk with Mary, and . . .'

'No, M'sieu! You have to decide tonight. Arnould wished to see you, I was to take you to him but I saw you would be obstinate. I had permission to make this offer, even . . .' She took her handbag from the settee, opened it quickly, and extracted a thin bundle of Bank of England notes. She counted them swiftly, lifting each one.

'A hundred pounds each, M'sieu—twenty-two, twenty-three, twenty-four, twenty-five! They are not dangerous, these notes, they are . . .'

'I wouldn't touch them with a barge-pole,' said Bruce brusquely. 'But I'll do the job, provided you bring all the cash in smaller notes when you bring the man you want me to look after. If the notes are clean, your man stays. If they're not, he doesn't. When is it to be?'

Lucille looked at him, and some measure of her relief communicated itself to him. He wondered whether it was relief at the thought that she had carried out Arnould's order, or at the solution of the smuggling problem.

'A thousand thanks, M'sieu Morely! Ring, please, we must have champagne, this must be celebrated! And then . . .'

'And then we go,' said Bruce firmly, 'after a quick dinner. I've arrangements to make. When is it to be?'

'Tomorrow—when else?' replied Lucille. 'But you have a heart like ice, M'sieu.' She looked towards the communicating door, and then at him with her bold eyes inviting.

Bruce smiled sardonically.

'Business first,' he said, 'and pleasure afterwards.'

Lucille laughed, but in it he fancied he detected a note of genuine disappointment.

.        .        .        .        .

The Pink 'Un smiled benignly on the Prime Minister, Marridew, Kershing and Glennister. The first he tolerated, the last two he liked, and consequently he felt that he could bear with them. Moreover Marridew was in a harassed, almost apologetic frame of mind. After all it was his first term of office, and the Allaway business could easily break him. That a trivial error on the part of a permanent official could even make such a disaster possible gave the little, black-haired Minister for War very human anxieties. He was, too, genuinely alarmed; the disaster could affect the Allies. He had everything to lose—his post, his self-conceit, and his easy conscience.

The three distinguished gentlemen had been at Number 10 when Holt and Glennister had arrived, and Holt wasted little time in preliminaries.

'Well, gentlemen, I've some news for you.'

'About Allaway?' exclaimed Marridew sharply.

'About the same case,' said Sir Robert, shaking his

head in benevolent reproof. 'Can't expect miracles to happen, you know, Marridew; got to give even Secret Intelligence time.'

'Holt, I need hardly emphasise the importance of this.' The Prime Minister's ascetic face was lined and troubled. 'It will be a disaster of the first magnitude if he is not found.'

Holt raised both hands.

'My dear Prime Minister, *everything* possible is being done, you have the police assurance that they can find nothing, *nothing*, and their belief that Allaway has been smuggled out of the country.'

'If he has . . .'

'I am simply emphasising the official viewpoint of the police. They can see no angle on which to work.' Holt's lips puckered babyishly. 'I *have* found an angle. To be strictly truthful, one of my men has found it. A brilliant young man, doesn't know the meaning of carelessness.' Holt dared a wicked glance at Marridew. 'I cannot promise that he knows where Allaway is, or who was responsible for the outrage . . .' Glennister had to bite on a chuckle, for Holt was imitating Marridew's precise diction superbly—'but he knows who has the Allaway Papers, and he is to make contact with that gentleman today.'

The Prime Minister stared incredulously.

'Are you *sure*?'

'Is this absolutely certain?' exclaimed Marridew.

'No doubt, no doubt at all,' declared Sir Robert genially. 'I'll have some word for you by midnight to-night.'

'It—it is a remarkable achievement,' said Marridew.

The Pink 'Un chuckled.

'I shall probably want an O.M. for my man after this, P.M. It's time the Service was acknowledged. Well, I'm off. Anyone coming my way?'

'I am,' said Glennister.

Outside, and walking through St. James's Park, the Foreign Secretary looked humorously at his friend. Glennister was tall and dark and some said saturnine, but he was a first-class man for his job.

'Are you really sure, Bob?'

'Sure I've got something, yes. Cheered them up a bit, least I could do when all's said and done. I'm going to seed, I felt almost sorry for Marridew. Engaged for dinner tonight?'

'No, Meg and I are dining at home. Can you come?'

'Wouldn't be away from Sloane Square tonight for a fortune.' The Pink 'Un lowered his voice. He told of a report Murdoch had telephoned, of the coming rendez-vous at Cliff Cottage, of the fact that Ted Angell and Mick Fuller would be near the spot, with two other agents also holding a watching brief. There would be no concentration of the police, since they had to make sure that Arnould was not frightened away.

'I'm going to bring Meg to Sloane Square for dinner,' Glennister said, 'and we're staying until news is through.'

'Welcome, welcome!' said the Pink 'Un in high glee. 'Glad to see Meg again, she's the only thing about you that makes me jealous. Nice lad, young Murdoch. Made him feel like hell on earth saying he'd pulled a boner which was as much my fault as his, and this is the result. He needed a little more motive power, which reminds me I've got to alter their contracts.' He beamed at Glennister, who was one of the few who understood the Pink 'Un's abrupt changes of manner and subject, and then chuckled. 'So Henrietta Allaway, bless her, won't be alone for long. How is she?'

'She's been nearly prostrate all day,' said Glennister soberly.

'Tell you a funny story,' said Holt.

'All right,' said Glennister resignedly.

'Murdoch wanted to third degree her,' rejoiced the

96

Pink 'Un, and slapped his thigh. 'Third degree Henrietta! Glennie, that boy's going a long, long way!'

.    .    .    .    .

Cliff Cottage was a genuine Tudor relic built for some absurd reason on the edge of the cliffs overlooking the Channel with a row of stately elms between it and the cliff edge, with the thinly-wooded Dorset countryside beyond. It was not far from Lulworth Cove, and had a tiny cove of its own.

Bruce and Mary had spent months of planning, working and scheming to make it what it was; experts had put their heads together to have modernisation without spoilation. It looked a delight from the outside, and was a delight in.

A warm sun shone at midday as Percival Briggs turned Bruce's Lagonda into the drive leading to the cottage. Percival wore a chauffeur's hat and coat, and had driven down with hardly a word, outraged beyond measure at being brought from Dorset to London and taken again from London to Dorset before he had had a night out.

As he pulled up outside the front porch, he turned slowly and deliberately in the driving-seat, and said clearly:

'Did you just wanter look at it, sir, or was you thinkin' of goin' in?'

Bruce and Mary laughed spontaneously. Percy's bright eyes twinkled as he stepped out.

'Offers me apologies, sir, no offence meant and none took I 'ope. Got the place all clean and tidy. I'll have some food in a matter o' jiffs, there's a coupler pieces o' rump steak in the fridge. I got it for me lunch day before yesterday. Chips or *sauté*, sir?'

'*Sauté*, tomatoes, a sausage or two and in a hurry,' said Bruce.

Percy took the car to the garage at the rear, while

Bruce turned the key in the lock. He felt a quiet joy when going inside with Mary. It was so much their home, and would be more so when their contracts expired and they could marry. The warmth, coupled with the keenness of the clear Dorset air, had brought a sparkle to Mary's cheeks and eyes. They entered the long, low-ceilinged lounge, illuminated at night by wall lamps cunningly hidden and revealing the oak beams and the panelling in all their solidity. The brown leather suite merged with the polished oak floor and the two bear rugs, one at each end. A fire was set in the red-brick inglenook fireplace, and Bruce stepped past a high chair to put a match to it.

'Good morning, Mr Morely.'

The words came as suddenly as that, without the slightest warning, or intimation of anyone's presence. A smooth voice, with clear enunciation but an unmistakable accent, and the sound of it made Bruce stop short, his heart missing a beat, and made Mary stifle a gasp.

Arnould was sitting in the high-backed chair, and on his knees was an automatic.

Bruce straightened up slowly. It was the first time he had seen the man in daylight, and he was no better impressed than he had been by night. The swarthy, immobile features, the thin lips twisted slightly at one corner, the narrowed, near-black eyes watching Bruce unwinking, held menace. Even sitting, Arnould's head was still lifted a little; for the first time Bruce realised that the reason was a slight deformity of the neck.

Bruce said evenly: 'Good morning.'

Arnould smiled thinly; his teeth were small and very white.

'You take shocks well, I will admit. Don't stand there, Miss Day . . .' He used the name Mary was known by at the cottage. 'You waited behind me once before, with unfortunate consequences. However, Victor is watching you this time.'

The curtains stirred, and the tall, saturnine Victor stepped out, without speaking. Mary dropped onto the couch and tried to quieten her heart.

'Just what does this mean?' asked Bruce.

'It means,' said Arnould carefully, 'that I wished to test your reaction to a flank attack, Mr Morely. Most satisfactory, I am happy to say.' He slipped the gun into his pocket and spread his hands out. 'Please light the fire.'

Bruce struck a match. Pitch-pine logs soon blazed and began to crackle, resin bubbled and seethed. Bruce stepped to a cocktail cabinet.

'A drink?'

'Thank you, no, I am a teetotaller. So is Victor. But please have one yourself.'

'I propose to,' said Bruce drily. 'Have you been here long?'

'Some twenty minutes.'

'You might have started the fire.' Bruce mixed a weak whisky-and-soda for Mary, a stronger one for himself. 'Does this indicate any change of plans?'

'It does not,' said Arnould, and his eyes narrowed. 'You are not considering any such alteration, I hope.'

'If I say a thing I mean it, but I don't like your methods.'

'I have always found them most satisfactory. But we need not go further into that. Can you provide lunch?'

'My man can.'

'Your who?' Arnould looked startled, and sat up.

Bruce chuckled, and said easily: 'You always forget someone, this time it's my man. He's in the kitchen, preparing lunch.'

'He wasn't here . . .'

'He drove us down. Listen to me, Arnould.' Bruce eyed the Frenchman soberly as he sat down opposite him. 'Lucille seemed well impressed by you, but I've been working in this business long enough to know you

99

are not a regular. Your mistakes come too often. What you're doing is no concern of mine, but it will be my concern if you make mistakes that bring police down here.'

Arnould's lips twisted.

'Your opinion of yourself has not altered, I see. No one will come here, except my friends.'

'How many?'

'Lucille, two men, and'—the thin sloping shoulders moved—'the passenger.'

'That sounds all right,' Bruce said. 'Very well, I'll tell my man to make lunch for four, but you'll have to do with what we've got.' He nodded, and went into the hallway and then the kitchen.

Percy, unaware of what had happened, was standing over the electric stove.

'Won't be long now, sir. Steak's a bit of all right.'

'Make it for four,' said Bruce, and as Percy stared added quietly: 'Visitors, and you won't like them. Don't show it. Do whatever you're asked to do, and remember I am Morely. Give the impression that your past is not blameless, and see what you can make of the man Victor, who will join you in the kitchen.'

'Gorblimey,' said Percy faintly.

'I won't have a chance of telling you what's happening, but Mr Fuller, Mr Angell and two others will be at hand if they're wanted.'

'Perish me innards,' gasped Percy. 'I—oh, all okey-doke, sir, suits you suits me. You would 'ave enjoyed all of that steak though.'

It was a strained meal, for Arnould made no conversation and blanketed the others with his silence. He ate stiffly and slowly, masticating each mouthful until Mary wanted to scream. Not until they were finished, and coffee had been served in the lounge, did he make more than a trivial comment.

100

'Well, Morely, you have a pleasant house here. A piece, it might be said, of old England.'

'It might,' agreed Bruce.

'And so convenient. A man of your—er—varied experience will need no telling that there is a great demand for conveyance out of England at this time, the sending of messages to ships outside English waters—that and many things. This would appear to be an admirable spot for such activities.'

Bruce eyed him stonily.

'I'm not so sure. We'll get this job finished first.'

'It is, I agree, the most important, but we shall come to terms for the future. What kind of experience have you had?'

Bruce met the narrowed, unwinking eyes.

'Plenty, thanks.'

'Always in espionage?'

'For the last three years.'

'For which master?'

Bruce said slowly: 'I haven't any master, I sell to the highest bidder *if* he's safe. I don't propose to have any master. I don't trust you, Arnould, and I won't until I've proved you're trustworthy. Am I understood?'

'You are,' said Arnould. 'We will discuss it later, your frankness is at least refreshing. Now . . .' He glanced at a fob-watch, and looked up. 'It is nearly fifteen o'clock. The others are due now. Until they have left, the bedrooms must be at our disposal.'

'You're not bringing invalids, are you?'

'That,' murmured Arnould, 'is my business.'

He broke off, and stepped towards the window. Bruce and Mary heard the hum of an approaching car engine, and followed the little Frenchman. They saw a closed Daimler car swing into the drive, and Bruce recognised Lucille in the back, but he had seen neither the driver nor the other male passenger before.

Two men, then, and Lucille.

101

Where was the third, the passenger?

He was startled by Arnould's voice in his ear.

'You show your curiosity, Morely, in your eyes. It is as well not to be curious. Go from the window, and wait until the car is empty. Do not forget,' he added suavely, 'that I have Victor as well as these two men, and Lucille.'

Bruce said: 'Before the passenger comes in here, I want twenty-five hundred pounds, half the agreed sum. Whether I see him or not doesn't matter.'

Arnould sneered: 'The money is in my bag, the bag is standing by your chair. Examine it, please.'

It was a small brown attaché case, and Bruce opened it, tightening his lips at the sight of the thick wads of money. He could not rid himself of his fear of Arnould, a feeling that the man was always thinking and planning something unspeakable—and unknown. But he showed no signs, and Mary maintained an outward calm.

The front door opened, although they had not heard Victor approach it; yet they knew the tall Frenchman was there. Lucille came sweeping through the doorway, dressed in a tight-fitting black coat trimmed with astrakhan, and with a small hat worn to one side. She lifted a hand towards Bruce and Mary.

'So we come, my friends. It is all right, Arnould, the journey has been a good one.'

'Entertain M'sieu Morely,' said Arnould sharply.

It was unquestionably an order, and Arnould went out, walking in his curiously furtive fashion and, seen from the rear, with his head raised more than it appeared to be from the front. He closed the lounge door, and Lucille unloosened her coat in front of the fire.

'It is cold, yes, but what you would call glorious? The sun—we were lucky for such a day. And this house, M'sieu, a delight in all ways. I am proud to have introduced you to Arnould. You have not . . .' She seemed

102

anxious. 'I imagine that he is a little less pleased than I had hoped.'

'I don't like Arnould,' said Bruce, 'and nothing he's done today is going to make me change.'

As he stopped, something heavy dropped in the hall, and a man exclaimed in a hoarse voice:

'Be careful, you clumsy lout.'

It was Cockney, but not Percy's voice, which intimated that Arnould recruited some help from the East End. But the words and the sound together made him and Mary realise that the two men were carrying a large box.

But there was no 'passenger'.

Footsteps sounded heavily and noisily on the stairs. There was a bump again, and a curse. A few seconds of silence, and then a thud as something was dropped on the floor in the room immediately above them.

Lucille was talking quickly, but only giving half her attention to what she was saying, and she broke off as Bruce moved towards the door.

'M'sieu—where do you go?'

'I'm going upstairs,' said Bruce evenly.

'You are not, you . . .'

'Lucille,' said Mary gently; and Lucille turned, to see an automatic trained on her, while Bruce reached the passage and hurried up the stairs. He saw a door standing ajar, and the back of a man bending almost double. He went further forward, until he was able to see the crate itself, which was opened, and from which a body was being lifted.

He had his right hand in his coat pocket, ready for any emergency, and he felt that the beating of his heart must surely be heard. But he forgot that, forgot everything in what he saw.

They lifted the body—alive or dead Bruce did not know.

It was not Allaway, for it was a woman.

Henrietta, her face grey, her eyes tightly closed, her lips compressed and with a predatory expression even in immobility, was raised from the crate and rested on the single bed.

## 11

# The Efficiency of Arnould

To pretend he had not seen her would be useless; even if he escaped downstairs unseen, Lucille would talk. Bruce stood by the open door, looking away from the woman and across the room to where Arnould was staring down. Arnould's face was expressionless.

'Is she dead?' rasped Bruce.

He had the satisfaction of seeing Arnould jump and the two men started violently. One moved his right hand towards his gun, but Bruce's was in sight, and Bruce said sharply:

'And don't try to be clever.'

Arnould moistened his lips.

'My orders . . .'

'No one gives orders in my house. You've got the wrong end of the stick altogether, and it's time we had a showdown. Is she dead?'

'No.' The monosyllable was like an oath.

'Then what is the matter with her?'

'She is drugged. Now go downstairs.'

'When I've made sure she's alive, I will,' growled Bruce. 'I'll harbour no corpses for you or anyone.' He put his gun back in his pocket, stepped to the dressing-table and lifted a hand-mirror. He leaned towards Henrietta, and held the glass in front of her lips. It clouded immediately, and he nodded. 'All right, Arnould. But remember one thing.'

'What is that?'

'You're not the only one with friends. Don't try any tricks while you're here, or you won't get away.'

He had never seen hatred nor malevolence so naked in a man's eyes; he would not have believed a human mouth could have turned back over his teeth to show the same snarling, bestial expression. He felt a clammy sweat at his forehead and the nape of his neck, but he continued to glare at Arnould.

Seconds passed.

Arnould drew a long, slow breath.

'You are very clever, Morely. I hope you will not be too clever. Who is near this place?'

'Friends of mine,' Bruce replied roughly, and turned to the door, ignoring the two roughnecks, who made way for him. He walked slowly down the stairs, and entered the lounge. Lucille, her expression strained, leapt from a chair and approached him, her hands raised as high as her breast.

'Did you see . . .'

'I saw the woman, yes. And you lied, you said a man.'

Mary was looking at him, but Lucille's back was towards her and Lucille could not see the sharp disappointment, mingled with surprise, in Mary's eyes.

'I did not know then,' said Lucille. 'I—Morely, you fool, you ten times a fool! You have disobeyed Arnould.'

'I can handle Arnould,' said Bruce sharply. He stepped to the window, and peered out into the garden, where a faint mist was creeping in from the sea. Beyond the elms he could see the blue-grey waters, for the sun was no longer shining brilliantly, being partly hidden by the mist. He leaned forward and opened a window, as if he needed a breath of fresh air. For three minutes there was no sound in the room, and then he turned back, ignoring Lucille.

'I can't get rid of a feeling that this job is too dangerous,' he said to Mary. 'I wish to God we'd never touched it.'

'But you have,' said Arnould.

The little man had entered with his uncanny, furtive silence, and he was alone. He shot a venomous glance towards Bruce but addressed Lucille.

'Why did you let him come?'

'The—the woman showed a gun.'

'It is not important now that it has happened. Morely, you may know now that the boat will be at the inlet at half past six, for the evening tide, and the woman will be transferred then. Did you recognise her?'

Bruce frowned.

'No. Should I have done?'

'Forget that.' Arnould turned to the fire and warmed his hands, speaking as he did so. 'You are efficient, and you have courage, but your mind is too much your own. I can use you, Morely, but I must have your implicit obedience.'

Bruce said: I've told you before, I work a lone hand. Anyone who works with me works for me, although I've no objection to a fifty-fifty cut if the stakes are high enough. How are you going to spend the time between now and half past six?'

'I can amuse myself.'

'I was thinking of myself. The bedrooms have easy chairs.'

Arnould stared, and then for the first time in Murdoch's hearing he laughed. It was a soft, clucking sound, seeming to originate in his throat, and although he was amused it did not make him seem a genial soul.

'Certainly, Mr Morely, you do not mince words. You will perhaps have some refreshments served upstairs. Come, Lucille.'

He went out after the woman, closing the door behind him. Mary stepped towards Bruce, but the latter went to the door, waited a moment, and then opened it.

Arnould was halfway upstairs. Bruce closed and locked the door, and then sat on the settee in front of the fire, his forehead wrinkled in bewilderment and disappointment. Mary pulled a pouffe close, and sat down.

'So we guessed wrongly.'

'About fifty per cent wrongly,' said Bruce gruffly. 'It's Allaway's sister. She knows something or Arnould thinks she does, about the Allaway Papers; and so we've scored half a point. Arnould and the others are satisfied with our motives, and that's also useful. But where the devil's Allaway?'

'Could they have smuggled him out of the country already?'

'If they have, why not use the same means for Henrietta? Mary, we're further forward, but not much. Arnould's our man, we've got to let him go and follow him. I signalled Ted, so Pinky will have word fairly soon. He won't be pleased.'

'Are any of us?' Mary shivered. 'Arnould's like—a ghoul.'

'I'm not sure,' said Bruce slowly, 'that he isn't one.'

.　　.　　.　　.　　.

Mr Edward Angell, who for some hours had been cramped behind a clump of bushes close to the edge of the cliff opposite the cottage, saw the right-hand window of the lounge open, and Bruce standing there. Mr Angell, who had a habit of commenting to himself in sepulchral tones, confessed that he was jiggered.

He scrambled down twenty feet of the cliff to a path that could not be seen from the cottage, then walked hurriedly along it until, after fifteen minutes, he reached a tiny hamlet which possessed a telephone kiosk. He telephoned Holt and was somewhat relieved to find that Holt was out, and that Gordon had instructions to take messages.

'We're all wrong,' said Angell glumly. 'Break the news gently to him, Gordon. Just say it was the sister not the man. And that I'm standing by for further word from our Mr Murdoch.'

'Very good, sir.'

'And make me some nice, strong, Indian tea,' said Angell, still glumly. 'It's perishing cold here, Gordon.'

'I'm sorry to hear that, sir.'

'You're not as sorry as I,' complained Angell.

He returned along the cliff walk but went some three hundred yards further along, scrambled up the cliff, and reaching the top, saw a rugged, square-jawed face turned towards him. This was of a man of medium height who looked short because of his unusual breadth of shoulder. Curly hair, the bane of Mr Michael Fuller's life, was tousled by the sea wind that was making the air chilly. About them were patches of mist, which seemed to be rising from the ground, and tufts of grass.

'How's tricks?' asked Mick Fuller, who could see the side of the cottage.

'Lousy. We've made a wrong guess, or at least Bruce and Pinky have, we didn't get the "rush to the rescue" sign, which means we'll probably be stuck in this perishing place all night, and can't even get a drink. Who thought of this?'

'Pinky, I expect. Ted, you're deserting your post.'

'I know, I hurried to the 'phone to take this five minutes, if I hadn't seen a face that didn't belong to a seagull I'd have gone crackers.'

'Gone?' asked Fuller pointedly.

Angell grinned, and went back to his post. Nothing else happened at the cottage, and slowly the shades of night closed down. There were no stars, and no moon, for dark clouds were scudding across the sky, to take revenge for the brilliance of the day. The wind was rising, the soft lap-lap of the incoming tide grew louder, and could be heard receding down the shingle. Angell turned the collar of his macintosh up, took a sip of whisky from a flask, and waited with considerable patience.

But from time to time he told the clump of bushes that anyone who worked for Sir Robert Holt was certifiably insane.

.        .        .        .        .

At a quarter past six it was dark, darker than on a normal night, for the clouds were thick, and a light rain was driving in the wind. At Cliff Cottage Bruce and Mary had been together in the lounge alone, from the moment Lucille and Arnould had gone upstairs. Occasional movements of the men above had disturbed them little, and Percy had been in but once, to say in an exaggerated whisper that he hadn't had a word out of the beggar yet: the beggar being the uncommunicative Victor.

If mystery surrounded the death of Devereux, there was no longer the possibility that Arnould and the Dees worked from separate angles. More, there was plenty of confirmation that Cole had sold the Allaway Papers. How Cole had procured them was not a matter for Bruce's attention just then.

Arnould probably worked for himself, not for an enemy Power; eventually he would sell to the highest bidder. But before he sold he would need Allaway's common denominator for the non-combatant countries; all he had to offer to date were the Papers. And if Murdoch judged the man aright, he would act cautiously until he had forced information out of Allaway. Once he had contrived that he would have a strong hand to use against either the German, British or French Governments, with Russia in the background as a possible buyer.

'All of which,' Mary said, 'is based on the assumption that Allaway was kidnapped by Arnould.'

'Since we know his sister has been, that's a more reasonable assumption than ever.'

'But not an established fact.'

Bruce grinned. 'Darling, since when have we been able to work on established facts?' He broke off, for there was a tap on the door. He went across and unlocked it, to see Arnould standing in the hall, his head cocked upwards and his eyes narrowed, the perpetual sneer on his lips.

'We are going to move, Morely. We shall want you with us to show the way to the inlet.'

'Yes, that's all right.'

'Miss Day, perhaps, will entertain Lucille,' said Arnould. 'As soon as the woman upstairs is safely away we shall remove ourselves.'

'Right,' said Murdoch. 'How are you taking her?'

'We have improvised a stretcher, that will be safe enough in the dark. There is just enough light to see without torches, but if you have one that complies with the regulations and will not attract attention I shall be glad.'

'I've several. Percy!'

Bruce went for the torches, while Arnould's two men came downstairs, carrying the unconscious Henrietta on a stretcher made of two bedroom chairs covered with blankets. From the kitchen came Victor, expressionless and unspeaking, a silent ghost of a man. Lucille entered the lounge, and sat down without a word to Mary. The Frenchwoman seemed on tenterhooks, as though afraid that something would go wrong.

'Hall light off,' said Bruce, after handing Arnould and Victor torches. 'Percy, stay in the hall with the door open, in case we need you. Come on, I'll lead the way.'

The faint glow of his torch shone downwards as he

stepped from the porch and along the short drive. The little party followed, Arnould and Victor on either side of the stretcher, and illuminating the ground so that the bearers should not stumble unnecessarily. As far as the gateway the going was easy, but then it was across rough grassland, and the men slipped and swore. Once Henrietta's head and shoulder were dropped, the stretcher hitting the ground with a thud. Henrietta's head, just visible in the ghostly light, jolted unpleasantly.

'Nom de nom, vous . . .'

Arnould's acquaintance with Montmartre oaths was comprehensive, and he spat the foulness viciously as the offender picked up his end of the stretcher. The man grunted but said nothing, and Arnould stopped, while Bruce felt that the night air had been polluted. Five minutes walking, which seemed much longer, took them to the rough steps cut into the cliff face. The wind whipped at their faces, gusts of stinging rain made the ground slippery, the roar of waves rolling on the shingle rose and faded against the strength of the wind.

'There's a wooden rail,' Bruce said, 'it'll give support but you'll need a man at each corner of the stretcher.'

'You will take one,' Arnould said, 'and Victor . . .'

'I'm going ahead, to make sure the steps are sound,' said Bruce. 'If we all fall we won't be much good at the bottom.' Inwardly he grinned at the discomfiture of Arnould, who took one corner of the stretcher.

It was a slow, perilous climb down.

The rough-hewn steps were greasy with the rain, and some had been eroded. Bruce kept himself braced all the time, for fear the others would fall and knock him off his balance. The breathing of all five men grew harder, the stretcher banged against the side of the steps. Once Arnould slipped, shouted, and would have fallen to the bottom but for Bruce, who turned in time to steady him. Even then the little Frenchman fell heavily on his backside.

112

'Ups-a-daisy,' said Bruce, and hauled him up. 'Be careful, we're only halfway.'

The climb seemed interminable, but at last they trod on shingle, and as they stepped forward the wind whipped a thick spray of sea hissing and falling about their feet. Twice Bruce shone his torch seawards, wondering if the boat had managed to reach the inlet; the entrance would be calm enough.

A blue light shone for a moment at the water's edge, not five yards from them.

'It is there!' snapped Arnould.

'Take it steadily,' Bruce said, 'the shingle gives.' Slowly, laboriously, they made their way to the blue light, and against the faint greyness of the sky they saw the figures of two men, with their oilskins glittering in the glow of the torch Arnould sent towards them. The torch also showed a fleshy face and a pair of thick lips Murdoch would not easily forget.

Smith—or Jem Dace—was with the boat.

No unnecessary word was spoken. Henrietta was taken from the stretcher, and two men chaired her to the boat, sitting her upright in the stern and then tying her, so that she would not fall overboard. Smith took the oars, the man with him sat behind the crook, while Murdoch, Victor, and the two men with Arnould, strained and heaved as they pushed the boat down the heavy shingle. Twice it stuck, but with the third heave the keel grated, and Smith dipped his oars in. Bruce had gone knee-deep in the sea; only Arnould stood high and dry.

'How far have they got to go in that?' Bruce demanded gruffly. 'There's a gale blowing-up, it won't live out there.'

'They will not be long, there is a launch.' Arnould turned back towards the steps, and for the first time was almost amiable. 'It has been well done, Morely. You see how easy it can be?'

113

'I can see,' muttered Bruce.

The testing time was coming, the time when things could really go wrong. He reached the top of the cliff, and turned right towards Cliff Cottage. The return journey was accomplished more speedily, and Arnould aimed to waste no time. Lucille was dressed ready for the journey.

'You will come with me, Lucille, Victor will drive. You'—Arnould turned to his two roughnecks—'will return with the Daimler. Morely, the balance of your money is in my car, you shall have it in five minutes.'

Everything was planned to the last detail, he was efficiency itself. The Daimler was taken away first, dimmed headlights forcing the driver to go slowly; Arnould's car pulled up outside the front door, and Victor handed out a bag which Murdoch opened and found filled with one-pound notes. Lucille stepped hurriedly into the back, and Victor let in the clutch.

Bruce, the torch in his hand, turned it deliberately towards the west, and swung it three times. No one saw him near the house, but as Arnould slammed the door sensation came.

The powerful headlamps of a car standing two hundred yards away stabbed out, bathing Cliff Cottage and the car in a sea of light that dazzled all but Bruce and Mary, for they were prepared for it. Holt's two reserve men were in the car. Angell and Fuller were nearby.

And from the side of the house came Percy, at the wheel of the Lagonda.

# 12

# Rush!

If there had ever been the slightest doubt in Murdoch's mind about the ruthless capability of Arnould, it was removed then. The emergency came with the suddenness of lightning, but the lights had barely shone across the garden and the nearby fields before Arnould snatched an automatic from his pocket. Bruce saw him lean forward, pull down the window, force Lucille back into a corner.

The headlights made the blue stabs from the automatic seem faint, but the roar of the shots were loud enough, there had been no time for fitting a silencer. A split-second—and the sea of light was halved, there was a crash as a bullet bit into the headlamp of the car which had been stationed there by arrangement—an arrangement calculated to make Arnould lose his head.

Victor let in the clutch, and the car roared off. Arnould was still shooting at the second headlight, and found his mark as the car swung out of the gates and into the secondary road leading to Lulworth village. Blackness descended.

Bruce and Mary jumped in, Bruce next to Percy.

'Keep on their tails, Percy, but don't catch them up.'

'Okey-doke, sir.'

What was happening by the stationary car, or to Angell and Fuller who were with it, Bruce had no idea.

115

His one object was to keep in touch with Arnould, to find that Frenchman's hideout. He had Arnould on the run—but the run had to last until Arnould led him to Allaway.

Could the ruse succeed?

It was then that Bruce had a shock.

The car ahead swung off the road before reaching the village, and turned into what Bruce knew was a meadow, one of the comparatively few not ploughed up since the war. The dim light crawled across the meadow, and then stopped.

'It ain't a hundred yards across . . .' Percy began.

'I know. Block the gateway, I don't like this. Mary, we'll go by foot.'

Bruce jumped out but did not wait for her, and stumbled towards Arnould and Victor, his mind filled with questions. But questions which did not long remain unanswered, for light came again across the darkness. The masks of the headlights of Arnould's car had been removed, and the beam bathed a small aeroplane, standing squat and ugly on the ground.

Bruce stopped short in amazement. Mary bumped into him.

'He's prepared a getaway,' snapped Bruce. 'The man's got genius! What is it . . .' He stood still, peering at the 'plane, as Victor and Arnould, short and long figures, rushed from the car towards the 'plane. Lucille appeared, but went in a different direction, soon swallowed up by the darkness. 'A Handley Page—no, it's a Gipsy Moth, single control. Plus a little something, for the propellor doesn't need swinging. Darling, loose a couple of shots at it, but don't hit anything for the love of Mike!'

The Frenchman had climbed into the cockpit; the engine had a self-starter, for its roar shattered the silence of the night. Bruce doubled back to the car, while Mary fired twice and then moved away from the spot. From

116

the Moth two bullets snapped towards her, but safely to one side. Then the 'plane moved forward, heading for the sea.

Bruce reached the Lagonda.

'Got it all set for you, sir,' said Percy.

'It' was a radio-transmitter built into the Lagonda for just such emergency, and Bruce tuned in. At his desk in Sloane Square the Pink 'Un heard the signal, took headphones and stepped to the transmitter-cum-receiver built into the wall.

'X1,' Bruce called. 'Calling X1, calling X1. Operator A3 speaking to X1 . . . right. Our man is heading almost due south from Cliff Cottage, heading due south by air in Gipsy Moth engine power and speed unknown. Have him blocked until I can get after him, keep him blocked until I can get after him . . .'

'Message taken,' said the Pink 'Un brusquely. 'Get off the air.'

Bruce obeyed, while the Pink 'Un tuned into another wave-length, contacting with the South Coast Divisional Air Squadrons.

'X1 calling, X1 calling—send chaser 'planes after Gipsy Moth position over Lulworth, Dorset, heading due south, keep Gipsy Moth from breaking through until further word, allow observation 'plane signalling A3 free passage, accept A3's instructions. X1 calling . . .'

'Message received.'

The operator of S.C.D.A.S. lifted a telephone and called the Divisional Commander, sent word for patrolling 'planes to concentrate over the necessary area, had the instructions confirmed by the Commander. Three chaser 'planes went up, within ten minutes of Arnould taking off, a dozen of them already aloft headed for the spot where the Gipsy Moth was flying.

Arnould found quickly that he could not get straight through.

Victor was at the controls, and Victor knew how to

handle them. He climbed to nine thousand until he was forced down by Spitfires rushing at him, went into a tail-spin almost to sea-level, tried to spurt through the cordon that was about him, saw it was useless, climbed steeply and fell into a falling leaf. In and out of the web of defence 'planes the Moth weaved its way, safe from disaster since the two were wanted alive, and Arnould knew that would be the case.

'They will not fire, Victor. Keep trying, keep trying.'

Victor obeyed, whirling, weaving, spinning, climbing, banking and falling; Victor manœuvred desperately for a chance of breaking through, while the dark skies were split by the powerful rays of searchlights, sometimes lost in the heavy clouds which were growing patchy now, and sometimes showing in the clear, starlit sky.

On land the air-raid warnings, among the first on the South Coast, sent hundreds of thousands of people rushing for the shelters, brought others, more foolish, to doors and windows to search the skies, fascinated by the spinning 'planes they could just see, and the web of searchlights shifting like magic and making a constantly moving pattern against the clouds and clear sky. The bright sides of 'planes caught in the glare showed for a few seconds and disappeared, showed again and were lost.

Word reached Fleet Street of an air battle on the South Coast, urgent calls were made to the Ministry of Information: while on the troubled surface of the sea a small boat made for a launch standing only half-a-mile off-shore, but ready the moment it transferred the passenger to get out of territorial waters. The boat drew alongside, the passenger was hoisted up, and Smith and his companion turned back towards the coast, alarmed by the brightly-lit sky above.

The launch gathered speed.

But hardly had it travelled a mile before a searchlight from a Coast Defence Patrol split the darkness, searched

118

round gropingly, found the launch and promptly fired a shot across its bows. The skipper of the launch knew trouble when he saw it, and hove to. In twenty minutes the launch was taken over by the Defence Patrol officers and turned into Weymouth, while Henrietta lay in a cabin, still unconscious, all unaware that she—although known only as Arnould's passenger and at the time believed to be her brother—had been allowed deliberately to leave the coast in order that Arnould should be completely deceived, and therefore better and more easily handled on shore. Had the passenger been Allaway, Bruce would never have allowed Arnould to leave Cliff Cottage except under escort.

Four Coast Patrol vessels had been concentrated on the spot.

As the launch started back for Weymouth, and while the searchlights swept the seas for the small boat, Bruce Murdoch, Mary Dell, Angell, Fuller and Percival Briggs had reached the nearest Air Squadron Base, where a cabin 'plane, pilot and observer were put at their disposal.

The 'plane took off and joined the others slipping between the searchlights; Bruce spotted the Moth and gave his pilot instructions.

In the Moth, and speaking into the telephone, Arnould said:

'We must get through, Victor. Find a way, find a way!' The little Frenchman's forehead was beaded with sweat.

Victor, expressionless and unspeaking, tried every trick he knew again—and then saw a chance of slipping through a gap left by the chaser 'planes. He widened the throttle, and the Moth went ahead at a speed much greater than one with a normal engine could have done.

Arnould held his breath.

The Moth got through, and Victor headed for a patch of cloud towards the south-west. With two screaming chasers behind them they were lost in the thick mists of the cloud, and Arnould drew a deep, satisfying breath.

'You can get through now, Victor.'

Victor said nothing, but kept heading south-west until, out of the clouds, he was able to make reasonably sure that the chase had been given up. He swung about, climbed to fifteen thousand feet, and in the open cockpits he and Arnould shivered as they tightened their leather flying coats about them.

At twenty thousand feet Murdoch's machine flew on the same course, since they were guided by the sound-instruments and the pilot knew that he need never lose his quarry.

But where would his quarry's flight end?

.      .      .      .      .

The Pink 'Un plucked at his double chin, and eyed Glennister across the small dining-table at the Sloane Square house. Glennister's wife had discreetly disappeared.

'Well, there it is, can't be any is—er,' Holt grunted, his spirits very low. 'Could have sworn the prisoner was Allaway, but this Arnould beggar has put something across us.'

Gordon appeared, announcing a telephone call from Weymouth. Pinky moved with startling agility.

'Won't be a moment, Glennie, only a moment.' He sped into his office, but Glennister followed him, watching him grab the telephone while leaning over the desk. 'Yes . . . yes, speaking . . . a what? A woman? A . . . I don't believe it!'

There was a crackle from the telephone, and the Pink 'Un repeated but with less emphasis that he did not believe it. Then he replaced the receiver, only to pick it up again without speaking to Glennister. 'Hallo . . . get

120

me Scotland Yard . . . I said Whitehall 1212, and hurry!' he glared at the Foreign Minister. 'These confounded girls, don't listen half the time. I . . . hallo, Superintendent Lawson, please, yes Lawson . . . all right, Inspector Wilson will do . . . Wilson, is that you? . . . Get over to Sir Frederick Allaway's house and find out whether Miss Allaway is in her room. If not see if she's in the house at all, and if she isn't, God help the policemen who were pretending to look after her.' He banged the receiver down and turned to Glennister, and his face had lost all of its chubby cheerfulness.

Glennister was staring wide-eyed.

'Not—*Henrietta*.'

'They say so. Said I didn't believe 'em, but they insisted. Well. We got the right family if the wrong branch. I'd better tell the P.M. right away. Henrietta's been drugged, she isn't fit to move, if we want to see her we'll have to go down there. Glennie, the more I see of this business the less I like it. In fact I don't like it at all.'

Nor did the Prime Minister, nor the Minister for War, who was so disheartened that he made no comment on the false hopes which Sir Robert Holt had raised.

The tall dark Foreign Secretary and the short, plump, pink Director of Secret Intelligence left Downing Street and walked past crowds of people who did not recognise either of them, and brooded on the consequences of the kidnapping of the one man in the world who might evolve a plan for effective neutrality for countries who wanted it.

About that time Lucille Devereux arrived by car at Frayle Manor, so well wrapped up in furs that she was not recognised by Holt's agent watching the Coles.

## 13

# No-Man's Land

Mary shivered, and hugged a borrowed Flight-Lieutenant's coat tightly about her. Her nose was red with cold, and her eyes were watering; her right hand was gripped by Bruce and tucked in his coat pocket. It was the only part of her that was really warm.

'It's nippy,' admitted Bruce, 'but if we're cold what is Arnould feeling like in that cockpit?'

'Perhaps,' said Ted Angell, who had a deep, at times depressing voice, 'he's frozen stiff. And his pilot. Just think—two arch-spies roaming in space with locked controls and an inexhaustible supply of petrol, and we can't go down until they do.'

Mick Fuller peered out of the windows of the darkened 'plane towards the apparently limitless blackness beyond, and asked:

'How far to Mars, pilot?'

The youthful pilot turned his head and grinned.

'We're about halfway there, sir.'

'You don't seriously tell me you know where that other 'plane is?'

'About five thousand feet below us, sir, flying nor' nor' east as nearly as I can tell you.'

'Huh.' This from Bruce. 'Over Holland yet?'

'We're as nearly over Copenhagen as makes no difference.'

'No-man's land,' said Ted Angell sepulchrally. 'I can feel it in my bones. Between two fires. Who'll take ten to one that we won't see the fair face of England again? With the green fields about us, and the trees bursting their buds, lambs frolicking and . . .'

'Munition factories at full pressure night and day,' put in Fuller sourly.

'A low, material mind. The new spring grass springing up, daffodils—doing whatever daffodils do, Wordsworth —young love triumphant, young men with many fancies fancying . . .'

'U-boats refuelling,' interposed Mick Fuller.

'Have you nothing artistic in your soul?' Ted eyed his friend reproachfully. 'I—going down, Lieutenant?'

Like Bruce, he had seen the pilot push the joystick forward, or at least seen the forward movement through the partition separating the pilot's cabin from the body of the 'plane itself. Through Mary's mind flashed surprise that a change from flippancy to seriousness could come so quickly, and that while fooling Ted had been watching the pilot so closely.

'Yes,' called back the pilot. 'He's dropped nearly two thousand feet, at a guess. And we're still dropping.'

'Over Denmark?' Bruce said.

'A little further nor' east, sir—Scovia.'

'Scovia,' said Bruce very slowly. 'Now I wonder . . .'

.        .        .        .        .

Bruce Murdoch was a democrat, and a democrat who was not satisfied that democracy in England was all that it could be. Scottish born and English bred, he had a deep affection for England with the ability to analyse its customs and characteristics, most of which he appreciated and admired, some of which he viewed with a tolerant amusement. He disliked the Party Whip system, and for that matter the then arrangement of the Parties

123

in the House of Commons, believing that some kind of system should be evolved which the actual voting powers of the people were represented in the House. The National Government had a preponderance of Members of Parliament far above the wishes of the electors. Looking, therefore, for something which represented his own ideals more completely, he had for some time seen in the Scandinavian countries something approaching—he thought—perfection.

Social conditions, cleanliness, free speech, comparative lack of poverty, a love of peace, friendship with their immediate neighbours: in them he saw the possible birth of a new world. They were being threatened, as the whole world was being threatened, and the first to suffer—if suffering was to come—would be Scovia.

It was a small state, little more than the size of Wales, lying close to the Baltic and with a superb strategic position—for a big sea power—over the Baltic. Its agriculture and industry were rationalised, its Government was Social Democrat, and its actual as well as nominal head was King Henrik, a middle-aged, happily married monarch whose two sons and one daughter seemed to be likely to carry out all the best traditions of the Maalburg dynasty, which had been flourishing for three centuries. Its people were tolerant, happy, mostly well-fed, clever, unambitious, slow to anger. Even the evacuation that had taken place from the bigger towns and cities—the total population being less than four million there were few big population centres—had been carried out with Scovian thoroughness and good humour, but beneath that easy-going acceptance of the necessary precautionary measures there was a grim determination to resist any kind of aggression to the utmost.

At one time it had seemed as if the maws of the Russo-German pincer, working together and yet ostensibly separate, would swallow Scovia, making the Aakon Islands, one of the highest prizes in the Baltic, with natural harbours of great importance as well as beauty an excellent starting-point for operations further south and south-west. Unexpectedly, Scovia had shown stiff resistance to diplomatic pressure, the other Scandinavian countries had made it clear that Scovia's interests were theirs, and—providentially—a small Balkan State had caused a diversion, enabling the Soviet to relax its pressure on Scovia while retaining its prestige.

In short, Bruce knew, Allaway's idea—as far as he understood it—had a practical demonstration.

There had followed a period of comparative quiet, while the Soviet, Germany, the Allies and the neutral countries were getting their breath back. Rumours of further pressure on the non-combatant countries were current at the time of the disappearance of the Allaway Papers, and the kidnapping of Allaway himself.

Now Arnould, if the pilot was right, was losing height over Scovia and might easily land there.

The nose of the 'plane was pointing downwards; Bruce stood up so that he could see the altimeter, to find that they were flying at a height of ten thousand feet, and dropping fast. Tension had suddenly come into the cabin; there were no quips from Angell or Fuller. Mary put her hand into her own pocket.

Five thousand feet.

Scovia looked just a mask of blackness, for blackout regulations were as strict there as anywhere in Europe, and the policy of illuminating the frontiers had been discontinued. As Bruce peered down, however, a stab of brightness came through the gloom, a searchlight crept slowly about the skies, concentrating on a level of some three thousand feet. Suddenly Bruce saw the sides of Arnould's 'plane caught in the blinding light, unable to avoid it. Two other searchlights joined the first, keeping the 'plane under observation all the time.

'Is he still going down?' Bruce asked.

'Must be about to land, sir.'

'Hmm. Can you have engine trouble?'

'I don't see why not.'

'Then have some when you get me to a point where a parachute would take me to about the spot where they're landing.'

Mary caught her breath, and the pilot looked startled. 'You'd be about right now.'

'Then I'm going down,' said Bruce, and Mary knew that he had reached that decision a while back, and that it would be useless for her to try to dissuade him.

'Alone?' she asked.

'Yes,' said Bruce. 'One of us will be enough. Get down yourself as soon as I'm gone, Lieutenant. The story for the authorities is that your passengers are newspaper people, they've all got their cards of identification.'

The pilot looked glum.

'Very good, sir.'

'Worried about internment for you and the 'plane?' Bruce asked. 'A pity, but it can't be helped. Get that door open, will you?'

The observer, also looking glum, nodded and stepped to the door. Mary gripped Bruce's hand, his pressure responded, and then he stepped to the door. The wind cut in keenly, making them colder than before, while Bruce checked on the strapping of his parachute, donned soon after taking off, and wondered whether it would open when the cord was pulled.

'Ready, sir?' The pilot looked round.

'Ready.'

'Luck, Bruce,' came from Ted and Mick, simultaneously.

Bruce looked at Mary, then quickly away. He climbed out slowly on to the wing of the 'plane. He knew the construction intimately, and chose the right place and the right moment. He dropped. The air seemed to come up to meet him. He turned a complete somersault twice, then fell head first, with the blood drumming in his ears,

126

a tightening band about his chest threatening to suffocate him. He waited for what seemed an age before pulling the cord; even then nothing happened, he continued to drop like a stone.

Down—down—down.

No awareness of anything but thunder in his ears, not even fear. Icy coldness, but heat at his eyes and mouth and nose, and blackness all about him. Faster, faster . . .

He felt the check as the great envelope opened.

It seemed incredible that he could begin to float so sedately, feet first; that he could breathe with comparative ease; that the pressure and the sharp heat disappeared. A black void was all about him and he realised that the searchlights had been put out; but with a suddenness that alarmed him, one shone again.

Searching for the 'plane he had left, of course.

It was within twenty yards of him and he felt a sharp fear that he would be seen, but it wavered towards the left, and the darkness beneath seemed deeper because of the light he had seen. He knew he had been dropping only for a few minutes, and yet it seemed like an unending space of time. He could not be more than a few hundred feet from the ground, for to his left the orb of the searchlight was growing bigger.

It disapeared, but the beam still showed.

He tensed his legs for the contact with the ground, and then felt the sharp jolt, a momentary one for he was lifted promptly by the parachute. He touched *terra firma* again, bounced up, then felt himself being dragged along. He stumbled, fell, picked himself up and stumbled again, this time cracking his head against the ground and feeling his senses reel. The movement was slow, and finally he stopped moving, his weight sufficient to hold the parachute as it collapsed.

He waited for two or three minutes, and then, realising how cold he was for the first time, laboriously sought for the whisky flask in his hip pocket. A sip of the spirit warmed him, and he replaced the flask, rubbed his hands together to get back the circulation, and then took off the straps of the parachute. When he started to walk, he went in the direction of the searchlight. In its reflection he saw a hedge, and under its cover took off his flying kit, bundled it in a ditch, and then forced his way through, into the field where the searchlight was stationed.

Now he could see lights.

Only a glimmer, and all of them shaded, but enough to tell him there were buildings ahead. As he drew nearer, a shaft of light from an opened door showed for a moment and in it he saw three people—a short man, a tall man, and a uniformed figure.

Arnould and Victor, going for interrogation.

It did not occur to Bruce that Arnould would have any trouble with the authorities; he was quite sure that the man would have made all the necessary advance arrangements, and did not believe he had come down in Scovia by accident. He walked towards the buildings, trying to pierce the gloom, afraid every moment that he would come across a sentry, but luck was with him. The light, dim though it was, suggested warmth and made him feel the cold more keenly, but he stopped thirty yards from it, watching lynx-eyed.

No more than ten minutes passed before the door opened again. Arnould and Victor came out, and a loud voice in Scovian was genial enough to tell Bruce that there had been no difficulty.

'You will need conveyance, Herr Klein?'

'If there is a car going into Litrakka . . .'

'It can be done, yes, it can be done. Guard!'

A man apparently responded to the speaker's summons, and there was a mutter of instructions too quick for Bruce to understand; his Scovian—language mingling German, Dutch and French in remarkable fashion— was not good, although it would suffice him later. Although darkness had descended again he heard footsteps, and knew they were approaching. He stood quite still, but jumped when a car door opened and, after a moment's pause, an engine started not ten yards from him. Small points of light glowed as the lamps were switched on, and he could see enough to know that the car was a large one, with an open back. The temptation to try to get on the luggage grid was strong, but he forced it back, and heard it pass him. He watched the red lights disappear, so that he could judge the direction of the road, and then turned his attention to the searchlight.

His heart leapt.

He saw the beam shining on the British 'plane, which was no more than a thousand feet up, and he could hear the spluttering of the engine. He waited until the 'plane landed, in the vortex of three searchlights, and then darkness descended again, and he turned sharply in the wake of the car.

All he knew was that Arnould, under the name of Klein, would be somewhere in Litrakka, the capital of Scovia; he had not even had the luck to overhear Arnould's rendezvous.

But in Litrakka were several of Holt's agents, including Herr Doktor Mureth, who knew Scovia as he knew the palm of his hand, and was considered by the Pink 'Un as the most efficient agent in Europe.

Murdoch felt comfortable when he thought of Mureth, and then uncomfortable, for he did not know whether he was two, ten or twenty miles from Litrakka, and he had forgotten—he seemed always to be forgetting something—to bring food or chocolate.

'Amazing that Mary let me,' he muttered to himself, and smiled, stepping out smartly as soon as he was through the hedge and on the road. He walked easily on a good surfaced road, wondering whether Arnould was yet at his hotel, warm and comfortable and eating. As the minutes flew he found himself dozing mentally, felt inertia due chiefly to the cold. His steps were automatic;

he felt his chin dropping to his chest, jolted up, went through it again.

Then out of the blue a car came towards him.

He jerked to wakefulness in a moment. He saw the lights next, but had no time to tell himself that it was moving at speed when it was on him. He leapt to one side, but the tail of his coat was caught by the wing, and he was flung against the hedge. He felt a sharp pain shoot through his shoulder, felt thorns tearing at his hands and face.

The car squealed to a standstill.

## 14

## Herr Doktor Mureth

Dazed, bewildered and acutely aware of the pain in his shoulder, Bruce saw vague figures come towards him, heard low-pitched voices and felt hands at his arms and legs. He drew a deep breath, called on all he knew of Scovian, and hoped that he had made a fair attempt to sound like a native.

'I—I am all right.'

A gruff voice sounded relieved.

'So, you are awake, that is good. It was foolish of you, Mein Herr, to take the middle of the road.'

'Hans, must you tell an injured man he is foolish?' The second voice was a woman's. 'You were going too fast, I had said so. A light. A light, shine the light . . .'

A shaded torch gleamed on Bruce's face, and the woman—tiny, as far as he could see—gasped.

'He is hurt, his face is all torn—a doctor, quickly to a doctor!'

'Freida, he is all right.' The man seemed bulky as he helped Bruce to his feet, and a quick spasm of amusement flashed through Bruce's mind as he realised that they were discussing him as they would had he been unconscious. But the word 'doktor' had pulled him together, and as he leaned against the driver, he said with an effort:

'I shall need—some attention, please, my arm is pulled. My doctor, Herr Mureth . . .'

'That is Litrakka. We go to Kohn,' said the burly man, and his face now looked like a mist of white in the darkness. Bruce opened his lips, but the woman spoke.

'Three-four miles, and you knocked him down, Hans. He goes to Herr Doktor Mureth, you understand.'

She might be small, thought Bruce, but she could handle her companion. Grumbling to himself the man helped Bruce into the car; with difficulty it was turned, and while the woman—her features still indistinct for the light inside the car was negligible despite drawn curtains—dabbed at the scratches on Bruce's face. He continually assured her that he was all right, the car sped towards Litrakka—and Doktor Mureth.

.　　　.　　　.　　　.　　　.

Like most of the Scandinavian towns, Litrakka was planned as towns should be planned, with an architectural simplicity that had a beauty of its own once the habit of comparing all cities with London, Paris and New York was forgotten. Its buildings were originally white, but with characteristic Scovian thoroughness dwelling-houses and hotels as well as public buildings and offices had been camouflaged with brown and green paint, a fact Murdoch knew although he entered the town for the first time in the utter darkness of the blackout. Some critics complained that the plan of the Scovian capital was like a maze—you entered one street, turned right and left and found yourself where you started from; and to a degree this was true. The centre of the city was a formation of squares, each square confined by a wide, two-way thoroughfare bisected at four points, allowing for freedom of traffic movement.

To simplify the situation the authorities gave the streets numbers, as well as names, and if one started from the furthermost corner from the Civic Centre and walked by numbers but retrogressively, one trod in every street of any importance in Litrakka. On the outer fringes were the residential quarters, closer to the centre itself were the shopping thoroughfares, mostly departmental stores run by competitive combines which contributed handsomely to the country's exchequer, a fair example of applied Socialism. The stores were privately owned but Government controlled, while reasonable—never exorbitant—profits were permitted. Closer still were the Embassies and Consulates, the bigger offices of public utility as well as private companies and, surrounding the Civic Square, wide, scrupulously clean, gloriously colourful in spring, summer and autumn, but primly grassed during the winter, were the Senate House, the Palace, and the more important municipal buildings.

In the residential quarters lived Herr Doktor Mureth.

In that quarter representing Litrakka's nearest approach to Mayfair, Mureth was a doctor comparable with a Harley Street or a Wimpole Street practitioner. He was neither too tall nor too short. He was fair, for a dark man was a rarity among Scovians, and he had dignity, aloofness, courtesy, a manner designed to suit the rich and the poor. It was Mureth's reputation that he treated royalty and cottager with equal consideration. He had regular features, with light blue eyes that were more often serious than smiling, and had a way of looking through a patient as though into his mind and thus to the truth. The nostrils of his long nose were thin and sensitive, his mouth was well-shaped but also long and thin, his chin was pointed but not over-long, while his cheeks were thin yet with high cheekbones which, in some lights, made him seem gaunt. His lips were very red, contrasting with his white teeth. He moved his lips little when he spoke, and smiled rarely.

He was consulted from time to time by most people of importance in Scovia, from King Henrik and Larsen, the Premier, to the landowners and storekeepers who, in that principality, had equal social and civic status.

Mureth was half-English, half-Scovian. His wife was pure Scovian, and a superb example of fair Scandinavian womanhood. She was as tall as her husband, with a pristine fairness, clear, vivid blue eyes, and a colour in cheeks and lips that needed no artifice to enhance. To the English eye she was a little too large-boned, her shoulders a little too square, her hands and feet perhaps too large. But to any eye as she sat opposite Mureth on the evening of Bruce Murdoch's descent on Scovia, she would have been a pleasure.

Mureth, in smoking-jacket but otherwise dressed for any urgent call, lifted a polished briar pipe from his lips and raised his eyes from an English copy of *Why Hitler Can't Win.*

'A nuisance, this blackout, Hilde. I would like . . .' He stopped, and Hilde's eyes danced.

'I know, to walk and keep walking, to get the smell of the drugs and antiseptics and everything out of your system. Derek, if this war comes to us, what will you do?'

He shrugged. 'Offer my services, what else can I?'

'But . . .' They were talking naturally and yet her manner as well as his suggested the subject was something known only to their two selves. 'The other work?'

'I shall have to leave what I can to others, if I am wanted.'

'So—your first duty is to Scovia?'

'Always, Hilde, you should know that.' She did, but she had wanted confirmation. 'Those in England know it too. I help where I can, but never to Scovia's disadvantage.' He studied the bowl of his pipe. 'Not that there need be. England and Scovia work so much in concert, and—well, she will be with us if there is war.'

'Even to declaring war on Russia?'

Mureth raised his eyes, frowning.

'I think even to that. But put it aside, Hilde, and put that tapestry aside . . .' On her lap was a tapestry of the

134

Virgin, almost finished, and in her hand a needle. 'We have so few evenings together, come and sit . . .'

There was a tap at the door as she started to put the needle away, and Mureth frowned as he said 'Come in'. A raw-boned girl, out-of-place in her cap and apron, entered the long, narrow, sparsely furnished room.

'The surgery, Herr Doktor.'

'No, Katerin, it is too late.'

'A gentleman insists, Herr Doktor.' Katerin spoke as if she were repeating a lesson. 'He is an old friend of yours, he says. His arm is dislocated perhaps.'

Mureth exchanged resigned glances with his wife.

'All right, I'll come.'

He changed his smoking jacket for a white coat, and hurried to the ground floor consulting-room. In the waiting-room two men, one burly and thickset and a slight acquaintance of the doctor's, the other tall, rangy and lean but at that moment dishevelled, were waiting. Mureth looked at the acquaintance, annoyed at the claim to be an old friend.

'Ha, Mureth, good of you to be so quick. Knocked a man down'—the speaker retained the habit of speaking of Murdoch as if Murdoch could not hear—'a patient of yours. I am in a considerable hurry, can you look after him?' The burly man nodded distantly to Murdoch, and stepped to the door. 'Send me your account, of course, provide the man with anything he needs.'

The burly man went out, without waiting for an answer.

Bruce, with his shoulder uncomfortable and a deep scratch on the back of his hand painful, felt like laughing. Mureth's cold appraisal stopped him.

'An old friend, I understood.'

Bruce straightened up on his chair.

'I'm sorry, Herr Mureth, it was important that I should see you. I . . .' He looked at the scratch, with the coagulating blood on it, then up into Mureth's eyes.

135

'You would hardly call that a Pink 'Un, would you?'

Mureth's head jerked up.

'Where there is pink there is usually red.'

'White and blue,' said Bruce.

He was not surprised when Mureth stepped to the door and locked it. The windows were already shuttered for the blackout and needed no further attention.

'I've a nasty feeling that I've put my arm out,' Bruce went on, 'it would happen! Will you see what's what while I get my bearings?'

'Yes.' Mureth took the other's coat off, cut the sleeve from his shirt, and fingered the shoulder. Bruce winced. The long, lean fingers of the doctor continued probing. 'Hold your breath,' he said, 'and sit still.'

Bruce obeyed. Mureth used both hands, and the sharp pain that followed forced a gasp from Bruce's lips, but as quickly as the gasp had come Mureth stepped back, smiling faintly.

'It will be all right, I will bandage it, and you will have little discomfort, although you must rest it. It was not a finished job,' he added grimly, and if he was curious he hid it even from the expression in his eyes. 'These cuts, I will dress them too. You look exhausted; when did you last eat?'

'I hardly remember. Oh, yes, lunch with Arnould.' Bruce felt a shock of surprise that so much had happened since that strained lunch. 'In England.'

'England!'

'Yes,' said Bruce. 'If you will listen . . .'

'First I will have some food prepared,' Mureth said, and he pressed a bell, unlocked the door and, when Katerin appeared, gave instructions. He sent word to Hilde that he would be engaged for some time, then re-locked the door. He smiled. 'All right, you may talk. First, who are you?'

'A3, Bruce Murdoch.'

'*Murdoch?*' There was a new interest in Mureth's eyes,

136

proof that he had heard of Bruce's exploits in the journey which had put Holt's seal on him as an agent out of the ordinary.*

'Yes—in the flesh,' grinned Bruce. 'I—oi! steady with the flesh. It's a long yarn, but here are the essentials . . .'

When he had finished, by which time Mureth knew most of what there was to know of Allaway's disappearance, Bruce was feeling more comfortable, although there was a dull ache in his shoulder. The irony of making the parachute descent without any damage and meeting trouble from a careless motorist did not immediately strike him. Nor was he concerned by the minor injuries. He was too relieved at his successful journey, the knowledge that Arnould was within a mile of him, and that the resources of an unusually capable agent were at his disposal.

'And so,' Mureth said, 'we must find Arnould, or Klein, immediately. Also you will want to know what has happened to your companions. You have your hands full.'

'And my middle empty,' said Bruce hopefully.

Mureth laughed, but even then his mouth did not open widely.

'A gentle reminder. You shall have dinner at once. One other thing, Mr Murdoch. My wife often helps me, although she is not officially in the service. Sir Robert . . .'

'Holt told me of her,' said Bruce, and remembered a description of flawless Scandinavian beauty. 'There's nothing she need not know, provided it doesn't bring her into the firing-line.'

'We have always worked together,' said Mureth, 'and I hope we always will. I shall introduce you to her, and then I start work. You interrupted a domestic evening, Mr Murdoch.'

There was nothing quite so attractive as a happily

*Dangerous Journey by Norman Deane

137

married couple, Bruce decided as he ate, with Hilde Mureth pretending to eat also. The Mureths did not shout their happiness, he had heard no term of endearment, yet they had that serenity which only contentment could bring. And Hilde *was* beautiful. He thought of Mary and the future, frowned, and then for no apparent reason thought of Lucille. He smiled.

'Amused, Mr Murdoch?' Hilde did not hesitate to use his real name, for the door was locked and the room soundproof.

'I was thinking of another beautiful woman,' said Murdoch cheerfully. 'Working for the other side. The last I saw of her she was running hell-for-leather across a rough meadow, and I was wondering whether she escaped.'

'A friend of this Arnould?'

'It seems so. I wonder . . .' He hesitated, and then slipped his hand into his breast pocket. He drew out a wallet, and from that a small photograph. It was one he had taken of Lucille at the Regal, with one of the tiny Leicas used by many of Holt's men. He handed it to her. 'If they are operating from Litrakka you *could* know her.'

Hilde took the photograph and studied it, a tiny and entirely charming frown of concentration on her forehead. At last she shook her head.

'It is not unfamiliar, but I cannot recall her.'

'I can't expect too much,' said Bruce.

'If you are like Sir Robert you always will.'

'So Pinky's fame precedes him!'

Hilde laughed, and was still laughing when Mureth came in. He sat down opposite the British agent. His voice was quiet, decisive, professional.

'Well, Mr Murdoch, I have some information. Arnould, or Klein, has registered at the Schohn Hotel, in Strasslinder, with his man, who is registered as Schmidt. Both have been there before, without being

138

well known. Their rooms are reserved for three days, and they are both in bed.'

Bruce frowned thoughtfully.

'No direct contact with Allaway, then. Are you having them watched?'

Mureth raised his brows.

'Of course. A reliable man will be on duty back and front, all the time. I shall be told if either of them moves from the hotel. The other matter was somewhat more difficult. The military authorities are reticent about the British 'plane that landed—in fact officially no such thing happened. But we are friendly towards Great Britain here. A 'plane lands, it should be retained according to international law, and its crew and passengers interned. At least the crew. But . . .' Mureth shrugged. 'Who saw it land? Who need see it take off again?'

Bruce stared. 'The authorities will let the pilot go?'

'I think so. Officially he has not been seen.'

'The passengers?'

'I understand they are newspaper correspondents,' said Mureth, 'and they are to be allowed to remain. Their passports are in order, they can obtain the necessary visas tomorrow. They are likely to stay at the Raboth Hotel for the rest of the night.'

Bruce began to smile.

'You've done a wonderful job—thank you. Now if you'll book me a room at the Raboth as Gustav Morenson, Swedish national travelling in books, we can start moving.'

'You need sleep and rest,' interrupted Mureth decisively. 'I cannot let you do anything more tonight without warning you that you will not be fit tomorrow. That arm needs a week, not a day, to get strong again. There is ample room in this house. I will telephone your friends.'

Bruce hesitated, and then stifled a yawn, and said: 'If I'm not putting Mrs Mureth to too much trouble . . .'

139

'Katerin will prepare a room immediately,' said Hilde. 'You look very tired, Mr Murdoch, and you have had a busy time.'

'And busier, I think, to come,' said Mureth. 'I am glad you are sensible.'

While Bruce, also glad that he was sensible, wondered whether he was wise.

.    .    .    .    .

The gentleman who was known at the Schohn Hotel, in Strasslinder, as Herr Rudolf Klein, put through a telephone call to Copenhagen. Herr Klein had been known to do such things before. There was some delay, until at the other end of the wire a man announced himself as Herr Vaaron.

'It is Klein,' said Arnould. 'I have arrived safely after a difficult journey, but I have not brought the consignment with me, Herr Vaaron.'

'Why?' The voice at the other end was heavy and deliberate, and Arnould's lips started that odd twist back over his teeth.

'It proved impossible, although everything was done.'

'I see. The other consignment arrived, why should this have been impossible?'

'My negotiations failed.'

'I see.' The heavy voice was silent for so long that it seemed the speaker had rung off, but Arnould knew differently. 'You have other negotiations, see that they do not fail.'

'I shall succeed with them, they are so much easier.'

'Take nothing for granted. Did anyone complete the journey with you?'

'There was no way they could have done.'

'So. Goodnight.'

Arnould replaced the receiver and stared at it for some seconds; and then he swore with the same cold, vicious obscenity that Bruce had heard near the cliff in Dorset. And Bruce, had he overheard that conversation, would have known three things.

First, that Arnould did not know he had been followed.

Second, that Arnould assumed Henrietta had not been successfully shipped from England, but that Allaway had.

Third—and Bruce Murdoch would have considered it most important—that in Copenhagen that night there was a man who could make Arnould afraid.

## 15

# Herr Gustav Morenson

Living near Covent Garden, in London, there was an insignificant little man who was known as 'Sam' to many of the brighter lights of the theatrical firmament. His full name was Samuel Augustine Webber, and he was such an artist at make-up that a number of temperamental stars refused to go before the footlights until he had put the finishing touches to their appearance. Sam, who was a man with a considerable national conscience, had by some devious route been introduced to Sir Robert Holt, and in that gentleman's hearing claimed that any man in the wide world—those with facial disfigurement or distortions excepted—could be made to look like three different people. More, that with patience and perseverance they could transform themselves by their own hand.

Which had interested the Pink 'Un.

By degrees, he had co-opted Samuel Augustine into the service of his department. Many men and women took a course of lessons from the make-up artist, who did not give them their certificate of capability until he knew they could always change their appearance at short notice, given the necessary equipment. He also talked a great deal about bone formation, but most important, he rammed home the essentials of disguise.

He had into Bruce.

Bruce awakened just after seven on the morning following the flight, and found Hilde Mureth herself standing by his bed, with a tea tray in her hand.

'Bless you,' he said. 'Tea and morning are inseparable. Is everything all right?'

'No reports have come through,' Hilde replied. 'Everything you want will be in your bathroom, through that door.' She went out, and Bruce drank tea that might have been made in England. At last he climbed out of bed, found himself painfully stiff, but better when he had had a hot bath.

Then he turned his attention to the make-up case opened on a table beneath the bathroom mirror. Mureth had assumed that Herr Gustav Morenson and Bruce Murdoch would not look alike and, having been through a course of Samuel's training, had one of Samuel's make-up cases available.

Bruce worked for twenty minutes.

Being fair, he had no need to dye his hair, but with an electric razor he cut it shorter at the sides, and then trimmed his eyebrows. That finished, he bleached his skin with a concentrated solution of hydrogen peroxide specially prepared for quick results, examined the effect and selected carefully a moustache that matched his hair. He fixed this, tapped it into position, nodded with satisfaction and then began the most tricky task—altering the lines at his eyes and mouth. He was so intent on the operation that he did not hear Mureth tap on the door, but heard his voice.

'Come in.'

'I thought you might need help,' said Mureth. He glanced at Bruce, nodded but did not speak, and took up the razor, trimming the back of Bruce's hair without asking whether the task needed doing. Bruce's opinion of Mureth went up even further.

'Klein is still at his hotel, with his man,' he volunteered. 'Your friends have had a good night, and the lady sends her regards.'

'Nice of her,' said Bruce, and glanced up, to find that Mureth had an unmistakable sense of humour. 'The pilot?'

'Was there one?' asked Mureth blandly.

'Long live Scovia!' Bruce waited for Mureth to finish with the razor, and then stood up, eyed himself critically, and nodded. 'Will it do?'

'Webber would be delighted.'

'Splendid! Clothes?'

'On your bed.'

'Pinky's right, you're almost too efficient,' said Murdoch, and added with a chuckle: 'I hope your patients think so! Have you had breakfast yet?'

'Yes, we keep early hours over here, but Hilde has waited. You will be quite safe coming to and fro here, but come to the private door, and avoid the consulting-room entrance. Katerin understands that I sometimes have private patients, she is quite trustworthy.'

'Thank you,' said Bruce. 'Will you tell your agents to send word of Klein to the Raboth, if Klein moves when I've left here?'

'They have had those instructions, and will act on them after nine o'clock. Oh—one other thing. If you should be held up by police, the words "agent political" will usually be enough to get you through.'

Bruce would gladly have lingered over breakfast, for Hilde was as delightful in the morning as she had been in the evening, but he conquered the temptation and, just before nine o'clock, entered the Raboth Hotel.

The hotel quarter occupied a part of the square of thoroughfares chiefly devoted to the large stores, although there were others in various places. The Raboth and the Schohn were within a hundred yards of each other, and the taxi that took Murdoch to the Raboth passed Klein's hotel.

144

Litrakka appealed to him.

Its spaciousness and its cleanliness were at first obvious, but both were emphasised by the comparatively few vehicles on the roads, the absence of crowds. He had not realised before that the Scovian capital had been so fully evacuated, but he saw clearly that despite the camouflage a dozen bombs on such a city would do far more damage than on London or Paris, and the authorities were wise to take no chances.

Policemen went in twos, he noticed, and occasionally an armoured car rumbled by, two light tanks made their cumbersome way across the path of the cab. At some corners, behind sandbag emplacements, were anti-aircraft guns, while on some buildings he saw smaller sandbag nests, and assumed they hid other big guns, or machine-guns. Many windows were boarded up, and it was typical of Scovian thoroughness that the wood was not bare, but painted green and grey, increasing the camouflage effect. Streets and pavements also had been coloured.

So had the Raboth Hotel.

Bruce went through, walking stiffly, and approached the reception desk. He booked a room, and while signing the register recognised Mary's writing: she had taken the wise course and signed herself 'Dell'. In the friendly neutral country it was safe enough. Angell and Fuller had used pseudonyms, the first Cartwright, the second Graham.

They had two rooms on the first floor.

Bruce was taken upstairs in a lift by a middle-aged man, and one of the things he had already noticed was the absence of young men, women and children. The hotel was very silent, few doors were open, he was passed by only one other attendant. He entered his room, signified his satisfaction, and waited for five minutes before going four doors along the passage to Ted and Mick's room. He tapped, and Ted Angell said deeply:

'*Intrer!*'

'Which I suppose is French for "clear out"?' said Bruce.

He pushed open the door, and grinned at Angell, who was standing near the window, with his right hand apparently negligently in his coat pocket. Ted lifted the hand out, and lifted it in greeting.

'Ho, Morenson!' They gripped hands. 'A nice job, Bruce, you look even uglier than usual.'

'Thanks. Where's Mary?'

'Just finishing off. Mick's gone for a stroll to see the sights. How are tricks?' He looked at the scratches on Bruce's face and hands, and lifted an eyebrow. 'Dropped among bushes, did you?'

'I got scratched! Arnould's at the Schohn. Get over there right away, will you, and keep your eye on him. There's no shortage of petrol, so you can use a cab if you need to take a longish journey. Try to make sure he doesn't see you.'

'Right,' said Ted, and made for the door.

Bruce saw another which communicated with Mary's room, opened it, and saw her standing by a wardrobe mirror, fully dressed, but quite unrecognisable. She was still dark, but her hair was done in different fashion, her cheeks were colourless and pasty, the lustre seemed no longer in eyes covered by horn-rimmed spectacles. She had a little too much powder on the right side of a nose that seemed shorter than it was, and her lips were not only painted but badly painted.

He stepped across and put his arm about her.

'How I like lipstick. I—ouch!' She had gripped his shoulder, making him realise it was not yet sound.

'What's the matter?' she asked in alarm.

He explained quickly, and outlined what he planned to do. It was easy to realise that he was lost in his part, and would be most of the time until the task was over.

'And so,' he said, 'we work on the assumption that Klein has contacts over here, and we take a contact

146

apiece. I'll be looking after him myself for a start.'

'Klein?'

'Sorry, *alias* Arnould. You'll stay put, Mary, until you have to move, and for the love of Mike be careful.'

'I will. Are you going to the Schohn now?'

'This very minute.' He gave her an almost impersonal kiss, then went out, knowing that neither Arnould nor Victor would recognise either of them. He went to the Schohn by foot, but did not register, merely waiting in the lounge-foyer where Ted Angell was already drinking lager. He sent a commissionaire for a *Scovia Tagblatt*, and was reading it with difficulty when the revolving doors opened and he glanced up.

He found himself looking at *Lucille*.

.    .    .    .    .

Lucille made no effort to disguise herself, and she had the air which Bruce seemed to have known all his life. Her bold eyes swept the foyer, and she stared into Ted Angell's eyes, winning a quick smile. Ted even started to get up, but she turned quickly, and addressed the reception clerk.

'Herr Klein, please. He expects me.'

'Yes, madam.' The clerk lifted a telephone, while Ted sat heavily back in his chair, covering his surprise that the beauty and Arnould were so closely associated. Bruce repressed a smile.

She waited, keeping her eyes from Ted, but looking with passing interest at Murdoch. The same latent invitation was there, and he was reminded of the dinner tête-à-tête at the Regal. His gaze was frosty rather than indifferent, and her lovely lips curved at the corners. Before he had time to wonder whether she was really little more than a well-dressed *cocotte*, the clerk turned to her.

'Herr Klein will see you, Madam. Room 18.'

'Show me, please.'

'At your service, Madam.' A commissionaire was called, for there were no pageboys, and Lucille swept towards the lift.

Ted went to the desk and inquired terms; he wanted a room that overlooked the Strasslinder. The clerk, polite but not obsequious, brought out a plan; and in three minutes Ted had made his selection.

It was Room 16, exactly opposite Arnould's; but there was no opportunity for using it then.

Five minutes after she had gone upstairs, Lucille reappeared. She was with Arnould who was not disguised, but as swarthy and vicious-looking as in England. They went out, walking quickly, but Bruce reached the door before them. He saw Victor at the wheel of a large Citroën opposite the main doors.

Two taxis, which looked like private cars, were standing nearby, and Bruce beckoned a driver. He climbed in, and as the man waited for his directions, said gruffly:

'*Agent political*. That Citroën in front.'

'At once, Mein Herr!' The cabby jumped into his seat, and passed the big car before it started. It was cleverly done, cabbies were cabbies all the world over. Bruce's man allowed the Citroën to get ahead at the first corner, and then followed without ostentation. Bruce wondered which part of the city they were heading for, but he was not left long in doubt. Arnould and Lucille travelled no more than a quarter of a mile, and the Citroën pulled up outside an imposing, once white but now camouflaged building, above which the Nazi flag was flying.

Arnould had come to the German Embassy!

．　　　．　　　．　　　．　　　．

Baron von Rintzen hal one thing in common with Sir Frederick Allaway. He felt that he had been passed over for lesser men. He should have been posted to America, or Italy, or a power of importance, instead of being buried in little Litrakka. It was the fault of a corporal, a house-painter, a . . .

At which stage in his thoughts Baron von Rintzen usually stopped and looked nervously about him. For he had spent three years in Berlin since Hitler had risen to power, and he had seen so many unfortunates who had been caught doing little more—apparently—than thinking. It was not safe even to think. And in Scovia, one had food in plenty; one's allowance came often enough to keep private debtors at bay and the beauties of Litrakka amiable. When the allowance failed, as it might one day for the Fatherland demanded service for very little, there was his income from England and America to fall back on, an income which reached him through so many devious routes. Safe routes. And he was doing his share, no one could deny that. Admitted, it was not in the best traditions of diplomatic privilege to organise and to control espionage, but what did tradition mean in the Nazi world?

Von Rintzen was a Prussian, short, thick-set, running to fat. He was fresh-faced and clean-shaven, and although his close-cut hair was jet black his stubble, on those mornings when he was indisposed and did not shave, showed grey. His nose was broken, the result of a student escapade. He could not do much to improve the fleshy, uneven features, the little porcine eyes that could glitter with fury when he was disobeyed or annoyed, the square mouth which was pushed forward a little, or the weak, receding chin. Except, of course, powder a little, and spray his ears with scent.

It angered him that he could rarely appear in uniform, since formal occasions in Scovia were few. He sat in a high-backed chair at a vast mahogany desk bare of papers but with a carved inkstand containing four quill pens, two telephones coloured to match the desk, and three large, closed books containing photographs. The

149

middle book, an especial favourite, had been open before a secretary had entered discreetly to announce Herr Klein.

'Klein, Klein?' He spat the words, and then started. 'Yes, Herr Klein. He may come in.'

'He is accompanied, Excellency.'

'Accompanied? Accompanied? By whom?'

'It may be Fräulein Klein, Excellency.' The secretary was tall and reserved, but understanding. Von Rintzen lifted a finger.

'Both may come in. At once, Müller, at once.'

Klein entered first, and Lucille was a step behind him. His Excellency the German Ambassador ignored the little, sinister Arnould, and waited to see his companion more clearly. She was dressed in black furs that fitted her superb figure closely, and made von Rintzen grope for the monocle which dangled at his chest. He appraised her slowly, his chin thrust out as far as it would go, from her neatly shod and neatly turned ankles to her full breast and her lovely, sparkling, expressionless face. Expressionless but for her eyes, violet and bold and inviting.

Von Rintzen stood up, clicked his heels, raised his hand.

'Heil Hitler!'

Arnould went through a mockery of the salute, and Lucille waited while Müller pushed a chair against her legs. She sat down, adjusting the coat of her skirt so that her leg showed to the knee.

'So!' The Ambassador sat down, and ignored Lucille. 'Herr Klein, my time is fully occupied.'

'A little, Excellency, only a little.' Arnould was transformed, he was no longer sinister but cringing, and von Rintzen's chest seemed to swell. 'On a matter of considerable importance.'

'You may speak.'

'Excellency . . .' Arnould's eyes darted about the room. 'Are there any to overhear?'

150

'I said speak!' bellowed von Rintzen, and looked to Lucille for approval. Her smile gave it in full measure. Arnould clenched his right hand, but spoke with the same obsequiousness.

'A matter of considerable importance for transmission to Berlin, Excellency, concerning'—he lowered his voice, hesitated, and waited until he had the Ambassador's full attention—'the Allaway Plan, Excellency.'

Von Rintzen opened his lips, readjusted his monocle —and even Lucille saw the change that came over the man. He took on a new dignity, a fresh importance. He had forgotten himself in his work, and when he was working he gave it his full attention: Lucille, for the time being, might not have been there.

'Are you serious, Herr Klein?'

Klein lifted his hands and hunched his shoulders, and then said very softly:

'I would not waste His Excellency's time. But it is a matter of great delicacy and importance. I act for others, others demand full evidence of His Excellency's interest in the Allaway Plan. There are people who would be prepared . . .'

'Do you know the plan?' von Rintzen snapped.

'The outline, Excellency, is carried in my pocket. The only man who knows it fully, Excellency, is Sir Frederick Allaway. He could be made available, for questioning' —Arnould leered—'at any time. He could, I believe, be persuaded to talk, but . . .' Arnould shrugged cunningly. 'It must be carefully, discreetly arranged, Excellency, and the Führer's interest fully assured. In money, Excellency.' Arnould was no longer cringing nor obsequious, but in some uncanny way had become sinister and threatening. 'Payment must be discussed first.'

# 16

# In Action

The German Embassy in Litrakka sent out a radio message which was picked up in Berlin. It was a message in code, none but those for whom it was intended could decipher it. A uniformed operator took it down, and passed it to a uniformed messenger, who hastened with it to another department in the big Wilhelmstrasse building, where three more ostentatiously uniformed men took it through three distinct phases of decoding. Each phase was separate, the first man knew nothing of the real import of the message, the second man knew little. But he knew the worls: *Allaway Plan.*

The third, a Kommandant of the Gestapo, also read the 'Allaway Plan' as well as the rest of the context, and pushed his chair back abruptly. Two uniformed attendants sprang to attention, expecting to be summoned. Instead the Kommandant stretched for a telephone, made a request, replaced the telephone and waited, staring at the instrument impatiently. In five minutes it rang, and he received permission for an audience with Herr von Hiddenthrop. He jumped up, strode out of the room as one of the men opened the door, walked several passages and several flights of stairs, passed innumerable guards and was constantly compelled to repeat the password; the interrogation grew more stringent as he neared the inner offices of the rulers of the Third Reich.

Finally he entered the huge room where von Hiddenthrop sat at a vast desk, which was covered with maps
and papers. Von Hiddenthrop was alone; a tall, pale-
faced, cold-eyed man with clearcut features and an arro-
gant expression.

'Heil Hitler!' snapped the Kommandant, and raised
his hand in a quivering salute. Von Hiddenthrop eyed
him glassily, and then lifted his hand carelessly.

'What is it?'

'A message from Litrakka, Excellency.'

'There are other means for messages to reach me.'

'Yes, Excellency, only one of the greatest importance would cause me to harass you. It *is* of importance,
Excellency.'

'Concerning what?' von Hiddenthrop considered his
fingernails, pushed back the quick of his index finger.

The Kommandant said hissingly: 'The Allaway Plan,
Excellency.'

Von Hiddenthrop's hands dropped sharply to the
desk, palm-downwards, and he glared up at the man.

'*What?*'

'It is so, Excellency, word of the Allaway Plan. I considered it essential none others should know.'

'Give me the message.' The German Foreign Secretary
snatched at the paper, and snapped: 'Wait.' He read
swiftly, and when he had finished, stood up. 'Wait!' He
stepped through a communicating door, where a uniformed secretary to the Führer was sitting at his desk
and looking important. 'He is disengaged, Schmidt?'

'For you, Excellency, I am sure he is.'

'Tell him it is urgent.'

Von Hiddenthrop waited for five minutes after the
message had been telephoned, then the door opened and
the gross figure of General Mulke appeared. Mulke
nodded genially and stood aside for Hiddenthrop to
enter. At a desk vaster than the Foreign Secretary's, but

153

bare of everything but one telephone, a blotting pad, and several pens, sat the Führer.

His sallow face held an unhealthy tinge, his dark eyes were brooding and yet feverishly bright. The lock of hair over his forehead was more lank than usual, a hand plucked nervously at his small dark moustache. He stared at von Hiddenthrop but did not speak.

The Austrian house-painter, the Bavarian champagne salesman, and Mulke, the only representative of the Junker class on the War Council of the Reich, were gathered together as the door closed. Von Hiddenthrop forwent the formality of a salute.

'I have word of the Allaway Plan.' He threw the words out as a challenge, and he was rewarded by a sharp exclamation from Mulke.

'*Donnerwetter!*'

The Führer, whom some knew as Mitzer, stopped plucking at his moustache and thrust his head forward, staring up into the Foreign Secretary's eyes.

'*The Allaway Plan?*'

'It is so.' Von Hiddenthrop lifted the decoded message and began to read swiftly: 'Baron von Rintzen to His Excellency the . . .'

Mitzer stood up and snatched the paper away. Mulke stepped round the desk and read it over the Führer's shoulder:

'His Excellency Baron von Rintzen to His Excellency the Foreign Minister of the Third Reich.

From a reliable and previously attested source comes a statement that the outline of the Allaway Plan is in his hands, a further statement that he has the person of Sir Frederick Allaway, which person can be available in Berlin or other place so desired for interrogation.

This reliable source is prepared to exchange the preliminary details for a consideration of fifty thousand American dollars, and the person of Sir Frederick Allaway for a further consideration of five hundred thousand American dollars.

His Excellency the Baron von Rintzen respectfully submits that the matter be treated with utmost urgency and suggests the radio-ing of permission to dispense fifty thousand dollars for the preliminary plan, which can be placed at the disposal of the Third Reich for forty-eight hours before negotiations need be completed for the ultimate destination of the person of Sir Frederick Allaway.'

'So,' breathed Mulke, 'the rumour was true. They have a plan for the neutrals . . .'

'They, they, they!' roared Mitzer. '*They* have a plan? *We* have the plan! Send word at once, have the preliminary papers flown to me at Berchtesgaden, lose not a moment!' He clasped his hands in front of him and paced up and down the room, his head thrown back and his eyes blazing. 'Why do you wait? Hurry!'

.      .      .      .      .

It was well known to the British authorities as well as the Scovian that there was a widespread espionage net throughout Scandinavia, directed chiefly against neutral shipping and to assist the ruthless prosecution of the U-boat campaign. But it was not known that the German Ambassador to Scovia played a part in it. Bruce Murdoch waited outside the Embassy for half-an-hour, in which time Arnould and Lucille reappeared, climbed into their car, and were driven straight back to the Schohn Hotel. As far as it was possible to judge, Arnould was pleased with his interview.

Bruce went immediately to Room 16, but Ted Angell was not there.

Ted, in fact, was in Room 18.

He was behind a large settee, out of sight and, provided he made no sound, reasonably safe. He heard the footsteps outside, saw the door open, and saw the high-heeled shoes of Lucille and the patent-leather ones of Arnould. Lucille dropped on to the settee heavily, and her deep laughter rang out.

'The fool, he is easy!'

'Von Rintzen is always easy,' said Arnould softly, 'but we have to deal with others. You will dine with the Baron tonight.'

Ted could imagine Lucille's lips curling.

'That man? Why do not others . . .'

'What difference does it make? He is a man. Be pleasant to the Baron, we may need him afterwards, Lucille. In any case they will take the papers. And the papers will make them want Allaway.'

'Are you sure you can get him into Germany?'

'Am I a fool? It can be arranged with ease.'

'Where is he now?'

Angell raised his head a fraction of an inch to make sure he lost no word. But he was disappointed, for Arnould only laughed, a clucking, unpleasant sound.

'I know. Vaaron knows. That is enough, Lucille. Remember when the Baron telephones you, you will arrange to dine, and you will be pleasant all the time, whatever he wants. That is understood?'

'*Nom de nom*, yes. He will be easy.'

'All right, then go. I wish to rest.'

Lucille stood up, a spring clanged loudly, but Ted made no movement as the door opened and closed. For some minutes Arnould remained in the room, and then went to a door leading from it to the bathroom. That too closed. Ted waited until he heard the creaking of a bed, pushed the settee forward enough for him to wriggle out, and reached the door. It was locked, from the inside, and the key was not in it. Ted took a pick-lock from his pocket and after three minutes of faint scratching un-

156

locked the door and stepped into the passage. He re-locked the door and stepped across to Room 16. Bruce was lying back on the bed.

'Everyone's tired,' Ted said with a grin.

'Anything?' asked Bruce.

'Lucille is about to seduce the German Ambassador, and she considers it will be easy. Arnould has offered the Nazis the Papers.'

'Is that certain?'

'Not a doubt. He expects them to buy at once. He's also planning to offer Allaway.'

Bruce jerked to a sitting position.

'Did you learn where . . .'

'No.' Ted grimaced. 'Lucille asked where Sir Freddie was, but only Arnould knows, apart from a man we haven't heard of before, by name Vaaron. Judging from Arnould's tone I'd say that Vaaron is a king-pin in the business. Does it mean anything?'

'Not yet. Well now, let's think. The Papers are in Arnould's room, and we could get them, we're strong enough to overpower him and Victor if necessary, as well as Lucille. But I'm not sure,' Bruce added thoughtfully, 'that we want those Papers. Arnould will have read them, and he can send copies or a fake enough to satisfy Berlin. A raid for the Papers will destroy any chance of locating Allaway. Agreed?'

'Elementary,' said Ted.

Bruce fingered 'Herr Morenson's' moustache, but before he spoke again he heard hurried footsteps along the passage. They stopped opposite, and a knock echoed loudly on Arnould's door.

Bruce eased himself from the bed. Ted opened his own door a fraction of an inch, and they could both see Victor. Victor's back was towards them, but his hands seemed to be quivering. There was a pause, and the door opened. Arnould was hidden by his servant but his voice rasped.

'Victor, I told you . . .'

Victor lifted his hands. There was a moment while his fingers fluttered, although he said no word. Bruce felt rigid, knowing that Victor was speaking in the only way he could, suddenly realising why he had never heard the man speak.

Victor was dumb, and using the deaf-and-dumb language!

A pause, and Arnould gasped:

'*Morley's* man! You're sure? I—come in!'

Victor stepped through, while Bruce and Ted eyed each other in consternation. For if Percy had been seen and recognised by Victor, all hope of working in secrecy was gone.

．　　　．　　　．　　　．　　　．

Von Rintzen listened, scowling, to the voice over the telephone. When Arnould had finished, he said sharply:

'It is bad, Klein, very bad. But I can allow you the use of three men, will that be enough?'

'Ample, Excellency, I am indebted . . .'

'They will call at your rooms.'

'Be advised, Excellency, have them meet me at the Strasslinder Park, in one hour. I can then give them their instructions.'

'I will arrange it.'

'A thousand thanks, Excellency.'

．　　　．　　　．　　　．　　　．

It was dark that night when Mary Dell left the Raboth Hotel and, two hundred yards along the Strasslinder, was met by Percival Briggs. Percy's Cockney face had not been disguised; Bruce had realised it was too late for that, and out of the mistake that had been made he had to re-establish safe contact with Arnould. Briggs walked close to Mary's side, talking earnestly and waving his hands.

On the opposite side of the road two men, agents of von Rintzen and now working for Arnould, kept pace with them. Immediately behind Percy and Mary was the third agent, for they were following Percy on Arnould's instructions. Through the gathering gloom they walked, passing the main gates of the Strasslinder Park. Outside a smaller gate, Mary hesitated.

'All okey-doke,' said Percy. 'You don't have to worry, Miss, I'll be okay.'

A car drew up in the kerb, without lights.

Two men were no longer walking towards Mary and Percy, but one was watching from the other side of the road. The big thoroughfare was nearly deserted, for heavy clouds had been blown across the city and it would soon be dark; blackout sent people indoors early and kept them there.

Percy moistened his lips.

The passenger of the car stepped out, approached Mary, and said very softly:

'Madam, a favour from you . . .'

Mary, still disguised as when Bruce had seen her that morning, drew back as the man's hand clutched at her forearm. Percy went forward, raising his clenched fist, and growled in English:

'Lissen, you, if . . .'

The spokesman did not release Mary's arm, and Percy struck savagely at him. His blow did not land. A blackjack descended on the back of his head, and he would have collapsed but for the quick supporting movement of the man who had struck him. Mary opened her lips as though to scream, but a gloved hand was clapped over her mouth, and the business end of an automatic poked against her ribs.

'Do as you are told, if you wish to live. It is too dark for help to come.'

Mary drew a deep breath, and tried to drag her arm away, but the pressure increased and the wielder of the blackjack grunted before using it on her.

In the semi-darkness Mary and Percival were pushed into the waiting car, and the three men who had been borrowed from von Ritzen followed them. Victor, at the wheel, swung the car round and drove swiftly back, past the Schohn and the Raboth Hotels, through the commercial thoroughfares and the residential streets. Darkness was almost complete as they went past the fringes of Litrakka, and made for the open countryside, in the direction of the airfield where Bruce had landed.

Behind them a second car followed, with Mick Fuller and two of Mureth's men, one of the latter driving. As they left the outer suburbs of the city he leaned back towards Mick.

'This road now runs for four miles, without a turning right or left. We can safely lag behind, and catch them up again. We are going either to Bohn or one of a series of little fishing villages on the coast, I can tell you that.'

'My bet is the fishing villages,' said Mick.

He was wondering what had come over Bruce Murdoch, whether the parachute descent was affecting his judgement. Why, demanded Mick of himself, let Klein's roughnecks collar Mary and Percival? Percy, in an emergency, was understandable, but to let Mary run her head into danger was a crime. He rubbed his prominent chin and scowled more ferociously while, at the back of his mind, he admitted that Bruce Murdoch rarely did things without a sound purpose, although he had an irritating habit of thinking two steps ahead of the next man.

Which had a disturbing effect on the next man's equanimity.

At the Raboth, Ted Angell was saying what Mick was thinking, for one of Mureth's men had reported the attack and its consequences.

Bruce heard him out. As Gustav Morenson his expression was normally cold, but the gauntness in his eyes belonged to Bruce Murdoch.

'Ted, right or wrong, it's the way I see what we have to do. We've got Klein on the run, and must keep him there until we find Allaway. He knows we're about, he believes he's stopped our next move, and he can go on believing that. Please God Mary will come to no harm while we're playing cat-and-mouse. Now . . .' He dropped the subject, and Ted shrugged. 'There's no point in letting the Papers go to von Rintzen if we can prevent it, now that we're known to be here. If Klein can't show his Papers it will slow the game down, and that's our chief immediate need.'

'Klein—oh, Arnould . . .' Ted scowled, always finding it difficult to think in *aliases*. 'He won't leave them in his room, will he?'

'It isn't likely, but we can make sure. As far as we know Klein isn't in his room, but Lucille's in hers. We'll arrange for one of Mureth's men to watch her, then get busy.'

Mureth had placed four men at his disposal, all of them agents acting under the Scovian representative, and knowing little about Holt—knowing, in fact, only that they were cyphers in British Intelligence. Bruce brought one up to Ted's room, gave him instructions, then stepped across the passage. Ted kept a lookout while Bruce worked on the lock.

He had it back in less than two minutes, and opened the door quietly. He heard no sound. He beckoned Ted, who joined him, and slipped quickly through.

And stopped on the threshold, facing two thick-set, square-headed men, both of whom were showing automatics fitted with silencers. Beyond them, the room was in the kind of mess Allaway's study had been in.

161

## 17

# The Cunning of Von Rintzen

The guns stopped all argument and made backward movement unwise. Bruce stepped through, with Ted at his heels, and at a motion from the nearer man raised his hands. Ted did likewise. The second man stepped past them and closed the door. He stood with his back against it, and his gun in his hand.

'What is the meaning of this?' Bruce spoke sharply and in Scovian, but without expecting an informative answer. He did not get one.

'You are not Klein.' The spokesman was a fair, bullet-headed Teuton, and his guttural voice also suggested the German.

'No, I am not Klein,' Bruce replied. 'What . . .'

'If you value your life, silence!' The spokesman snapped a question which made it impossible to obey his order. 'Did you come here with Klein?'

'We have just arrived,' Bruce said. 'He sent for us.'

'*Donnerwetter*, he is the fool!' To the military-trained German mind, Bruce knew, anyone who did not act as the German wanted it was a fool; it was part of the Nazi creed. 'What is it you know?'

Bruce licked his lips. He was acting like a man badly scared and trying not to show it, and Angell was taking the same line.

'Not—not much. Klein needed help, and sent for us from Denmark.'

'You know nothing of what he is doing?'

'He does not confide in us.'

'It is good. Understand, we are looking for money, we . . .'

'Kurt.' The man by the door spoke sharply. 'They should be sent to His Excellency. It is the only safe thing.'

'Perhaps. But how to get them there? Better they believe we are just thieves. Or for them to tell Klein that.'

The intelligence of Kurt, thought Bruce, was a long way below par.

Von Rintzen had sent two men to try to steal the Allaway Papers. It would be much cheaper to steal than to buy. It had probably occurred to him that Berlin would be delighted to save fifty thousand American dollars, but if that were so then he had seen no further—had not realised that a doublecross might prevent the deal over Allaway in person, a fact which explained the Baron's presence in Litrakka instead of a capital of a bigger power.

'Who,' Bruce said, 'is His Excellency?'

'Silence!'

'We might, perhaps, be of assistance,' Bruce insisted.

The man named Kurt stared, and the other by the door uttered a sharp exclamation.

'It is so. Telephone His Excellency, Kurt . . .'

Kurt turned away, approached the telephone stiffly, and dialled a number. The man by the door did not move his gun. There was silence for some seconds, and then Kurt talked rapidly. The conversation lasted for fully five minutes before he rang down.

'It is approved, His Excellency will see them. Remember'—he glared—'His Excellency can use men who know how to keep silent and obey orders. We have finished here, we will go at once. Downstairs, to a car standing outside. Remember we shall hold the guns in our pockets.'

163

'I shan't forget,' said Bruce feelingly.

The man by the door went out first, Bruce and Ted followed, Kurt brought up the rear. Ted glanced at Bruce with a sardonic smile in his eyes, and muttered in English:

'Nice work; so we get to see their Boss.'

'We might learn something . . .'

Although they were walking along the brightly-lighted passages of the Schohn, a gun poked into Bruce's ribs, and he stopped speaking. In twos, the Germans behind, they hurried down the stairs and through the revolving doors. From light to darkness the change was disconcerting, but in that moment they could have made a dash for safety.

Would the men have shot them down?

In the darkness they might have done so without much risk, but it was not worth the chance. Bruce stepped to a car, the vague outlines of which he saw, and stepped into the back. Ted followed and Kurt joined them, nursing his gun. It did not seem to occur to him that they would make a break for safety.

It was impossible to tell where they were going, but easy enough to guess. The big car pulled up outside the German Embassy. Bruce and Ted were ushered in, taken to a small reception room and left with the man who stood by the door at the Schohn, until Kurt returned.

'His Excellency will see them.'

'Good! This way, quickly.'

They were led through the large halls of the Embassy, and up a wide staircase. Kurt tapped on a door, but it was little more than a formality, and Bruce was pushed inside. As he went he heard the laugh, deep-throated and unmistakable, and as he entered he saw the obese Prussian behaving in a way no Ambassador should have done.

For von Rintzen was patting Lucille's bare shoulder. Lucille was by the door leading from the Ambas-

164

sador's private study into his bedroom, and she wore only a silk negligée which had slipped down. She waited long enough to glance at the two men who entered and then, with another laugh, went through. Von Rintzen rubbed his hands together and then realised that the men were in the study.

He stiffened, the square lips tightened and were pushed forward. Bruce saw his broken nose, his dyed hair, his powdered face.

'You did not knock!' roared von Rintzen.

'Excellency!' Kurt looked scared. 'I knocked, I swear.'

'You did not!' bellowed von Rintzen. 'Would you call me a liar?' He glared, groping for his monocle, and then peered through it at Bruce and Ted. His lips twisted. 'Who are these?'

'The men I informed your Excellency of. They work for Klein and arrived when we were looking for the Papers . . .'

'Silence!' von Rintzen swaggered up to Bruce, lifted his ugly face, and sneered into Bruce's. 'Why do you work for Klein?'

'For money, Excellency, why else?'

'Money, money, always it is money! But . . .' von Rintzen levelled a stubby forefinger. 'Others than Klein have money. Understand?'

'Your Excellency's generosity is well known,' murmured Bruce, and von Rintzen preened himself. He was a pitiful imitation of a man, Bruce thought, cunning perhaps but certainly not clever. He stepped to his desk, and sat down stiffly.

'Klein has brought a man from England. Where is he?'

Ted went rigid. Bruce hesitated and then said slowly: 'It is not known, Excellency.'

'But you know of such a man?'

'Yes, Excellency.'

'So,' said von Rintzen, and his arrogance and vanity

165

seemed to drop away from him, he was deep in his purpose again, and Bruce knew suddenly why the interview had been granted. Now von Rintzen was suave and courteous; he pointed to chairs, pushed cigars towards them. 'We can come to an arrangement, understand, an arrangement. You can continue to work for Klein, but for information leading to the discovery of the man from England you will receive . . .' He paused, portentously, and then jerked himself forward. 'Twenty thousand German marks, *each*. Twenty thousand German marks —*each*!'

Bruce licked his lips.

'Excellency, Klein is a dangerous man. The risk is . . .'

'Twenty-five thousand—*each*!'

Bruce looked at Ted. Ted nodded. Von Rintzen rubbed his hands, clapped them resonantly, stood up and approached them. He beamed at them, showing his teeth to be small and wide-spaced. Bruce was reminded of a puppet or a ventriloquist's doll.

'You are wise men. There is Klein's money to receive, and that from me. Now—this man from England. Understand I want only to know where he is, nothing else, afterwards I can make all the arrangements. But . . .' He tightened his grip, and his eyes were suddenly hard and cruel. 'Do not attempt to make tricks, gentlemen, you will be watched very carefully, you will be overheard if you tell Klein of this.'

'We shall be faithful, Excellency.'

'Faithful, ha!' Von Rintzen glared at Bruce, and then laughed harshly. 'Faithful, that is good! It pays, eh, Kurt? And now, I have business.' Deliberately and blatantly the Ambassador winked, and jerked his head towards the closed door.

.        .        .        .        .

They were driven back to the Schohn, where Kurt left

them with an urgent reminder that they must not hope to escape attention—they were not to be surprised if they were followed at times. They went up to Ted's room, and the tall man sat slowly on the bed and peered up into Bruce's face.

'Mr Murdoch,' he said gently, 'who *are* we working for?'

Bruce grinned.

'Berlin, Mr Angell, and we shall be faithful. But von Rintzen won't take us on our own valuation, he'll have his men looking through our rooms. You'd better remain Cartwright for the time being, and leave your Cartwright identity card and passport where they can see it. I'll do the same as Morenson.' He smiled. 'Lucille *is* busy, isn't she?'

'Cat and mouse all the time,' Ted said. 'That fat little swipe is trying to get information from her, she's trying to get it from him. What I like about this job is that it's all so nice and straightforward. Are you going to look through Klein's room for the Papers?'

'Yes, although Kurt won't have left much undone. I'll tackle Klein's, you look after Lucille's.'

The Nazi agents had looked through every drawer and cupboard, while clothes were dropped about the floor, their pockets turned inside out, their linings torn. Arnould—whom Bruce was thinking of with increasing frequency as Klein—was not going to be pleased when he returned.

Apart from a railway ticket a week old, and some loose money in Scovian dinars and German marks, there were no papers of interest at all. But in one of the pockets was a photograph, apparently a postcard enlargement of a snapshot. Arnould was not in it, but Lucille and Devereux were there, with Cole and his wife. The background was a herbaceous border and a six-foot brick wall—or as nearly six foot as Bruce could estimate. The

167

quartette were standing on a lawn, and all of them seemed to be happy.

Bruce scrutinised the back of the card but there was no indication of a date. It suggested only that the Coles and the Devereuxs had, at one time, been socially acquainted. He found himself puzzling about the Coles as he locked the door behind him, and tapped on Lucille's. Ted opened it at once.

'Results?' asked Bruce.

'Only that she's got so many clothes here that she must have had them before she arrived yesterday.'

'It wasn't yesterday, it was this morning.' Bruce glanced at the pile of silk and satin lingerie, neatly folded on the end of Lucille's bed. Every drawer was open and empty. 'You've an orderly mind, she'll be pleased about that anyhow. So there's nothing at all?'

'Unless you call this something,' said Ted.

He handed Bruce a postcard photograph, a print identical with that Bruce had already found.

'Odd, Arnould has one too.'

'Are you going to try Victor's room?' Ted asked.

'Yes,' Bruce said, 'although we're not likely to find much there. You slip up to it. I'll wait in case we have a call from Mick.'

Ted was down again in twenty minutes, and his smile was at once rueful and puzzled.

'Nothing at all—except a photograph identical with the others,' he said. '*If* we can call that anything.'

Bruce frowned. 'It's odd. Mr Smith, *alias* Jem Dace, whom I'd almost forgotten, said he was looking for a photograph and some papers. I wonder if the man could have been telling the truth? And I wonder . . .' He stepped abruptly to the telephone, and called Mureth's house. Hilde's husky voice answered him, and he went on quickly: 'Mrs Mureth, how quickly can I have a photograph copied?'

'It should not take long. An hour, perhaps. We have

168

everything needed here.'

'I'll send a man over with one,' said Bruce, 'and I'd like it back as quickly as I can.' He rang off, and handed one of the three photographs to Ted. 'Take it to one of the boys downstairs, and tell him to hurry.'

'Dare I ask why?' asked Ted.

'I want a copy but I don't want Arnould or Lucille to know we're interested. It's less an idea than a hunch, old man, and taking nothing for granted.'

Ted shrugged. 'Myself, I think you're going batty.'

But he took the photograph, and in fifty-five minutes it was back, with three damp copies. While the man had been at Mureth's, both Victor's copy and Lucille's had been returned. Bruce took Arnould's back, and laughed on his return.

'That room looks as if it's been struck by a hurricane.'

He stopped, and the glint in his eyes was very hard.

'Ted, it did pass through my mind before, and it's come again more emphatically. Was Allaway's room upset in a fight or on purpose? Was that room really upturned to show signs of a struggle? If it was . . .'

'Allaway *could* have faked it, you mean.'

'Pinky's quite sure Allaway's not trying tricks.'

'Good God! You're not suggesting that Allaway *isn't* a prisoner?'

'Not suggesting, no. Just wondering.'

That was when the telephone rang sharply.

He stepped towards it, and in a moment recognised Mick Fuller's voice, and Mick spoke in German, a language used a great deal in Scovia.

'Mary and Percy are in a house by the sea here— lonely as Cliff Cottage. We had a hell of a job finding it.'

'Is Klein there?'

'Oh, yes, Arnould's around, and Percy's been yelling like the devil. More hurt in dignity than anything else, so far. Seriously—it's a gruesome spot, I don't like the idea of Mary being here.'

169

'No.' Bruce hesitated. 'Can we find it on our own?'

'Mureth's bloke—gosh, the man's got eyes in the dark!—says that Mureth will know it. Reikmann's Folle, the local white elephant, believed to be empty.'

'Wait for me,' Bruce said, and turned to Ted. 'You keep Lucille under your eagle eye if she comes back.'

'You're not forgetting the Ambassador's bodyguard?' Ted said.

'They can believe I've had orders from Klein,' said Bruce quickly. 'Get Mureth on the line.'

.　　　.　　　.　　　.　　　.

Reikmann's Folle had been built twenty years before by a wealthy Scovian with repressions and phobias—one of the latter being a hatred of big towns and any kind of neighbour. The Folle, Mureth said, had been built on a small peninsular which at high tide was almost submerged, and after Reikmann had died no one had bought the place, nor lived in it. It was still furnished, and the sheds and stabling were used by fishermen during the spring and summer. Due to the cold snap there had been little fishing of late, normally the Folle would be empty and desolate.

'Do you think Allaway is there?' Mureth asked.

'I don't, but he could be. I'm taking your two men out there, and we might have trouble. Meanwhile come over, will you, and see Angell in Room 16. He can tell you of the latest developments.'

Mureth said 'at once' and Bruce told Ted to get the local agent's views on von Rintzen. Then he went downstairs, and over a drink at the up-to-date American bar told Mureth's men to have a car outside in ten minutes. As he talked, he was aware of the interested gaze of Kurt, and as they left the bar he beckoned the German.

'I am called to Herr Klein, and must go at once.'

'Where?'

170

'I do not know—those two men will take me.'

'Guard your tongue,' snapped Kurt, as though he knew the prospects of following Bruce in the blackout were small. Bruce grinned to himself and hurried out, to find the car waiting. He sat back, smoking cigarette after cigarette, while the car sped towards the peninsula.

There were no stars, only the faintest grey light showed from the sky. Somewhere not far off Bruce could hear the lapping of the waters on the shores of the Gulf of Scovia, that gulf so badly wanted both by the Russians and the Nazis.

He knew the taller of his two companions as Dirksonn, the shorter as Hendrik. Hendrik was driving. The car went slowly over uneven ground, and then stopped altogether. All the lights were switched off, and Hendrik said softly:

'We are near the edge, sir, it is not wise to drive further. If we show a light we may be seen from the house.'

'Can you guide me?'

'Of course, did not Herr Doktor advise you? We can get inside without difficulty, it has often been done.'

Bruce asked: 'Are you sure?'

'Just follow me,' said Hendrik. 'Dirksonn will be best to look after the car.'

Bruce nodded, and through what seemed utter darkness Hendrik led him with unhesitating sureness of step. The lapping of the waves grew louder, although there was no other sound. But gradually the outlines of the house formed itself against the sky, a tall, square building perhaps thirty yards away. Hendrik took his arm, turned right, and then stopped.

'The door to the cellar is here, sir, we can get through.' There was a sound of metal on metal, the grating noise of a key being turned. A squeak, as a door opened. 'Now,' said Hendrik.

Bruce stepped into an unseen passage, walked quietly

along it until Hendrik said that it was safe to show a light. The beam of his torch showed on coils of rope, bundles of fishing nets, lobster pots, and the regular equipage of coastal fishermen. The walls were white, and as he looked round, Bruce saw that apart from some trestles, with a table top, and half-a-dozen wooden benches, there was only fishermen's equipment in the cellar.

There was a door directly opposite that through which they had walked. Hendrik stepped towards it, listened at the keyhole, then opened it. In darkness again they entered a smaller cellar, from which a stone staircase led upwards.

'I have left the doors open, in case of hurry,' said Hendrik. 'They will be likely to be on the first floor.'

'We'll find out. But what about my friend and your two men?'

'On the other side, sir, they would not hear us approach.'

'Can you get back for Mr Fuller?'

'Of course.'

'Bring him as far as this, and then warn the others to prevent anyone getting through from the house. Can that be done?'

'We can try,' said the well-disciplined Hendrik.

He disappeared like a wraith, while Bruce went up the stairs and opened the door at the top. It led to a small room, the door of which was locked from the outside. Bruce located the lock with his torch and then began to work on it, seeing that the bolts were on the inside and that once the lock was back the door would be open.

The lock clicked at last.

He opened the door a fraction of an inch, and saw a crack of light coming from a door at the end of a narrow passage. He heard the mutter of voices, and believed he recognised Klein's. Certainly he heard Percy's.

' 'E ain't 'ere, an' that's flat, see.'

There was a snapped command, and Percy swore. The oath was sharp and sudden, more an exclamation of pain than swearing for swearing's sake. Percy growled something which Bruce did not hear, and then Mary said steadily:

'Aren't you satisfied yet, Arnould?'

'Be quiet, you!' This time Arnould's voice was raised and clearly audible. 'Where—is—Morely?'

Percy gasped again, and Mary exclaimed:

'He doesn't know, and nor do I! We were to meet him at the Raboth this morning but he didn't arrive.'

'Yes?' snarled Arnould. 'You little bitch, I'll make you talk, I'll . . .' He broke off, and Bruce could almost see the malevolence in his dark eyes. 'Why did Morely follow me?'

'He wanted to find out what you were after.'

'Why?'

'I'm not in his confidence!'

There was the sound of a blow, and another oath from Percy; obviously Arnould had struck Mary. Bruce tightened his lips, and shone his light down the steps. As he did so he saw a moving shadow, and a quiet voice called:

'Bruce?'

'Up here, in a hurry,' urged Bruce, and his voice travelled clearly although it was no more than a whisper. Mick reached his side. 'Arnould's trying some third degree.'

'What do we do?'

'Get Mary and Percy and try to put some fear into Arnould,' snapped Bruce. 'Let's move.'

The light coming from beneath the door was enough to show the way, and both men slipped automatics from their pockets as they hurried. Arnould's heavy breathing was audible, and Percy was muttering to himself.

The door was on the far side of the hallway. Bruce spared a moment to see that the big front door was locked; Arnould would consider himself safe.

But how many men did he have with him?

'Three, as well as Victor,' grunted Mick. 'Are you going to burst in?'

Bruce gripped the handle of the door, turned it, and pushed. The door opened a fraction of an inch, and the light grew stronger. He heard Arnould say very suavely:

'I don't care how much I hurt you, you bitch. I mean to know who Morely works for. It will do no harm to him or to anyone.'

'No,' said Bruce, in the guttural voice that might have been expected from Gustav Morenson.

He stepped through, the gun pointing at Arnould and Victor. Both were in front of Mary and Percy, each of whom was bound to a chair. Percy's shirt was torn from one shoulder and there were red-brown marks of cigarette burns on the flesh.

Mary looked distraught and dishevelled.

Three of von Rintzen's men were lounging by a fire of logs burning brightly in a large open fireplace. But it was not at them, nor the prisoners, nor Arnould and his man, that Bruce stared—with such surprise that he gave Arnould an opportunity of turning the tables.

For he was looking at a man lounging back in an old-fashioned easy chair, a man who should have been in England. A man with a leonine head, grey hair with one streak of black, a fresh complexion, grey eyes that stared towards him in consternation.

He was looking at Cole, of Frayle Manor.

Cole—here!

# 18

# A Suggestion of Terms

The room was large, high-ceilinged, bare and cold-looking although the fire threw out a considerable heat. There was electric light from a powerful bulb in the centre of the ceiling, and the light was not shaded. About the room six men stood—for as Bruce entered Cole leapt to his feet—like actors in tableau, while Percival Briggs gasped, and Mary's eyes were suddenly filled with hope.

Bruce stepped through, Mick on his heels.

Mick kept by the door, his gun covering the assembly, while Bruce pocketed his automatic and took out a knife. He looked expressionlessly at Arnould while he cut the cords that fastened Mary, and then those of Percy Briggs.

Percy muttered: 'Ta.'

Arnould recovered first, wasting no time; his head was cocked upwards and his eyes very narrow. His face was expressionless and hardly a muscle moved.

'So Morely has more friends.'

'More than you realise,' said Bruce, retaining the voice of Morenson and speaking in German. 'Get their guns, Graham.'

He intended to use Mick's alias for the time being at least, and he wanted to make Arnould believe he was not Morely. His own gun kept the others inactive, while Mick collected a miscellany of weapons. Victor, who was holding a cigarette, muttered sibilantly, the only one who protested. Percy Briggs moved quickly from his chair.

'Don't come it, see?' He jabbed a short-arm punch to Victor's middle, and the dumb man gasped and doubled up, dropping his cigarette. Percy seized it, made as though to push it against Victor's neck, but drew back and then leered. 'I'll teach you, you long streak o' sin. Burn me, would you . . .'

Percy's outburst was easily excusable, but Bruce motioned him back, and the Cockney obeyed, touching one of the cigarette burns on his shoulder gently.

Cole sat down slowly in his chair.

'What—have you come for?'

'Friends of mine, and of Morely,' snapped 'Herr Morenson'. 'And *you*?'

Arnould said softly: 'There are many of us.'

'Words won't help you.' The last of the guns were collected, the men were harmless, and Bruce felt fully in the ascendant, although even then Arnould's sinister eyes seemed to hold an unspoken threat. 'Klein, we are going to report this to the authorities, it will be serious. You are connected with espionage, you have kidnapped two English people—in every way it will not be good hearing for the police. Is that clear?'

Arnould's tongue crept along his lips.

'And you . . .'

'You've nothing against us. We have come merely for our friends.' His eyes glittered frostily. 'They allowed themselves to be kidnapped; your men were followed.'

Cole snapped: 'Why?'

'Herr Morenson' turned slowly towards him.

'Because you are not the only people who would find Sir Frederick Allaway profitable. Where is he?'

'Say nothing!' cried Arnould.

Bruce lifted a hand, with the thumb bent, in Percy's direction. Percy stood up with alacrity, and tapped

Arnould on the top of his long, thin nose. The tears sprang to the man's eyes; he looked absurd and no longer sinister.

'Let this be understood,' Bruce said. 'We want Allaway. If we don't get him the authorities will have the story of what you have done tonight.'

'And what *you* have done,' said Cole slowly. His German was fluent, almost that of a native's.

'Don't waste time,' said Bruce impatiently, 'I said before that words will get you nowhere. Where is Allaway?'

Cole said: 'Not here, nor anywhere in Scovia.'

Bruce had not expected for one moment to find the stolen Diplomatic Adviser at Reikmann's Folle, but it might serve a purpose if he pretended disappointment. He saw a glint of satisfaction in Cole's eyes, and Arnould's.

Arnould sneered: 'You expected it very simple. I . . .'

'Keep quiet,' said Bruce. 'Allaway's valuable, and I've Morley's permission to come to terms—if you look like keeping any agreement. We want a share, is that understood?'

'Yes.' Arnould licked his lips again, and seemed much less troubled, while Cole seemed to lose the tension that had tightened about him. 'We can perhaps arrange it. We might even use you and Morely again, even if he did lie and trick us.'

'Don't be all of a fool,' said Bruce. 'He had no idea of what was to happen. You had been watched. Anyhow, we are discussing Allaway.'

'Arrangements are being made for a financial transaction,' said Arnould softly. 'If you interfere, it might well fall through. It is a rich prize.'

'How rich?'

'Half-a-million American dollars.'

Bruce gasped—partly with genuine surprise.

'As much as that?'

'One quarter of which can be yours,' said Arnould suavely. 'The papers have already been sold for fifty thousand American dollars. Our buyer is serious.'

Bruce narrowed his eyes, and then motioned to Percy. 'Briggs—see what Klein has got in his pockets.'

Percy jumped up with even greater alacrity, but Arnould struck out at him as he touched his shoulder. Percy stopped him with a short-arm jab to the stomach, a favourite punch of his. Cole stood glaring as Percy took a wallet, some papers, loose change and a watch from Arnould's pocket, and handed them to Bruce. Mick kept his gun levelled while Bruce went through the papers, stuffing them in his pocket when he saw they were not what he wanted. He turned to the wallet— and heard Arnould gasp.

A moment later the Allaway Papers, written in the fine sloping writing that he had seen on the half-finished letters to Lucille, were clutched in Bruce Murdoch's hand!

.　　　.　　　.　　　.　　　.

Bruce looked up at Arnould, and his smile was of sheer enjoyment.

'Thank you,' he said gently. 'I shall keep these to show earnest. Miss Day—Briggs—go to the door. Klein, these Papers are yours—for one fourth of Allaway's ransom you can buy them when you like.' He glanced at Mick. 'Is the key in the lock, Graham? Take it out, we will lock them in while we get away.'

Arnould shouted: 'You shall have a quarter, a half! I must have those Papers now, I must . . .'

'Later,' said Bruce.

He slipped out, and Mick locked the door on the six men inside. Percy was grinning like a Cheshire cat, and Mary gripped Bruce's arm.

'That was wonderful! But . . .'

'All buts later,' said Bruce. 'We can do a deal worth

178

doing with these things, and we've got Arnould on the hop. Not to mention Cole.' He was leading her towards the staircase and the cellar, speaking as he went. 'They gave you no idea of where Allaway is?'

'No. Bruce, wouldn't it have been wiser to have tried to make Arnould talk?'

Bruce laughed. 'Why not fly to the moon? No, darling, Arnould has bad points but talking isn't one of them. We've got him in a spot where he has to bargain with us, and he will. Then we'll have him in another spot he doesn't know anything about yet.'

'Do you?' asked Mary faintly.

'You'd be surprised,' said Bruce.

.　　　.　　　.　　　.　　　.

Sir Robert Holt sat rigidly at his small desk, which was as untidy as usual. He was alone, and breathing stertorously. In front of him was a message in code, received half-an-hour before from Litrakka, and by its side was the decoded rendering.

'Have possession of Allaway Papers stop have reason to believe Allaway in Scandinavia stop Arnould known here as Klein negotiating with Berlin through German Scovian Ambassador for exchange of Allaway for money stop am unofficially assisting Ambassador while ostensibly working for Klein stop could sell Ambassador Papers over Klein's head thus forcing Klein to deal with Allaway in person and offer evidence of his well-being and whereabouts stop alternatively could compose false papers for Ambassador but not considered wise stop radio permission to Mureth for me to deal in genuine Papers if possible urgent stop woman Lucille and man Cole also here stop how the blazes did Cole get out of the country stop Signed A3.'

179

The Pink 'Un read it again, gulped, began to pluck at his chin, then slowly began to smile. A seraphic smile which lightened his keen eyes and twitched his babyish lips, and a smile which spread until it became a chuckle, and from a chuckle to a laugh. He laughed for fully three minutes before he pressed a bell for Gordon.

'You rang, sir?'

'Eh?' The Pink 'Un was so busy chuckling that he stared at Gordon blankly. 'I—of course I rang, you damned fool, what else would you be here for? The car, Gordon, and telephone the Prime Minister that I would like to see him, then telephone Glennie, the Foreign Minister, Gordon, and advise him that he might be wise to go to Number 10 straight away. Got all that?'

'Perfectly, sir.'

'Then what are you waiting for?' Holt waved Gordon out and lifted a telephone, being connected on a through line with the Secret Messages Department at Whitehall. 'Hallo—hallo, S.M. Holt speaking. Holt—H—O—L—T —I should think you had got it! A message to A3 at Scovia S1. "Suspend operations stop advising yes or no within the hour stop it must be Cole's double he's still at Frayle Manor stop you are reprimanded for impertinence stop Signed A". Got that?' roared Holt.

'Yes, sir.' The man at the other end repeated the message but omitted 'you are reprimanded for impertinence'. Holt chuckled.

'Put it in, put it all in, everyone in this world doesn't take me seriously, thank God.'

He pushed the telephone away from him and hurried downstairs. His car was drawn up three doors along, and he climbed into it, forgetful of hat and coat although the night air was cold. He stepped out briskly and entered Number 10 with his expression set and serious. Glennister was already there, and they were taken into the Prime Minister's study immediately.

Holt saw the P.M.'s lined, worried face and forbore exuberances.

' 'Evening, P.M. I've word from young Murdoch. He has the Allaway Papers, thinks he might trade them—in a manner of speaking—for Allaway himself.'

The Prime Minister's head jerked up, and Glennister drew a sharp breath.

'Can you be sure?'

'Yes, yes,' said the Pink 'Un, 'Murdoch's just sent a cable.' He took the decoded message from his pocket and spread it out in front of the Prime Minister. 'Murdoch does work fast, I didn't expect this, but there you are.'

There was a silence for some minutes, before the man at the desk looked up, thoughtful and intent.

'So Murdoch wishes to sell the genuine Papers to Germany in the hope of tracing Allaway through the Ambassador?' It was indicative of the Prime Minister's feelings that he made no comment on the evidence supplied that an Ambassador to a neutral country was occupied in espionage. 'Is it not somewhat involved?'

'Yes,' said Holt, 'but obviously he can win a lot of confidence by producing the genuine article. Murdoch knows what he's doing, and what he wants to do. Thing is, P.M., how much damage will the showing of the Papers do?'

Glennister said quietly: 'They give practically nothing away beyond stating that Allaway believes he can get the non-combatant countries in line with each other. Word of the Allaway Plan will certainly have reached Berlin by now.'

'Just what I think,' said Holt.

'Yes.' The Prime Minister fingered the message, adjusted his glasses, and cleared his throat. 'The matter is increasingly urgent. I have word through this evening that great pressure is being put on Scovia, Aravia, Shrinland and Lenmark. Of course, the rumour of Allaway's plan explains that. At the moment we can offer nothing to offset the demands being made, except'—he shrugged —'our armed assistance. We can, in fact, do little. But the subjection of the Scandinavian countries'—unconsciously the Prime Minister was slipping into the precise, lucid manner he used in the House—'by threats or by armed force will be equally disastrous for them, and will make our own position immeasurably more dangerous. We must stop that—if it can be stopped.'

Holt nodded slowly. The P.M. had a way of putting known facts in such a way that their urgency and importance became overpowering.

'Murdoch should handle it as he thinks best,' Glennister said. 'He can do no harm. He might find Allaway, who is the one man who can stop—or might stop—the collapse of the Scandinavians.'

'Yes.' The Prime Minister hesitated, looked at Holt gravely, and tapped the paper. 'I should consult the others, but—the urgency could hardly be exaggerated. Murdoch may act as he thinks fit.'

'Good man,' said Holt, and without asking for permission he grabbed a telephone. He gave the Sloane Square number, and then: 'Give me Secret Messages, Gordon—right . . . S.M., this is Holt. Message to A3 at Scovia S1. "Proceed immediately as circumstances demand stop fail and you're fired stop Signed A1".' He replaced the receiver and stared owlishly at the Prime Minister. 'Murdoch won't fail after that.'

Glennister covered a smile. The Prime Minister looked puzzled, and then openly chuckled.

'Of course Murdoch will be far less concerned about failing his country than being fired, Holt!' He lifted his hand, then pushed his chair back and stepped to a cabinet against the wall, a cabinet in which there was a bottle of brandy. 'Holt, you are an astonishing fellow, and I know you have much to put up with, but I do wish you would be a little more discreet at times.'

'Discreet!' gasped Holt, and accepted a glass, savoured the brandy and sipped, his hands cupping the glass as if in reverence. 'Hear that, Glennister, the man says I'm not discreet! Now if I'd told Marridew what I really think of him . . .'

The Prime Minister smiled.

'Spare us that! At all events . . .' The P.M. looked up from his glass, and the expression on his face was almost haggard. 'We must save the neutrals. If we don't the world *will* be torn to pieces, it won't stop at Scandinavia.'

Holt said: 'Saving the neutrals and finding Allaway being synonymous, we're in Murdoch's hands.'

'Yes—yes, I think we may say that,' the P.M. admitted.

'Then God help him,' said Holt soberly.

# 19

# Item by Item

Bruce Murdoch had returned to the Schohn Hotel by the time Doktor Mureth received Holt's message and sent it, decoded, by hand. Ted Angell reported that Lucille had not yet returned, and was presumably at the Embassy. Mary and Percy were at the Raboth, and Mary had dressed Percy's two burns, both inflicted at Arnould's orders by Victor, as a means of persuading him to say where 'Morely' was.

Percy was with Mary, while one of Mureth's men stayed in the next room, to make sure that there was no surprise attack.

Bruce, Ted and Mick were in Ted's room at the Schohn, while a local agent would telephone them as soon as Lucille or Victor reappeared. Two of Mureth's men had been left at Reikmann's Folle, with instructions to try to follow Cole.

'And Cole,' said Bruce as he ate sandwiches of true Scandinavian lusciousness, 'is our main personal problem. If it *was* him . . .'

'It was the man I was watching at Frayle Manor,' said Mick.

'You're sure?'

'Or his double.'

'He had Cole's voice,' said Bruce slowly. 'More likely the man at the Manor is the double. Anyhow, Cole may have to wait. We've got the Papers, and permission to handle the situation as we think fit.'

'You're going to von Rintzen with them?'

'Yes, as soon as Lucille's back. We've got to wait on her for the time being, and meanwhile'—he smiled—'I'll go and have a talk with Mary. You wouldn't agree that the risk I took with her has justified itself, would you?'

'If there's one man I can't bear,' said Ted Angell distastefully, 'it's the man who is always right. You'll do, go and whisper pretty things.'

.　　　.　　　.　　　.　　　.

There was much of the gentleman about von Rintzen, Lucille was prepared to admit. He had a charm of manner not suggested by his powdered face and piggish eyes. In some ways he was clever. He talked a great deal about the Allaway Plan, yet said nothing to intimate whether Berlin had accepted or turned down the offer. As Lucille put the finishing touches to her make-up, sitting in her negligée in front of the dressing-table mirror, she wondered just how clever von Rintzen was. Did his overwhelming vanity really represent the man or was there real intelligence beneath his bullying arrogance to underlings and his courtly manner with her?

Her task had been to estimate von Rintzen's capabilities, and she was not sure that she had succeeded. Arnould would not be pleased.

In his private study Baron von Rintzen reflected on a pleasant interlude, but also with a vague feeling of dissatisfaction. She was charming, she had that 'something' so few women possessed on first acquaintance, she seemed somewhat butterfly-headed yet he had a feeling that she was deep. She was, of course, simply Klein's *aide*, but then such things were understood. She would have had instructions to learn what she could and—the

185

Baron chuckled in self-satisfaction—she had learned little.

He could not rid himself of an impression that she could have told him more than she had. Her eyes were so inviting yet at times tinged with—could it be?—mockery. As if she had been laughing at him. He even went so far as to wonder whether, had he approached her in the right way, she would have said more about Klein. That was it—she gave the impression that she did know more, although his astute questioning had been unrewarded. She had admitted that she knew Klein had the papers and Allaway, but had denied any knowledge of where to find either.

Money? Was money the key? In so delicate a situation, of course, he was not thinking of trifles. She was the inducement submitted by Klein for friendly transactions: but could her allegiance be bought? Klein! He would soon learn that the room had been searched for the papers, and at the Ambassador's instructions. That also was in the game. One only paid money if there was no other means of obtaining what one wanted.

He pulled open a drawer in his desk and studied some figures. They were not encouraging; expenses were remarkably high and for two months nothing had come from Berlin. For a matter of this importance, however, he might safely draw on those secret, private resources.

*Could* he buy her allegiance from Klein?

She tapped discreetly on the door, and the Baron sprang to his feet, clicking his heels as she came through. He groped for his monocle, stuck it in his eye.

'Lucille, you are so quick!'

'I knew you would be busy, Hans.' Her smile was languishing, von Rintzen had a disquieting impression that she was thoroughly at home. 'Perhaps tomorrow you will be less harassed.'

'Tomorrow, tomorrow.' The monocle dropped. 'Lucille, I have been thinking. Klein—do you like him?'

186

Lucille laughed, deep in her throat.

'How could I? It is profitable to work for him.'

So that was it, thought von Rintzen, and he congratulated himself.

'Profitable, yes, profitable. Others . . .' He shrugged, and looked away. 'But I must not talk of business to you, Lucille, even Klein's business.'

'No,' said Lucille softly. 'It would be unprofessional, Excellency.' She *was* laughing at him, and he took the plunge when he was assured of that.

'These Papers—why should Klein receive fifty thousand dollars, Lucille, and give you—how much?'

'Perhaps five,' she said.

'Fifteen would interest you more?' He seemed casual.

Lucille lifted her hands slightly, rested them for a moment on his arm.

'May I see you tomorrow, Hans?'

'Tomorrow,' murmured von Rintzen, and nodded slowly. 'I shall be living for it. I will send the car for you. No others need know, *hein*?'

'Why should they?' asked Lucille.

When she had gone, von Rintzen sat back in his chair and pondered. Fifteen instead of fifty thousand dollars would be a fine bargain. He need put only forty thousand dollars against the expense item for payment by Berlin. As for the possibility that Klein would hedge on the main business of Allaway, there was no fear of that. The half-million was Klein's interest, the fifty thousand a preliminary in which von Rintzen had come out best. *If* she obtained the Papers.

'Yes, who is that?' He heard the tapping at the door and barked the words, to hear Kurt and to tell him to enter.

'What is it?'

'The Swede, Morenson, Excellency. He has been to see Klein, somewhere towards the coast, in the darkness he could not be followed. He is now back at the Schohn, Excellency.'

'His rooms were searched?'

'He is what he claims, and the other is an Englishman named Cartwright. I have seen the papers.'

'Address me as Excellency!' roared von Rintzen. 'All right, you may go.'

The door closed promptly, and the Ambassador thought of Gustav Morenson. He, too, might have access to the Papers, and perhaps could be bought for less than fifteen thousand dollars. Von Rintzen scowled. Was this diplomacy, or even espionage? Was it not like banking, saving a small sum here, a smaller one there? The Baron's lips curved distastefully and he groped for his monocle before opening the favourite photograph album on his desk.

.        .        .        .        .

Cole, or the man who looked like Cole, was the first to move after the door at Reikmann's Folle had been locked on its occupants. He had Cole's manner, at all events, and he spoke in English and a voice Murdoch would have recognised. The three men from von Rintzen did not know the tongue.

'Arnould, you told me that Morely was working on his own.'

'At the time I believed so.' Arnould's fingers were plucking at a button on his coat. 'Victor, unlock that door! I don't think so now,' he added.

'Mistakes of that nature are important,' Cole said. 'And you also told me that no one had followed you to Scovia.'

'That was impossible.'

'Then how did they find you?'

'Have you not seen the possibilities?' There was venom in Arnould's voice, enough to startle Cole and to make him stare.

188

'What possibilities?'

'How else could he have located me so quickly, unless he had agents here? How could I have been recognised here unless my description was given? How else but by radio or cable? How could Morely call on so many *private* assistants?'

Cole drew a sharp breath.

'England . . .'

'Holt's men perhaps. Or French, or even Russian. It could be American. Anyone's,' snapped Arnould. 'There is no other way in which it could have been contrived. We are not fighting Morely, we are fighting someone much stronger.'

'Can—can you . . .' Cole seemed to have lost his confidence.

'Find out who? Of course. But we shall soon see if he is English or French, we shall soon know more. He may try to sell the Papers to von Rintzen, no Allied agent would do that. *Sacre diable*, it gets worse! Allaway himself must be kept quite safe—can you be sure he is?'

'Quite sure,' said Cole, and he became the confident, aristocratic Englishman he had seemed to Bruce Murdoch. 'I shall go to Bohn, you will get back to Litrakka and deal with the Swede and the others. Telephone me Lucille's report. She is quite trustworthy, I hope?'

Arnould's expression was not nice.

'She knows what would happen if she was not, you need not fear that. Victor, open that . . .' He broke off, for Victor had forced the lock, and opened the door. 'Let us go,' he grunted.

With the three men borrowed from von Rintzen, and Victor, he started back for Litrakka. While Cole headed to the second largest city in Scovia, which was also the biggest port—the city of Bohn.

Doktor Mureth's men followed him.

.        .        .        .        ɪ

189

Sir Frederick Allaway sat in a chair as comfortable as any he had used in his life, stared blankly at a mezzotint on a wall otherwise bare of pictures, and drummed his fingers on his knee. He was remarkably like Henrietta, with the same predatory nose, the same intense and fiery eyes, the same taut mouth. His face was pale, his eyes seemed feverish, and from time to time his lips parted, as though he wanted to speak but could not.

He was alone.

He did not know where.

He was alone, with his thoughts for company, and they were not pleasant thoughts. He had failed, failed once again, to achieve an overwhelming ambition, and he had not only failed but he had endangered his life and possibly the lives of millions of others. For all his ambition, Allaway was not essentially a vain man. The plan for the neutrals had to be submitted to practical test before it was proved effective. But a lifetime of experience in diplomatic *affairs* convinced him that the scheme was not only workable, but could be arranged quickly.

He had heard the news bulletins from England twice since he had left Norton Road, and there had been no mention of him. He wondered whether it was known that he had disappeared. He remembered, as a man would remember a nightmare, the attack that had been made on him by the insistent Arnould. Arnould who for all his menace and threats had an ingratiating way with him, Arnould who had dangled as a bribe certain political advancement, and then finally come to the point: he wanted particulars of the Plan.

Allaway, of course, had sent him about his business. Or so he had thought. And then Arnould had made other suggestions.

He remembered to this moment with a terrifying vividness the revolver that had leapt into the Frenchman's hand after their talk.

190

Then, the blackness . . .

What had struck him on the head he did not know. When he had awakened he had been at sea, the rolling of a small boat had left him in no doubt of that. Since then he had been treated with exemplary courtesy, while being transferred to a rowing-boat and taken to a country that might—for all he knew—have been England. It had been pitch dark.

A journey, neither long, nor short, by car.

Terrifying darkness . . .

This house, which he had not seen. A room sumptuously furnished by day, a comfortable bedroom, everything he could wish in the way of food, even a bathroom suite—it might have been a luxury hotel. But it was silent, so silent that at times he switched on the radio for the sake of hearing a human voice.

No one had been to see him except a soft-footed servant who uttered no word, but attended his wants without being asked, brought food and cleared away. Outside the door, he had seen a shadowy-looking man carrying an automatic.

There were no windows, no other doors; and the one was always locked. He did not know that he sat sometimes for half-an-hour in a state of semi-consciousness cunningly calculated to bring him more quickly to breaking point. He knew, of course, that he would be asked for the full details of the Plan.

Allaway stirred and muttered: 'Damn them, I won't!'

And then he continued to stare ahead of him.

While he stared blankly, his sister was lying in bed at a Weymouth nursing home. She had recovered consciousness some hours after being brought ashore, but had not spoken. Friends who lived near had hurried to the bedside; they identified Henrietta beyond doubt, yet obtained no sign of recognition. Her fiery eyes were dulled and lifeless, her pallid face looked that of a corpse.

191

Local doctors diagnosed 'shock'. Bournemouth specialists confirmed it. Sir Randolph Weir, who flew from London to Weymouth at the express desire of the Prime Minister, flew back and said to Sir Robert Holt:

'Shock.'

'How long will it last?' Holt wanted to know.

'Forty-eight hours or a fortnight. It could be even longer, and she might not get over it. In my opinion, Holt, she received a severe mental shock some forty-eight hours before I saw her, and that in addition to mild morphine poisoning to induce sleep was sufficient to unbalance her.'

The Pink 'Un plucked at his middle chin.

'Mentally unbalanced, eh?'

'It could be.'

'So she isn't likely to talk sense when she does come round?'

'Judging from parallel cases I would say it is unlikely.'

'Hmm,' said Holt, and stared at the specialist for some seconds. 'Well, thanks, Weir, thanks a lot. How soon can she be moved to London?'

'I don't advise moving her until she shows more signs of animation,' said Weir. 'There's just one thing that might help her. She's always been very close to her brother. Has he been to see her?'

'No,' said the Pink 'Un promptly.

'I suggest that he does,' advised Sir Randolph Weir, and he did not know that when Gordon had shown him out, the Chief of British Intelligence demanded angrily of his long, low room whether Weir could suggest a way in which Allaway could be spirited back.

'Oh, damn and blast it!' roared Holt as the door opened and Gordon came in. 'Don't stand around like a tailor's dummy, go and make some tea. Hurry! Oh, Gordon . . .'

'Yes, sir?'

'Wherever I am or whatever I'm doing, see that I'm

192

told of any message from Mr Murdoch without a moment's delay. Not a moment, do you understand?'

'Perfectly, sir.'

Gordon went out to make tea.

While in Litrakka Bruce Murdoch and Ted Angell left the Schohn Hotel by a side door, succeeded in eluding the man Klein had put on their heels, and at the German Embassy begged an interview with Baron von Rintzen. He was shown into a cold waiting-room with Ted, and they were left to cool their heels, for the Embassy was a hive of industry.

Von Rintzen had received fresh instructions from Berlin—instructions virtually presenting an ultimatum to the Scovian Government.

# Ultimatum

Von Rintzen in uniform was a different man, and he wore uniform whenever the opportunity presented itself. Such an opportunity came that night. As a Colonel of the Imperial German Guard, he was driven from the Embassy while Bruce and Ted were in the waiting-room, reached the Scovian Senate House, and was shown immediately to white-haired Larson, the Premier, whose whole life had been spent in perfecting the democracy of Scovia. Larson was seventy-one, but physically fit, shrewd, clever, cautious and patient. He was clean-shaven and his skin was very fair and smooth. He had the gentle manner and the soft voice of an apostle and those who saw him for the first time gained an impression of spiritual calm and assurance which was only partially justified, for Larson was often strongly materialistic.

He shook hands with von Rintzen, almost against the Baron's will.

'It is an unexpected pleasure, your Excellency. May I offer you . . .'

'There is no time,' said von Rintzen stiffly. 'I have a matter of extreme urgency and importance to discuss. I am requested to send a reply to Berlin within twenty-four hours. It is a simple matter, Herr Larson. The deplorable frequency of accidents on the high seas, where Scovian vessels have unfortunately been sunk due to the obstinacy of their captains, is concerning my Government. You see, I am most frank.' Von Rintzen groped for his monocle, finding it among an imposing array of medals. 'I am able to offer Scovian ships escort and secure transport to German or Russian ports, but am requested to advise you that any other destination is undesirable and, in fact, the shipping of goods to other countries than those will be considered a hostile act. Is it understood?'

Larson looked from the Prussian's powdered face to his desk. He had been expecting another move from Berlin, but the naked threat underlying these words came as a shock.

'Is it understood?' demanded von Rintzen again.

Larson looked up, his blue eyes shadowed.

'Yes, your Excellency, it is understood. Is there any other consideration?'

'To further the safety of Scovian shipping and to insure Scovia against attacks from other countries, it will be necessary to establish naval bases, aircraft bases and garrisons in coastal towns, Herr Larson.' Von Rintzen shrugged. 'That can be arranged afterwards, it is not important.'

Larson's head jerked up, his blue eyes no longer shadowed but cold and angry.

'Indeed, Excellency? Were your instructions such as to make it necessary for you to transmit this *démarche* in so arbitrary a fashion? Have you forgotten the established canons of diplomatic precedence? Am I'— Larson lifted his hands sharply, a rare gesture from so quiet-mannered a man—'am I to be bellowed at by one whom I had believed to be a gentleman?'

Von Rintzen gaped.

'Herr Larson, this matter is not one for idle talk.'

'You have been badly misinformed if you have been told that Scovia is unable to defend itself, equally misin-

195

formed if you believe that so impertinent a demand can be presented and answered within twenty-four hours. Have the goodness to submit detailed particulars of your Government's astonishing communication, and to leave this building.'

'But . . .' Von Rintzen was too astounded to be out-raged.

'The communication,' snapped Larson.

'I was instructed to present it verbally.'

'I can only suggest that you refer to your Government for fresh instructions,' said Larson coldly. 'Goodnight, your Excellency.'

He pressed a bell, three times. Two secretaries and two uniformed members of the Scovian Civil Guard entered promptly, and Larson said: 'Escort Herr Baron von Rintzen from the building.'

Like a man in a dream von Rintzen walked out, down the stairs, through the wide halls of the Senate House, and into his car. His chauffeur drove off immediately, and von Rintzen struggled for breath. By the time he reached the Embassy he was in a choleric rage. He ranted, cursed, swore and called damnation on the head of Larson and all Scovians. Into his presence, terrified more than ever he had been, entered Kurt, who stood stiffly to attention by the door.

'What is it?' roared von Rintzen. 'Am I to be annoyed by a white-livered fool of a man who . . .'

'It is of importance, Excellency. The Allaway Papers.'

'Get out!' roared von Rintzen. 'They are not impor-tant, they are not important. Get out!'

'Yes, Excellency.' Kurt retreated, hesitated outside the door, and hurried downstairs to tell Bruce and Ted that there was no likelihood of an audience. He communi-cated something of the Baron's rage.

'It *is* of vital importance, Kurt. Where has he been?'

196

'To the Senate House. He has seen Herr Larson.'

'I see,' said Bruce gently. 'Show me his room, will you?'

'*Donnerwetter*, it would be suicide to try to see him! He is in the main study, but—*mein Gott!*'

For Bruce drew his hand from his pocket, and showed a gun. Of all things Kurt had expected, to be held up in the Embassy was the last. Ted stepped to the door and found the passage empty. 'Lead the way,' said Bruce, 'and don't make any mistakes.'

Kurt, his powers of resistance already weakened by von Rintzen's rage, submitted at once. Gun in pocket, Bruce followed him. They passed several minor officials, including one little group of people huddled together and discussing the Ambassador's rage, the worst paroxysm he had been known to have. An atmosphere of nervous apprehension filled the Embassy, and seemed to culminate in Kurt.

'You—you will not say who . . .'

'I'll go in without you,' Bruce said. 'And Kurt . . .'

'Yes?'

'This gun can kill von Rintzen as well as you.'

Kurt swore by the Fates that he would stand outside the door and not move. Bruce glanced at Ted.

'Better watch him.'

'What are you going to do?'

'Find out what's happened,' said Bruce. He smiled but did not feel amused as they stopped outside the oak door of the main study, and he tapped. He heard a roar of 'Keep out!', tapped more loudly and, when the roar was repeated, flung the door open and stepped inside.

Von Rintzen was pacing up and down the room, his eyes wild and his hands beating the air. He did not see Bruce until the latter had reached the desk. On it were several papers, including one marked *For His Excellency's Private Attention—Urgent.*

197

Von Rintzen was about to turn. Bruce watched him while slipping the paper from the desk and stuffing it in his pocket, with a conjuror's skill. Von Rintzen saw nothing but the man by his desk.

'*Mein Gott!* Did I not say keep out?'

'Excellency!' Bruce took a step forward, cringed, lifted both hands as though in supplication. 'It is of the greatest urgency. I have obtained the Allaway Papers!'

'They matter nothing! They—*what*?'

'I have them, Excellency! At great personal risk . . .'

Von Rintzen gasped.

'You—you *have* the Papers? Now? Here?'

'It is so, Excellency . . .' Bruce thrust his hand deep into his pocket and drew the memorandum out. Von Rintzen snatched it, stared down, and his lips moved as he read the English slowly. Two sentences sufficed him, and he stepped sharply to the desk, his rage disappearing completely. He lifted a telephone.

'Berlin—at once! Morenson—where did you get these?'

'From Klein. The opportunity came . . .'

'How long have you had them?'

'No more than an hour, Excellency.'

'It is good.' The Baron rubbed his hands together, and a smile began to twist his lips. 'It is very good work, Morenson, I shall not forget.'

'Excellency, the reward . . .'

'Ach, you will receive it, there are other things you will be doing for me. Go now, return early tomorrow.' He even stepped to the door and opened it, while Bruce went through, Ted and Kurt scuttling out of sight. 'To-morrow, Morenson.'

The door banged. The key turned in the lock. To try to get back and to overhear the text of the call to Berlin would be a waste of time, and Bruce said:

'Bring Kurt along, Ted.'

'Mein Herr!' protested Kurt.

'Don't argue,' said Ted Angell mildly. 'Do what Uncle Morenson tells you, and mind my gun.' He kept it in his pocket but poked Kurt in the ribs. The trio hurried out, into the waiting car, and with Bruce driving reached the Raboth. Mary was in her room, and she opened the door promptly at Bruce's knock. If she was surprised by Kurt's presence she made no comment.

'Push Kurt in the other room, Percy can look after him,' Bruce said. 'Mary, you read German much better than I do. Can you translate this?'

He handed her the crumpled paper, and she began to read aloud. Within four minutes the purport of von Rintzen's message to Larson was known to Bruce, Mary and Ted. Mary had not finished reading when Bruce reached for the telephone, and as she read the last word he was speaking to Mureth.

'Advise A1 to stand by for an important message. I am coming over at once.'

'I will do it immediately,' said Mureth easily. 'The man you had followed from Reikmann's Folle, A3, has gone to a house in Bohn. Is that urgent?'

'It will be, after this. Keep him watched, please.'

Bruce rang off, and turned to Mary and Ted. Both were appalled by what they had heard, knew that the neutral countries were about to be submitted to a pressure almost too strong to bear. It was an ultimatum; and if the usual Nazi methods were to be followed, within twenty-four hours the attack on Scovia would have started.

For Scovia would undoubtedly reject the *démarche*.

In those minutes, vivid and crystal clear, the three people there seemed to hear the roaring of enemy aircraft over Scovia, hear the violent explosions as the bombs dropped, see the fires that started, the panic spreading in the streets, the tortured cries of men, wo-

199

men and children. It had happened in Warsaw; it could happen here.

But why the sudden decision?

A Nazi *putsch* into Scandinavia could mean one of two things. Action in concert with the Soviet, or action to prevent the Soviet's influence spreading. The threat to Scandinavia had been expected from Moscow, not Berlin.

'Ours not to reason why,' said Bruce wryly. 'At least they'll have early warning in London. They . . .'

He reached the door, but it opened before he touched the handle. He dropped his hand to his pocket but did not touch his gun, for Klein *alias* Arnould was standing on the threshold with an automatic levelled, and Victor was supporting him. Two other men, one a stranger, were in support of Klein's party. The second newcomer was Smith, *alias* Jem Dace . . .

And his thick lips looked moist as if with anticipation.

'So, the three of you together,' Arnould said, leading the others in. His slanting eyes, upturned for his head was no longer cocked upwards, but seemed to have hunched into his narrow shoulders, looked at Bruce and glittered with malevolent anger, the worse because it was so cold and undemonstrative. 'You, of course, are Morely.'

'Guessing won't help you,' Bruce said. He was aghast at the failure of Mureth's men downstairs, who should have warned him of this approach. He wondered fleetingly whether Percy and Mick, at the Schohn, were safe —and then Klein snarled:

'The Papers, where are they?'

'Too important for you to play with,' retorted Bruce.

'I will give you one minute to produce them. If they are not in my hand by then I shall shoot, not only you but all three of you.'

Bruce said tensely: 'They hang murderers in Scovia.'

200

'There is no one to catch me, no one to find your bodies,' snarled Arnould. 'You will be taken to the Folle and thrown to sea, I . . . Half of the minute has gone.' He glanced again at his wrist-watch, and the tension in the room became unbearable.

## 21

# Prepare for War

'You were right, Larson, it was the only way you could have acted. Von Rintzen is . . .' King Henrik of Scovia hesitated, and then said slowly and dispassionately what he thought of Baron von Rintzen. The three members of the Scovian Inner Cabinet heard and agreed, while Henrik lifted his hands helplessly. 'What can we do but prepare for war?'

'Can Russia help?' asked Ekkra, the Foreign Minister.

'Moscow will expect us to ask, but will only present other demands,' replied Larson.

'It must be tried,' said Henrik. His thin, ascetic face, the face of a dreamer, of a man with ideas of Utopia which had nearly come to being in his little kingdom, was pale and harassed; his eyes were filled with unhappiness. 'But we must prepare for war. Thank God the garrisons are as strong as they can be, and the towns are evacuated.'

'England and France?' said Lykoff, Minister for Interior Defence. 'They have been told, your Highness?'

Larson looked at him wearily.

'We have tried to connect with them, but all known radio-wavelengths are jammed, the Germans must have prepared this well in advance. We can only keep trying. Twenty-four hours gives us such little time.'

'We have sent word by air?' asked Lykoff. He was a small, wizened-faced man, with protuberant black eyes and a loose, fleshy mouth.

'Two machines attempted to leave the coast,' Henrik said slowly. 'One was shot down outside territorial waters, the other was forced back. German ships control the coast, German 'planes are patrolling the whole coastline from the air. We are imprisoned in our own country, Lykoff.'

'It is impossible!' Lykoff threw up his hands, and paced the room furiously. 'We must get word through. What of the other Scandinavian countries?'

'For all we know, they may be placed as we are. Since eight o'clock, less than an hour before von Rintzen came, we have been unable to communicate beyond the frontiers. In time, of course, we shall get word through, but time is vital. In twenty-four hours the whole of Litrakka can be in ruins.'

Lykoff stopped, swung round.

'And you say fight?'

'I say prepare for war!' corrected Henrik. 'Berlin has given us twenty-four hours.' He broke off, and looked at Larson. 'What can you tell me of the Allaway Plan?'

'There was word of it, but no comfirmation. London has been silent on the matter. I have been speaking with Sir Hugh d'Arcy, but he has no word. No Embassy, British, French, Italian—no one can get word through to the capitals.'

Larson stopped.

Into the Council Chamber of the Senate House there came a droning sound that was familiar and yet in some ways different from anything they had heard before. Deep-toned, ominous, menacing. It drew nearer and louder. Henrik stepped swiftly to a window, pulled the heavy curtains aside, and peered into the night. The others crowded after him. Against the lighter greyness of the sky they could see the dark shapes of aeroplanes flying in formation.

Then suddenly a flash of flame, near them, revealed three 'planes clearly. The echoing reverberation of an anti-aircraft gun, started by a commanding officer who had taken it on himself to open fire. Another *boom!* another and another. The flames were bursting about the craft that flew towards the centre of Scovia in constant succession now; other batteries opened fire, the air was filled with the thunder of the guns.

A high-pitched siren sounded, wailing through the rare moments of silence. In the streets what few people had been walking rushed for shelter. In a matter of minutes mobile anti-aircraft units were rushing through the nearly-deserted streets, Air Raid Precaution commandants were in action.

The droning of the aircraft drew nearer to the Senate House. In the reflected glare of the fire about them at least a dozen were visible; black, ominous shapes. Louder, louder, closer, closer . . .

They saw nothing drop.

But the King of Scovia and his Inner Cabinet heard the mighty tongues of flame that sprang up not two hundred yards from the window where they stood, red and yellow flame that billowed outwards. Hardly were their eyes blinded by the flash than the thunder of the explosion came, a gust of wind sent Lykoff swaying off his feet, a splinter of glass cut Larson's forehead.

The walls of the building shook as in an earthquake.

'Away from the window!' Larson cried. 'Away, Highness, and downstairs . . .'

'Wait,' said Henrik.

They could see only his profile. He stood rigidly to attention and appeared to ignore the thunder of explosions while bomb after bomb dropped, some near, some further away. The flames from them illuminated the Civic Centre of the city, made the blackout a mockery for the time being—while by then searchlights were shooting towards the hostile 'planes, a dozen Scovian fighters took to the air.

The walls of the Senate House seemed to be constantly a-tremble, but still Henrik stood like a figure carved from stone. There was a scratch on his right cheek, and the blood trickled down. In the lurid glow that began to spread over the city, he saw the gaping masonry of a building that had been hit and came crashing into ruins. He heard the shouts of the few who had braved the night and not taken cover, heard the rushing of the mobile units, saw the pitifully few shells that burst near their objectives.

A *boom!* much louder than the rest was deafening.

A heavy picture thudded from the wall, and smashed against the Table of State. A vase toppled, fell slowly, smashed.

'Highness, come please!' Larson pleaded.

Henrik turned stiffly, while the droning of the 'planes began to fade. The first wave of bombers had passed the Civic Centre but there was no telling how long they would be gone—nor how many others would come. In front of the eyes of the ruling monarch the destruction of Litrakka, and of Scovia, had begun. It had come within six hours of the presentation of a twenty-four hour ultimatum, proving the desperation of the attackers and their treachery.

He was halfway to the door, with Lykoff, Larson and Ekkra about him, a little frightened by his stiff, automatic movements, when a telephone rang. It seemed a shrill, weird note after the thunder of the bombing, and amidst the lesser bark of the A.A. guns which were still active.

'See who it is,' Henrik said.

'Highness . . .'

'The danger is past,' snapped Henrik, and he reached the telephone and lifted it. He listened, and they saw the bleak expression in his eyes although they could not hear the words that came from a long way off—from the inner offices of the Führer of Greater Germany.

*'His Highness is reminded that little time remains for his acceptance of demands presented through the German Ambassador. His Highness now has some intimation of the uselessness of resistance, and is reminded that the protection of the Reich is offered to Scovia.'*

Just that and no more.

The voice at the other end stopped. Hendrik spoke one word, but he knew that the line was dead, that it was another, newer method of terrorising the smaller nations.

Must he submit?

Or be crushed?

Henrik said quietly to Larson:

'Send word to von Rintzen that he will have his answer in a few hours—by noon tomorrow. Ekkra, make every effort to send word to Britain and France, by any channels. Lykoff, have the army, navy and airforce prepared for immediate resistance, flood the south and south-west frontiers, complete the evacuation of the towns. In short,' said Henrik of Scovia very softly, 'prepare for war.'

.    .    .    .    .

The droning of the approaching aircraft came as Klein looked at his watch for the second time. If they heard it, the men in the Schohn Hotel, and Mary, ignored it. The windows were shuttered, and kept out the sound, they had no idea of the nearness of the raiders. Bruce felt that he was face to face with death, unavoidable because he had given the papers to von Rintzen.

The seconds ticked by.

'The Papers,' said Arnould very softly.

*Boom!*

The sound of a gun was clear, the walls of the hotel

shook in the repercussion, and then another came, a third, a fourth. In that moment all seven people in the room were startled by the suddenness of it, Victor's mouth opened, Smith half-turned. A crash that seemed to be about their very ears added to the din, another brought pictures toppling, sent them off their balance. There was a constant thunder of falling masonry; something crashed against the boarded window, thudded again, smashed its way through. The lights went out with sharp suddenness and dust and smoke filled the room.

*Darkness!*

Bruce's hand flashed to his pocket, Ted gripped Mary's arm and they leapt for the door. Arnould had fallen, and Bruce's foot struck him in the face. Victor was gibbering incoherently, Smith had dropped his gun. But it was Smith and the other newcomer who jumped towards the door to block it. Bruce closed with the man, tried to strike his chin with his gun but failed. Smith aimed a bent knee at Bruce's stomach, but the blow slid off the thigh. Bruce grunted, jabbed a punch to the man's middle, and heard the gasp.

He struck again, savagely, to the chin.

Smith dropped back, his teeth clicking. Ted reached the door, smashing his fists towards the fourth man. There was a red glow about the room from the bursting shells outside—and from a fire that was not far away. In the glow they could see each other. Bruce saw Arnould moving, saw him reach for his fallen gun. Bruce kicked backwards against the man's elbow, and Arnould gasped in pain as he drew back.

Ted went bald-headed for his man.

From her bag Mary took a small automatic. As coolly as if there had been no emergency, as if hell did not reign outside, she fitted a silencer. As Victor regained his self-control and touched his gun, she fired. The bullet went through the dumb man's wrist.

Ted dragged at the door, but it had jammed. Bruce

joined him, while Mary watched the men who were on the floor and helpless against her gun. Victor was staring up, while the face of Arnould seemed that of the devil, with the red glow on his snarling lips, the insane glare in his eyes.

'Jammed completely,' Ted muttered. 'We can't do a thing.'

'The window,' Mary called.

'Keep away from it!' Bruce snapped, and as he spoke another crash came from nearby, and dirt and debris rushed in, a stone caught Mary's forehead and sent her staggering against the wall. 'Keep pulling, Ted.'

He was exerting all his strength when the door opened with a suddenness that made him fall back. Ted also fell, while Mick Fuller and Percival Briggs staggered in, Mick in the lead.

Bruce scrambled up.

'What's it like outside?' he demanded.

'Lousy, but it's nearly over.'

'The roads?'

'You can get out I think.'

'Bring Arnould, leave the others.' Although he implied that one of the others should handle Arnould he yanked the man up himself, then sharply and deliberately brought the butt of his gun down on his head.

'Try and get that door shut and locked again,' Bruce urged. 'There's one thing . . .' He seemed to change the subject with an effort, then continued: 'There won't be many people about.'

Arnould was on his feet with Bruce's hand gripping the back of his coat collar, and Mary at his side with her gun. She had hardly spoken at all, but Bruce could see the strain in her eyes and her pallor. Ted and Mick pulled at the door, had it closed tightly with an effort, and turned the key. Victor, Smith and the unknown would not get out easily.

Percy was standing more or less at ease, and anxious.

'Any instructions for me, sir?'

'A lonely job, Percy. Stay here, and do what you can to stop that precious trio getting out. If I can find one of the local men I'll send him up to join you. At the slightest sign of trouble, make yourself scarce and report'—he lowered his voice, making sure Arnould did not hear— 'to the house of Doktor Mureth.'

'Okey-doke, sir.'

'Luck, Percy!' Bruce smiled fleetingly, and then hurried Arnould along, with Ted, Mary and Mick following. The passages and landings were deserted, and as there was only one floor it was not worth using the lift. The entrance hall of the hotel was almost deserted. One of Mureth's men, a short, stocky Scovian with humorous brown eyes, was smoking a cigarette and talking to a stolid commissionaire.

Bruce jerked his head upwards; the Scovian nodded.

'You go out, sir?' asked the commissionaire, eyeing Arnould curiously. The Frenchman did not appeal for help; even he knew that he was as well off in Bruce's hands as the authorities'.

'Yes, it's urgent,' Bruce said. 'What is it like outside?'

'Quieter now, sir.' The man seemed faintly contemptuous. 'They'll soon be coming out of the shelters.'

They pushed through the revolving doors and stood for a moment on the steps of the Schohn, all of them startled, Bruce and his friends appalled.

A lurid red glow spread over that part of the city, while almost immediately opposite them a store had been hit by a bomb, and a great hole gaped in the front of it. Smoke and flames were rising slowly, not helped by the absence of wind, and an increasing body of firemen were attacking the flames. Fire-engine hooters were sounding in the distance, and coming nearer.

Arnould was bundled in the car, but before Ted had released the brake a policeman approached them.

'No one goes out, please!'

209

'*Agent political*,' said Bruce, and put his hand to his pocket as if to show his papers. The policeman waved them on, and that open sesame provided by Mureth again proved invaluable.

'Do you know the way?' Bruce asked Ted.

'We'll find it.'

The car started off, threading its way through traffic coming towards them in contravention of the one-way traffic rules. Three times they were forced to mount the pavement in order to avoid yawning craters in the road-way, twice they passed demolished buildings which were already on fire. But the droning of the bombers' engines had stopped, only an occasional A.A. shell exploded in the dark heavens. The lighter drone of Scovian fighter and chaser 'planes was some distance away, towards the sea.

Arnould sat back, breathing noisily.

The journey took twice as long as Bruce wanted, for they missed their way twice and had to consult a street plan which Ted had procured. But without being challenged by the authorities they reached Mureth's house.

For the past quarter of a mile they had seen no evidence of damage. The bombs had been dropped, deliberately of course, as close to the Civic Centre as possible. People were in the streets, many moving towards the Centre, others clustered together and talking with nervous excitement.

The Frenchman appeared to be unconscious as they lifted him from the car and carried him to the private door of Mureth's house. Bruce knocked, to have the door opened almost at once by Hilde Mureth. She showed neither alarm nor surprise, but stood aside and let the party in.

'Where is he?' asked Bruce.

'I will show you. Are there others to come?'

'No.'

Hilde nodded, closed and bolted the door, then led

the way to the sitting-room where she had been with her husband on the night of Bruce's arrival in Scovia. Mureth was standing in front of a cabinet which stood open and revealed a radio-transmitter built cunningly into the wall. He turned, unhurriedly.

'So you got through, my friend.'

'Can *you* get through?' Bruce snapped.

'No.' Mureth turned round, and his eyes showed that he was worried even though his expression and his manner were calm. 'I managed to send the first signal, but after that I have had no answer from London. We have, I imagine, been subjected to strong interference.'

He switched on the receiving-set, and a loud crackling, almost as noisy as the gunfire, filled the room.

'Could be interference,' agreed Ted lightly.

Mick grinned, Bruce cocked an eyebrow, and Mureth's lips curved a little. But:

'I am afraid this is not amusing. Do you know what has happened?'

'Mitzer has pushed through an ultimatum but it looks as though he's not going to wait for it to be rejected,' said Bruce. 'I wish to God I'd told you over the 'phone. This might be a solitary raid, just to add a little pressure. Do you think your country will fight or give way?'

'Fight,' answered Mureth simply. 'If it can be called fighting.' Something of what the man was feeling revealed itself in his voice suddenly, a bitter hatred for the people who had started this horror. 'A generation of peaceful, vital work destroyed, the society of decades smashed in a few days by a madman!'

'Keep trying London, sending out word of what's happened, stress the fact that there's a twenty-four-hour ultimatum,' urged Bruce, 'and try to get Sir Robert on the air. But first find me a soundproof room, will you— I know there is one here.'

Mureth raised his brows. 'For interrogation?'

'Interrogation,' agreed Bruce bleakly.

211

He hated the task, but it had to be done. If it were humanely possible Arnould must be forced to reveal the hiding-place of Sir Frederick Allaway. If there was a chance of stopping the holocaust of war spreading to Scovia and thus to the other Scandinavian Powers, it had to be taken.

The soundproof room was on the top floor.

It was barely furnished, and there were two bright lights, both without shades. Several hardwood chairs, a table, and two trestle-beds made up the furniture, and there was no window. It had been used in the past for temporary accommodation of prisoners wanted for interrogation.

Bruce pushed Arnould into a chair, and tied him to it loosely. The scene was remarkably like that at Reikmann's Folle. Mureth touched Mary's arm, and she went out with him. As the door closed Arnould's eyes flickered open, but closed again.

Bruce struck him, flat-handed, across the face.

'Arnould, understand that you are going to talk before you leave this room. Where is Allaway?'

Arnould widened his eyes, and sneered, but he said nothing. Bruce struck the other cheek.

'Where is Allaway?'

Arnould's eyes narrowed to slits, and his lips set obstinately. Bruce pulled the movable lamp above the prisoner's head so that the glare was in front of his eyes. He drew the brim of his own hat low, and as Arnould tried to evade the glare, jerked the man's head up with his left hand, and struck him on the chin with his right.

'Don't make me really hurt you,' he said.

Arnould might have been as dumb as Victor. Bruce felt a tight band about his heart, a sickening distaste: and yet it was still possible to avoid a repetition of the bombing. Countries with nothing to win and only horrors to meet might be spared destruction if Arnould talked.

*If* he talked.

Bruce said: 'I'm not wasting time. Where is Allaway?'

He waited for ten seconds, and then said: 'All right, strip him right down, we'll have to be rough.'

His voice was as harsh as his eyes were bleak, and he watched them strip the clothes off the little Frenchman, who made no effort to resist. He looked thin and under-nourished even as they forced him face downwards on the table, Ted at his shoulders, Mick at his feet. Both men looked away as Bruce picked up a chair and deliberately smashed it on the table edge close to Arnould's face. In a few seconds he was holding the leg of the chair, and he struck the Frenchman's rear, heavily. Arnould jerked—and jerked again at the second blow. Bruce gritted his teeth and struck the man across his thin shoulders, and Arnould shrieked, a sudden, ear-piercing cry of pain and fear. Bruce forced himself to strike again, knowing that the remorselessness of it as much as the pain would serve—and at the fourth blow Arnould tried to twist round, sobbing in his native French:

'No, no, I will tell you! I will . . .'

'Let him up,' Bruce ordered.

They jerked him from the table, and he stood trembling in front of Bruce, an under-sized, naked, pitiful little man shorn of his menace and his ability to strike fear.

'At—at Bohn, with Vaaron . . .'

'Whereabouts in Bohn?'

'Akkrassa, four . . .'

And then the door was flung open, Mureth and Mary leapt into the room; Mureth roused out of his poise, Mary wide-eyed in alarm.

'What is it?' Bruce snapped.

'The house is surrounded by the Civil Guards and military,' Mureth declared. 'They are demanding admission.'

Bruce felt himself go cold.

213

'Is there a way out?

'Only by fighting.'

And as Mureth spoke, as a realisation of what had happened came to his mind, Arnould burst into a high-pitched cackle of laughter.

## 22

# Akkrassa, Four?

It was the laughter that made Bruce realise the possibility that he might have been tricked. It was of triumph more than fear, the triumph of a man who knew that he was safe. Bruce swung round sharply, to see Ted and Mick shielding the little man from Mary, and apparently trying to force him to dress. The absurdity of that moment eased Bruce's tension.

'I'm sorry.' He looked at Mureth. 'It makes it bad for you.'

'That cannot be helped. But you . . .'

'The only thing to do is to try to persuade the authorities that we're on a pro-Scovian task,' said Bruce. 'You know them well enough to get a hearing. If we fight we would prejudice any chance we might have. We'll all go down.'

Mureth looked greatly relieved.

'Quickly then, please.' He widened the door, and they could hear the urgent knocking downstairs. Hilde, her fair hair turned into a halo against a light behind her, was standing halfway up the stairs.

'Open the doors,' Mureth called.

'All right, Derek.'

There was no hesitation on her part, her trust in Mureth was complete. Between them, Mick and Ted had contrived to get Arnould into some clothes, but Bruce felt a chill premonition of coming disaster, for if it were possible for Arnould to swagger he was swaggering then.

Had *he* somehow contrived to bring the authorities?

As they reached the ground floor, three soldiers and an officer had entered, men in drab grey uniform, tall, stolid, with an obvious fixity of purpose. Mureth stepped forward.

'Herr Doktor, you and all the occupants of this house are requested to accompany me.'

'I understand, Lieutenant, but . . .'

'I have no time for discussion, Herr Doktor. Strong forces are about the house, resistance will be useless and unwise.'

'I should not dream of resisting.' Mureth said nothing more, while the two other men—one in plain clothes— came in from the street. Bruce had seen the man in plain clothes before: it was the burly, grumbling Good Samaritan of his first night in Scovia.

He said *sotto voce*: 'Who is that, Mureth?'

'Berenz, Larson's First Secretary . . .'

The Premier's Secretary . . .

And then Arnould stepped forward, and Berenz lifted a hand towards him in friendly greeting.

'Hallo, Klein, I am glad we had your word, and watched the house. What is happening?'

Bruce could not have spoken for a fortune, the others stood rigidly by as Arnould gave that queer, unnatural laugh, and then said:

'One of them, Berenz, has sold the Allaway Papers to von Rintzen, enough to explain the ultimatum, no? Be advised again, handle them quickly. If they are not Germans they are paid by Berlin.'

And Arnould turned, looked into Murdoch's face, and laughed again.

.  .  .  .  .

216

A short drive through the streets lightened a little now with the red glow of fires that were gaining a hold despite the efforts to check them. A silent drive, with Bruce and Mary in one car, Ted and Mick behind, Mureth and Hilde in a third. Each pair was accompanied by two soldiers as well as the driver, while Arnould and Berenz were in the leading car.

Searchlights weaved their way above the city, people were abroad in greater crowds than earlier in the night, and from the spots where bombs had fallen came a mutter of many voices.

The convoy of cars stopped outside the Police Bureau, and one by one the prisoners were taken in. Bruce had had time to face the facts, and he knew that the odds were heavily against them getting clear. Scovia was virtually at war, and even if they would be over-run within a week, there would be short shrift for spies during those seven days.

And Klein, *alias* Arnould, was working for Scovia.

Working, of course, on his own as well, espionage either for personal gain or for Berlin, under cover of operations for Scovia. It explained the ease with which he had been driven from the airport, explained so many minor factors.

Arnould had acted so well, both at Mureth's house and here. He had been expecting the interruption, even his screams had been faked, he had played a winning hand superbly. Useless for Bruce to wish that the blows had been harder, to remind himself that he had been surprised at Klein's easy capitulation. So many men were afraid of physical pain, he had thought Klein one of them. Klein—Arnould. Arnould—Klein.

Berenz was gruff and blunt as they were escorted into a large room at the Bureau, and a uniformed Inspector bowed stiffly to the Premier's Secretary.

'Political prisoners,' he said. 'I will interrogate them myself. Now . . .' The Inspector went out immediately, only three armed guards, Arnould and Berenz were in the room. 'The story, Klein.'

'I have told you most of it.'

Berenz seemed to laugh with his eyes, not pleasantly.

'We need corroborative evidence.'

'There will be plenty. Madame Devereux saw them with von Rintzen this afternoon, and heard their offer. They are the so-called newspaper correspondents who came into the country two days ago. Except the Mureths —who have long since been Nazi spies.' The narrow eyes glowered. 'Do you need more?'

'The house is being searched,' said Berenz, 'and Madame Devereux can identify them.' He looked at Mureth, and he seemed to be sorry. 'You, Mureth, are the last I would have expected.'

'It is absurd,' said Mureth quietly. 'There is a great mistake, Herr Berenz, and it can be proved.'

Berenz pulled his lower lip.

'Klein doesn't make many mistakes.'

'This time he has.'

'Herr Doktor of course defends himself,' Arnould put in suavély. 'I will go for Madame Devereux and others—members of von Rintzen's staff who will testify to their dealings with the Nazis. Who'—Klein lifted a quivering hand, pointed at Mureth—'who have started already to destroy Litrakka! I demand an immediate trial, they should be shot, they . . .'

'There have been other captures, there will be an Emergency Court sitting within an hour, it is sufficiently close to war to work quickly, Klein.'

Bruce started: 'Herr Berenz, I . . .'

'That man!' cried Arnould. 'That man stripped *me*, brutally flayed me, he and two others! You understand, Berenz, that they will lie and lie again! And will Mureth keep papers to incriminate himself—no, a thousand nos! There will perhaps be a radio-station there, who knows? But'—the man stepped towards Bruce, his head raised

218

stiffly, his lips turned back—'no messages can go out. They are condemned!'

'All right, Klein, get Madame Devereux and the Embassy officials.' Berenz was appealingly casual, but Bruce did not hear what he said. Nor did the others, for they had heard Arnould, and they knew the real meaning of 'No messages can go out'.

*There was no way of proving any story they told!*

A claim to be working for England could have been investigated, but on a night when quick communication was impossible, there could be no early corroboration. Anyone in their position would make such a claim, in the desperate hope for reprieve. But Klein would assemble such a weight of evidence that there would be no reasonable doubt of the truth of his accusations. He *could* prove that von Rintzen had received the papers from Bruce, and that in itself would be enough to condemn them.

Condemn them . . .

And at the same time condemn Scovia to devastation, Scovia and the Oslo Powers, for this would not stop at one country, once the Nazi beast had reared its head it would not stop until the helpless were all under its domination. The only faint chance of preventing that disaster had rested with Allaway—and Allaway was a prisoner, he . . .

Two words entered Bruce's mind.

'*Akkrassa, four* . . .'

Could Arnould have told the truth?

Was it possible that he had been so certain of himself that he had dared to say where Allaway was?

Even if he proved that Klein was really Arnould it would not matter, Klein would have business in England, that would easily be understood. And now the little swine was standing in front of him, gloating and gibbering, virtually sounding their death-knell.

Suddenly Klein moved, out of the room.

Berenz turned heavily in his wake.

'Would you prefer to be together, or shall the ladies be separated?'

'Together please,' said Mureth quickly. 'And Herr Berenz . . .'

'You can talk at the Special Court, not before. There is plenty to be done tonight.'

'More than you know,' said Bruce, and he lapsed into English.

The simple trick made Berenz turn sharply, and look into the face of a man who looked like a Swede and yet spoke in English with unmistakable naturalness. Bruce called on everything he knew to sound convincing.

'You don't know, for instance, that Klein is working with Berlin.'

'Nonsense! He is . . .' Berenz stopped himself, and then shrugged. 'It need not worry you. He is the Director of Scovian Secret Intelligence, that is a fact.'

'He is negotiating with Berlin. He has offered Berlin the person of Sir Frederick Allaway for half-a-million American dollars.'

Berenz rubbed his jowl, his deep-set eyes boring into Bruce's.

'Absurd!'

'Allaway was kidnapped by Klein, or Arnould as he called himself then, and taken to Bohn. The Allaway Papers were stolen by Arnould, regained by me, and handed to von Rintzen.'

'So you admit that?'

'Because only by producing the Papers could I make von Rintzen listen. I had to learn where Allaway was. But . . .' Bruce shrugged, and looked away. 'This is only wasting time. There is a radio at Mureth's place, of course, but no papers, the British Secret Intelligence would not be so effective if papers were left behind.'

'The what?' Berenz stepped back, stopping no more than a foot away from Bruce. He was the bigger man but they were of a height. His eyes were green, unmoving.

'We came on instructions to find Allaway. The only way we could do it was to follow Klein *alias* Arnould.' Bruce believed he was making an impression, making Berenz stop to think. He might even carry conviction with Berenz or others, while Arnould was absent. Arnould could destroy all the good he was doing, the only thing that remained was to make as good an impression as possible while the Scovian Secret Service leader was unable to mock and scoff. 'Herr Berenz, you can prove what I say.'

'How?' demanded Berenz.

'By finding Allaway in Bohn.'

'You *know* he is in Bohn?'

'I know that Klein said he was, when under considerable pressure. Akkrassa, four . . .'

Berenz jerked his head up.

'They are the Bohn Headquarters of the Intelligence!'

Bruce said softly: 'I wonder if Klein is on his way there now?'

Berenz stared, puzzlement and uncertainty in his eyes, while Murdoch said without emphasis:

'All this is true, Berenz.'

'Can it be proved?'

'By contact with England.'

'Which is impossible,' said Berenz roughly. 'Your name is . . .' He looked at Bruce.

'In England, Murdoch.'

'Murdoch and Mureth will be good enough to accompany me. The others . . .' He spoke to a guard. 'Advise the Inspector that the ladies shall be made comfortable.' He put a hand on Mureth's arm, another on Bruce's, and led them out of the room. Bruce was feeling a queer sense of elation, one which he was afraid would be deflated at any moment. Berenz did not take unnecessary chances, for two guards followed them, and he chose the middle one of three waiting cars.

221

'The Senate House,' he ordered.

The journey was a slow one, for they had to go through the Civic Centre, and there were many unavoidable detours. But in fifteen minutes they entered the House; in twenty-five they stepped into a long, stately room, hung with dark curtains, filled with a church-like silence.

The man at the desk in the centre of one wall emphasised that impression, for his white hair and pale face seemed that of a saint. No Primate could have better looked his part—but Bruce recognised Premier Larson immediately, and Mureth knew him as a patient.

Mureth also knew the man who was standing by Larson's side. Tall, ascetic-faced, with a scratch on one cheek not properly healed. His expression was gaunt, and yet determined—Bruce felt the regality and the latent strength of the man.

So this was Henrik of Scovia.

And Berenz had considered this story likely enough to submit it to the Premier and the King!

All three men bowed. Henrik waved a hand, indicating Larson and Larson looked intently into Bruce's face as Berenz gave his name.

'So—it is Herr Murdoch. There was an affair in the Balkans early last year, I recall—Herr Murdoch, who worked for England, received considerable praise.'

'I was fortunate, Excellency.'

'Yes. Strange if you were to prove fortunate again. If you *are* Herr Murdoch . . .'

'Doesn't look much like him.' A breezy voice, squeaking a little, came from one end of the room. Bruce stiffened and could hardly believe his ears, while the voice went on: 'Probably that's due to Sam Webber. Good man Webber. Yes, it's Murdoch, no doubt about that, seen him in the same guise before. And Mureth—haven't seen you for a long time.'

And Sir Robert Holt advanced, pink and smiling

222

seraphically, with his hands outstretched, while Larson picked up a telephone.

'Advise the Chief of Police to detain Herr Klein and Madame Devereux. The matter is urgent.'

.     .     .     .     .

'Did the only thing I could,' said Holt gruffly. 'You can thank the Prime Minister for it, he asked me to come in person. Had to find Allaway, and . . .' The Pink 'Un grinned. 'He wasn't too anxious to leave *every*thing to you. Can't say I blame him. I've been here no more than half-an-hour, blasted 'plane was shot at, too. Well . . .' He stopped smiling, and looked more grim than Bruce could remember. 'It's bad.'

'Yes.' Bruce was recovering. 'I sent a message for you to stand by, I wanted to tell you of the ultimatum.'

'I picked it up in the air. Waited for the second message but as it didn't come I thought there was something wrong. Now I'm in Scovia and can't get out. Nor can you—nor can any one of us.' Holt was sublimely indifferent to Henrik or Larson, and talked as if he were in his own office. 'Bruce, things couldn't be much worse. Blocked all the way round—air and sea. Radios all jammed. But—this damned plucky little country isn't giving way.'

Mureth swung round towards Henrik.

'Highness, I had prayed that you would fight!' He looked excited, and Henrik smiled gravely.

'We cannot submit, Doktor Mureth.'

'Does anybody else know this?' said Bruce slowly.

'It is unlikely that much is known outside the country.' Henrik sat on the corner of the desk, swinging his legs. 'But there are a quarter of a million soldiers prepared, the country is ready, and word will soon reach outside. It can only be hoped that we shall get assistance. If not . . .'

He shrugged, and Bruce knew the horror that was passing through his mind.

'Well,' said Holt. 'What's this about Akkrassa?'

'Klein said that Allaway was there.'

'The building will be searched,' said Berenz, speaking for the first time. 'We shall have word very soon. But he would hardly tell the truth in such circumstances.'

'No,' said Bruce, and then spoke very softly. 'There is one place where Klein might go, one man he might tell the truth to, and that's not far from here. He's been negotiating through von Rintzen.'

'Von Rintzen is not available,' said Henrik slowly. 'He is the Ambassador to Scovia. The Embassy is, however, being closely watched . . .'

'Diplomatic privilege still covering sins,' said Bruce, and he had forgotten who was in the room, who had just spoken. 'Give me—and my friends—a clear passage into the Embassy, and we'll find out what the Baron knows.' He looked at Henrik with urgent appeal. 'Highness, if we can find Allaway . . .'

'No man can work miracles in a few short hours.'

'Allaway has!' snapped Bruce. 'Haven't you seen the reason for the ultimatum, for tonight's outrage! The Nazis have been afraid of Allaway's Plan, and now they believe that he is unable to work on it, that even if he's not in Germany he can't put his Plan forward. The Germans are working to make sure that he never will, whether they know the details of his scheme or not. He conceives a *bloc* of neutral countries from the Baltic and the Balkans, even further afield. What no one knows is the way Allaway hopes to bring them all together. If there is no group of independent, neutral Scandinavian Powers, no plan can operate successfully.'

'Upon my living say so!' gasped the Pink 'Un, 'Bruce, you're right!'

Henrik said: 'You may go to the Embassy, Herr

224

Murdoch. Berenz, arrange for the others to join Herr Murdoch—and you, Mureth?'

'With your permission, Highness.'

'It is granted.'

'Just what are you going to do, Bruce?' Holt asked sharply.

'Be unorthodox,' said Bruce briskly, and he bowed before turning towards the door. 'I shall do everything possible, Highness, and report as soon as I can.'

He went out, with Mureth. In ten minutes he had met Mick and Ted—the women, at Berenz's suggestion, remained at the Central Bureau for the time being. Mureth drove them towards the Embassy, a cordon of armed police forced a passage for them through the thick, angry crowd which had gathered outside. The Nazi flag was hauled down, bricks and stones hurtled against their car as they went through. Only the strength of the police enabled them to reach the front doors of the Embassy, and they were forced to wait for ten minutes before they were admitted.

And, approaching them from the stairs, was Lucille— Lucille in furs hugged tightly about her, Lucille, looking afraid.

## 23

# Death of a Diplomat

Three members of the Embassy staff, all carrying guns, had been in the doorway when the four had been admitted. They stood hesitantly as Lucille hurried down. She glanced up and saw them, recognised Ted as well as Herr Morenson. What little colour she had fled from her cheeks, and she stopped on the bottom stair.

Bruce stepped to her swiftly, speaking to the men by the door.

'Madame will not be going yet.' He gripped Lucille, his grasp apparently friendly, actually tight. 'Upstairs, I want to talk to you.'

He believed he saw terror in her violet eyes.

'Please, no. We must get away.'

'Upstairs,' repeated Bruce, and nodded to Ted and the others. They fell in behind, him and Lucille was thrust up the stairs. Bruce thundered on von Rintzen's door, and when there was no immediate answer turned the handle. The door was locked.

'Get it open,' he said.

Ted pointed his silenced gun towards the lock. Bruce felt Lucille trembling under his grasp, and for a moment he thought she was going to faint.

After three shots, the door sagged open.

Bruce had expected many things, but not von Rintzen on the floor, bound hand and foot, mouth against the carpet. His clothes had been torn off him, there were red weals across his back and shoulders, and his face was lacerated as though he had been struck time and time again with a nailed board. He was moaning, but the sound hardly passed his lips, and when it did lost itself in the thick carpet.

The room was in shambles.

Against the window leaned Kurt, eyes staring, mouth agape. The tunic of his uniform was stained with blood that was still spreading, and his arms were bent at an odd angle beneath him. By the Ambassador's desk was a second man, crumpled up with his back to Bruce; there seemed no top to his head.

Lucille gasped: 'I tried to stop them!'

'Was it Arnould?' demanded Bruce.

'Yes. He and Victor came, they . . .' She began to shiver, and Bruce believed she was as horrified as she seemed. 'They stopped me from getting out.'

And then, abruptly, she fainted.

Bruce eased her fall but left her on the floor and knelt down by von Rintzen. He eased the man's head round. The lacerated face was a dreadful sight, and all the dislike and contempt he had felt for the man disappeared. In his right hand something was crumpled, and Bruce took it away gently, while Ted brought water from a carafe, wetted a handkerchief, and made some effort to cleanse the dying man's mouth and cheeks: for von Rintzen *was* dying.

'A little in his mouth,' Bruce murmured, looking at the thing he had taken from the clenched hand. 'I— Good God!'

'Things?' asked Mick, from behind him.

'That photograph again . . .'

Von Rintzen was clutching a copy of the snap of the Devereuxs and the Coles. It was torn almost in half, and there were stains of blood on it, but it was instantly recognisable. The surprise was still in Bruce's mind when the Ambassador's voice sounded; the words—in German—came clearly.

'I—tried—Excellency. I—tried!'

It was an agonising cry; there was loyalty in the man, loyalty unto death in a mistaken cause. The words tailed off into incoherent muttering.

Mureth was trying to bring Lucille round, and she stirred but did not open her eyes. There was a stench in this room of horror, of newly spilled blood.

Bruce had von Rintzen's head in a more comfortable position and water trickled into his mouth. He swallowed some, and his voice strengthened again.

'Klein—where is he? Where . . .'

'*Mein Gott!* So close! Akkrassa . . .'

The voice trailed off again, but Bruce's head jerked up, he knew that Klein had either lied to von Rintzen or else the headquarters in Bohn really held the kidnapped diplomat. He damped the cut and tortured lips again, but suddenly a shudder ran through von Rintzen's body.

He was dead.

Bruce straightened up.

'Bring Lucille round,' he said hoarsely. 'There must be some more sense in this, somewhere, she's the only one who might know. Try the 'phone, Mureth, tell the Senate House of the second mention of Akkrassa.' He turned to Lucille, who was breathing evenly, and sharply slapped her face. Her eyes began to open.

'Where is Allaway?' snapped Bruce.

'I—don't know. Arnould said Akkrassa . . .'

'What happened here?'

'Arnould had told von Rintzen about Akkrassa. Then he came back. He wanted money. Von Rintzen would not pay, there was a fight, and—and Arnould went mad! I tried to stop it, I swear . . . *nom de nom, nom de nom!*'

She started to scream, and Bruce straightened up, knowing that whether it was genuine hysteria or whether she

228

was acting he would get no more sense out of her for the time being.

Klein *alias* Arnould had given von Rintzen the Akkrassa address, then had returned to kill him.

For money alone?

Lucille had said so, but Lucille was capable of duplicity even now. The reasons for the maniacal attack on von Rintzen, Kurt and the other servant were unimportant compared with the whereabouts of Allaway.

'Sir Robert wants you, Murdoch.' Mureth spoke crisply from the telephone, and Bruce took it, squatting back on his heels. Quite unconsciously he said:

'Yes, Pinky.'

'Damned young pup!' growled Sir Robert Holt. 'Bruce, I think you're right, but you're late, Allaway was at Akkrassa but he's gone. The place has been searched and a room located—some writing including Allaway's signature was found. Odd thing, too.' The Pink 'Un's uncertain voice, high-pitched one moment and low the next, was like a cool wind on a hot day to Bruce Murdoch. It was so essentially sane, when everything else seemed mad. It was at that moment that Bruce realised how coolly and naturally he had accepted Holt's presence in Litrakka. 'Odd thing too,' repeated the Pink 'Un. 'He wrote the name "Lucille" over and over again.'

'She's here,' said Bruce. Von Rintzen's dead, and so are others. But Arnould's flown and the Bohn house is empty.' He felt as if his heart had dropped out of place. 'So we can't do another thing.'

'Wake up,' Holt urged. 'You've got Lucille.'

'She might be dead for all the use she is.'

'How much have you offered her?'

Bruce stiffened. 'What?'

'Good God!' exclaimed the Pink 'Un. 'She won't have scruples or morals, wake yourself up. Start at five thousand and work upwards, promise her her freedom,

229

promise her the whole damned world but find out what she knows. We must have Allaway in less than twelve hours. Understand?'

'Yes,' Bruce said, slowly. He replaced the receiver, and turned to Lucille, who was watching him from narrowed eyes. Still sitting back on his haunches he looked as if he had all the time in the world at his disposal.

'Why did you kill Devereux?' he asked.

She had been lying full length. She rose to a sitting position, still looking distraught.

'*Kill* him? He is alive!'

'He was killed before I left England. At the flat where you met Allaway so often.'

'It isn't true!'

'It's true all right.' The fact that she did not know startled him yet had no lasting effect. He was thinking of Allaway's letters at the London house, and the mention of Lucille's name in the room where the diplomat had been imprisoned here. He had to find out her true relationship with Allaway. Recollection of Henrietta was in his mind. Uncertain, uncomprehended factors thrust themselves urgently into his mind.

Allaway—Lucille—Devereux—Henrietta Allaway.

Klein *alias* Arnould.

'You wanted to frame Allaway, of course.' he said casually. 'You wanted it to seem that he had killed Devereux, because Devereux was married to you. You needed a weapon against Allaway and that was it. You . . .'

'Great fool!' she said, and her eyes glared. '*Nom de Dieu*, to me Allaway is everything!'

And then Bruce began to see the truth.

'All?' He laughed, and his voice echoed mockingly in her ears. 'You sent Devereux to his death and Allaway to his . . .'

'Allaway will live! And he will come to me. While he was important to his country that woman could hold him, now—he is *mine*. Understand? Why else should I help Arnould?'

'And Arnould has promised that Allaway will live,' Bruce said. 'He is on his way to Berlin. You know what happens to obstinate people in Berlin. Or have you never heard of Schussnigg, of . . .'

'Berlin, you fool! He is with Vaaron at Reikmann's Folle!'

And then she stopped, realising that she had given the truth away, while Bruce felt a surge of hope, almost elation.

'Thank you, Lucille! Mureth, the Senate House again! Ted, you and Mick get downstairs. You're coming with us, Lucille . . .' He jumped up as Mureth called him, and heard Pinky's testy voice. 'Reikmann's Folle,' he snapped. 'The others there will know it. Lucille says that Allaway is there. Have the place surrounded by land and sea and if necessary air.'

'You're sure?' howled the Pink 'Un.

'Every woman has her price,' said Bruce, and he laughed.

But he laughed a moment too soon, for Lucille was standing facing him and Mureth, Ted and Mick had left to get the path cleared. Lucille had an automatic in her hand, while her eyes were blazing. Her lips were working, her words trembled and yet were clear.

'He won't go back to England, he won't! Tell them you're wrong. Pick up the telephone and say you're wrong! Or . . .' She moved the gun, and he knew that her finger was trembling on the trigger, that a moment's hesitation might be fatal. 'I'll kill both of you!'

Very slowly, Bruce reached for the telephone again.

## 24

# Reikmann's Folle

Bruce knew that Allaway could never be taken far from the Folle. By now the military would be on the move, 'planes on the way, destroyers converging on the peninsula. Nothing he could do or say into the telephone would alter that. The issue now was whether Allaway would be recovered alive or dead; and between his own life and death. His life was in the hands of the woman standing there, a woman with a distraught yet unearthly beauty. She was breathing quickly, her lips parted and her teeth pressed close together.

He touched the telephone.

'Hurry!' she cried.

Bruce took the telephone, and as he lifted it, hurled it towards her, dodging to one side. She fired, and he felt a sharp stab of pain in his right shoulder. She was no longer beautiful but ugly with rage, and he saw the gun move round towards him.

The next moment it was spinning from her fingers, and she was gasping with pain. Mureth had used his gun and his aim was good. The pain and shock stopped her from moving, and Mureth jumped towards her and stooped for the gun. As he straightened up he gripped her arm and looked at Bruce.

'Are you all right?'

'I can manage, thanks. Get her downstairs.'

232

Now that the crisis was past and she had lost, the spirit died in Lucille. Bruce moved towards the door, conscious of the pain in his shoulder. At the door, Ted appeared.

'All right downstairs. Bruce! What's the matter? You look dreadful.'

'It'll keep.'

They hurried downstairs, past the scared staff who were far more worried about the hostility of the crowd outside than what was happening in the Embassy. The door was ajar, but kept on a chain, and the police were forcing the crowd back. A brick crashed against the wood as Bruce slipped through, a piece of iron clanged. There was a scuffle in the crowd as the police grabbed the assailant, and under cover of this Bruce's party reached the car. With police on the running boards, and four men with linked arms leading the way, they drove through the crowd, past wild, angry faces close to the windows, hearing missiles crash against the glass and bodywork. It was a nightmare passage but at last they were able to drive at fair speed towards the Civic Centre. They arrived as Holt, Berenz and Larson hurried towards a waiting car. Holt saw Bruce jump out, stopped and hurried towards him.

'All right, my boy?'

'Thanks. Yes. Where are you going?'

'Front line,' grinned Holt. 'Bruce, I'm enjoying myself, been stuck in that office too much. How much did it cost?'

'It didn't,' grinned Bruce. 'I've got her in the car, she'd better come to the Folle.'

'All right. Follow us.'

There were four cars in the procession, one in front and one behind filled with soldiers, to ensure a quick passage. Here and there fire-fighters were working under the glare of headlights. As they passed through the outer fringes of the city they heard the roar of aeroplanes ahead, and nearer to the Folle they drove alongside small detachments of the military mobile units. Here and there headlights cut through the darkness, and the first car of their convoy was ignoring the blackout regulations for that night; speed was all essential.

At last, they saw the headlights of a dozen cars, and three mobile searchlights, shedding their brilliance on Reikmann's Folle. Because it was a landmark that might have been recognised from the air it was camouflaged green and brown, but illuminated from the ground as it was light shone on darkened but unshuttered windows, on a square, gaunt outline. From the sea, which ran along two sides of the little peninsula, motor launches were adding their lights to the others. Twenty or thirty beams stabbed through the night and converged on the Folle.

Lucille stepped out, still listless.

Bruce thought: And it's all for Allaway, all for the Allaway Plan.

In fact it was not, of course. Rightly or wrongly Great Britain—and in fact the world—had come to the conclusion that Allaway could produce the rabbit out of the hat, could make sure of the continued neutrality of the non-combatant countries, could prevent the chaos and destruction from spreading to every corner of the world. Europe, or its major Powers, were in the grip of the spectre of war; death, panic, horror and starvation stalked side by side. Each day the conflagration threatened to spread, already Scovia had felt the hot breath of Mars.

All this was the final effort to stop the spreading.

And it was centred on one man—a single, solitary human being, a creature of hopes and fears, bitterness and disappointment, thwarted ambitions and dangerous ability.

He was in there with Klein *alias* Arnould, the mysterious Vaaron, Victor, and perhaps others. They

234

must know that there could be no escape, but what would their reaction be?

Surrender, and the chance of life?

There was little chance, Bruce knew, they were already condemned to the firing-squad. They had only one weapon to use, and that was Allaway. Allaway dead would be useless to Scovia and the Allies. They could barter his life for their own.

The Pink 'Un hovered near.

'Damned impressive, but I don't like it. Not a sign of life.'

'I'm going in, Pinky, with Lucille, Ted and Mick,' Bruce said.

'How?'

'Front door first,' said Bruce. 'A hand grenade will break it down, and we'll soon know whether they're going to try to fight or come to terms. Yes—and we'd better have tear-gas and masks. We'll approach by car, if they start shooting we'll have some kind of cover. Back in there, Lucille.' She obeyed and the others followed her, while the Pink 'Un talked to Larson and Berenz, who made no fuss. Both men knew that no direct attack could save Allaway's life. Bruce was the only one with any chance of success. He had to try. Ted drove slowly as the car approached the front entrance of the Folle. Every light was turned towards it, they felt as if a thousand eyes were watching them, and in fact a thousand were. They went slowly, and two soldiers—each armed with hand grenades—walked behind them. The droning of the 'planes in the air, the rumble of cars and mechanised units approaching was a distant thunder.

'Near enough, I think,' Ted said.

'Right.' Bruce signed to the men in the rear, and one left the cover of the car, approached the front door and hurled two grenades in quick succession. He dropped flat as he waited for the explosion. Two vivid bursts of fire, a roar, and then the rumble of the collapsing masonry about the door. As the door itself crashed in Bruce, gripping Lucille's arm, and the others left the car and rushed forward. They leapt over the rubble into the wide hallway, a hallway illuminated by an unholy light because of the white glare outside. Their shadows showed in sharp relief against the bare walls, they looked like waxwork models animated by some clockwork mechanism.

The Folle seemed silent.

But it was not empty, for from above them—from a landing approached by a wide staircase of stone, uncarpeted and covered with dust, came Arnould's voice.

'I expected you, Morely.'

Bruce called: 'That's fine. You're through, Arnould. Give up now.'

'A mistake, believe me.' The voice, coming out of the air, with no sign of the little Frenchman, was uncanny. Also it was suave and well controlled, Arnould was in no panic. 'Go back to the fools outside. Tell them that if they refuse us free passage they will get Allaway's body.'

So that was the way they would fight: the obvious one.

'It won't work,' Bruce said. 'They're more concerned with stopping you from getting away.'

'You think so?' Arnould laughed, that high-pitched clucking sound. 'An error. There is a single wave-length available, Morely, and on it I can contact Berlin. The moment Allaway dies Berlin will know, and within an hour the 'planes will be here again. Believe me they won't leave much of Litrakka. But if Allaway is *alive* . . .'

Bruce did not speak, and the others waited in silence, half-guessing what was coming and yet hating the very thought of it. From the door two other shadows appeared, of the Pink 'Un and Berenz. They made no sound as they approached, as Arnould's voice continued:

'But if Allaway is *alive*. Morely, that makes it different. Even if he comes with us. The Allies will negotiate, don't you think? Negotiate for his person. In fact he is for sale, a million American dollars, and a free passage for all of us here. Cheap, don't you think?'

'Go on,' said Bruce.

'Delighted,' said Arnould. 'The free passage first, and negotiations afterwards. Simply a financial transaction, you understand. Allied money will be more reliable than German.' He laughed, and the sound was diabolic. 'Take that message back, Morely, I want an answer in half-an-hour. Don't make any effort to get up here, we are nicely placed for seeing everything, and the lights outside help so much.'

Bruce said evenly: 'You haven't a chance in the world of getting away with it. Allaway alive or dead makes no difference. We want him quickly or he won't be of any use. I doubt if he's any use now, it's too late. Take your choice of a trial or being blown to pieces.'

'Take the message!' snarled Arnould. 'If you haven't left in thirty seconds I'll slit Allaway's throat myself!'

And then Lucille moved.

Bruce had believed she would, had waited for that moment. He knew that there was a power in the woman that was beyond her own control, a passion beyond all understanding for Sir Frederick Allaway. He had brought her here for this one purpose.

She leapt for the stairs and raced up them, screaming.

In the moment of diversion, Bruce hurled a tear-gas bomb up the stairs, where it burst ahead of Lucille. The first fumes of gas came as she reached the spot; she gasped and tried to get forward, but staggered and collapsed. Arnould's voice stopped in the middle of a word and he gasped. Bruce waited long enough to push his gas-mask on, then leapt after the woman. He caught a glimpse of Arnould rushing towards a room with an open door. He hurled a second bomb against the wall. Arnould was lost for a moment in the cloud that billowed out from it. He heard a dozen cries, and the pounding of feet behind him, but he reached the doorway first.

Arnould was stretched out on his face, gasping for breath. Back in the room were four men, Victor—with one arm bandaged and useless—Smith, Cole—Cole!— and a fourth who was sitting back in an armchair, his chest heaving as the gas bit at his nose and throat.

*Allaway!*

Cole seemed less affected than any of the others. He had an automatic in his hand, and was levelling it towards Allaway.

Bruce fired simultaneously with Cole.

Allaway gasped, and he slumped down in his chair. Cole's gun went clattering against the wall, blood poured from his wounded forearm. But the effort had taken him too long, the gas was taking effect, he was heaving for breath and his eyes were watering. Bruce ignored him and reached Allaway, as Ted arrived.

It was then that Cole, less affected by the gas than the others since he had been nearer the window, slipped a gas-mask on to his face and—while Bruce and the others were by Allaway—moved for the door. Once outside he raced to the ground floor and made for the cellars.

Bruce did not know this at the time, nor did he know that Cole was not Cole, but Vaaron.

.　　　.　　　.　　　.　　　.

Allaway was conscious, but too weak to speak. Blood was coming from a wound in his arm.

'Get him outside,' said Bruce, his voice muffled.

Mick and Ted lifted the diplomat bodily from the

238

chair and carried him outside. Mureth, masked and hideous to look at, exclaimed:

'We can leave them now!'

'We've got to find that transmitter,' said Bruce. He was standing in the middle of the room, looking at what seemed to be bare walls. In one of them there was a crack, and he stepped towards it. As he went Mureth exclaimed:

'Look out!'

Bruce swung round, and saw Arnould.

The man was on his knees, tears were streaming from his eyes and his breathing was convulsive, his face a hideous, distorted mask. But in his right hand he held a hand grenade or something like it, and as Mureth called he flung it towards the wall, towards Bruce Murdoch. It curled through the air, the fuse sending a streamer of smoke in its wake, and in that moment time seemed to stand still.

Bruce leapt.

It did not pass through his mind that there was courage in what he did. His outstretched fingers tightened about the bomb, as they would a cricket ball, and he hurled it back, over Arnould's head and towards the stairs. It burst in the air, and the blast swept into the room, a piece of steel hurtling past Bruce's head. He lost balance and went sprawling, but was up again in a moment. Mureth had fired twice at Arnould, making sure there would be no more trouble.

Bruce reached the crack in the wall, and he saw the white-painted knob that might have been a door handle, sticking from it. He pulled, without effect, then pushed sideways; and a panel in the wall slid open. In front of him was a powerful radio-transmitter!

'Can you handle it?' he asked Mureth.

'I think so.' The man stepped forward, pressed a switch and then another. He started to speak from behind his mask after what seemed an age; and then in

239

German a voice came through the ether.

'*We are waiting, we are waiting . . .*'

'They—they're standing by for word,' Mureth said.

Bruce went forward, taking his mask off. The tear-gas, weaker now but powerful enough to make him gasp and bring the tears to his eyes, had to be risked. He put his lips close to the microphone and began to speak in German . . .

. . . . .

Mitzer, von Hiddenthrop and General Mulke were gathered round a receiving set in the Führer's vast study. There was a crackle, and then a sharp voice said:

'The Scovian Station, Excellency.'

'Switch on, switch on!' ordered Mitzer. He turned his bloodshot eyes towards von Hiddenthrop. 'You see, they came through, they were to kill Allaway and advise when he was dead, there is no need to fear the Allaway Plan. Everything is ready for the attack on Scovia.' He began to pace about the room. 'We shall crush them—crush them!—if they dare to fight.'

A voice came over the ether in fluent German, and yet not a German voice:

'*Allaway is now free and safe in Scovia. Allaway is now free and safe. Details of his Plan are to be broadcast from London and Paris within twelve hours. Details are already with the neutral Governments concerned . . .*'

Mitzer reared up, Mulke clapped both hands to his mighty paunch, von Hiddenthrop stood motionless. Then suddenly Mitzer stood up, snatched the revolver from Mulke's holster and hurled it at the set. Glass smashed, but the voice continued:

'*Details of the Plan are already known . . .*'

Mitzer took the gun again, and fired at the radio, six bullets smashing into it. On the fourth the voice was

240

silenced, and yet it seemed to echo through the vast, high-ceilinged room.

Mulke looked at von Hiddenthrop, who nodded, and they both backed out. They heard the Führer shouting and raving, but the paroxysm was short lived, and they turned back. Mitzer was sitting at his desk, his hands clasped in front of him, his eyes staring as if at nothing.

'There is still time . . .' began von Hiddenthrop.

'There is time for nothing! If each country acts in concert it would be unsafe, before we strike we must know what the accursed Allaway has done. Send word at once to Litrakka. I have just learned that a squadron of bombing aeroplanes, acting against orders, attacked the capital. Extend my apologies, assure the Scovian Government that the pilots and men will be severely punished. Say also that von Rintzen is to be withdrawn immediately for exceeding his instructions. The fool. The fool!' shouted Mitzer and raised his hands beseechingly towards the ceiling. 'Do I wish to plunge the whole world into war? Let those at peace remain at peace!'

Von Hiddenthrop and General Mulke clicked their heels together and bowed as they withdrew.

# 25

# The Allaway Plan

Bruce Murdoch was aware only of the biting pain in his eyes and nostrils, for the gas had taken strong effect. It was Mureth who hurried out of the room to find Berenz and the Pink 'Un advancing cautiously at the head of a company of masked men—Berenz and the Pink 'Un recognisable only by their figures.

'Murdoch has sent word to Berlin,' said Mureth quickly, and explained. 'Is there nothing else that can be done?'

'Can't see anything,' grunted the Pink 'Un. He pushed his mask up an inch, to scratch his chin. 'And we've got the whole gallery of them, have we? Except this Cole fellow. Arnould?'

'Arn . . . oh, Klein. He is badly wounded, it was necessary to shoot him. The others can be taken away.'

'Get 'em out, will you?' Holt asked Berenz.

The gassed men and Lucille were carried outside and loaded into ambulances brought for emergency. It was then that Cole was missed: and despite a widespread search there was no sign of him.

Larson approached the Pink 'Un, his dignified white hair and face vivid in the glare concentrated on Reikmann's Folle.

'Sir Frederick is not hurt badly,' he said. 'What happened inside?'

Holt told him, and: 'They'll either have a go at you, personally, or withdraw, and I think they'll withdraw. If you find that the wave-lengths are free again, you've won. We've done all we can, we've just got the odds and ends to clear up.'

In an hour they knew that the pressure on Scovia had been relaxed, while for the first time word came from Moscow that the Soviet considered the absolute integrity of Scovia essential in the present circumstances. Scovia was not to be devoured for the time being by 'peaceful' aggression. The interference on the radio relaxed, word went out to the European capitals, and with it the rumour that through Sir Frederick Allaway the British Government was presenting a Plan to the neutrals which would ensure their continued neutrality.

With the rumours went hope.

Mureth examined Allaway, who had recovered consciousness. There was no reason, he said, why Allaway should not be flown back to England.

'I'll take him with me,' said the Pink 'Un, smiling at Allaway, who seemed dazed yet was little troubled by a flesh wound in his arm. 'Not going to lose you again, old man. Between now and London you've got to think a good one up.'

Allaway started.

'You knew . . .'

'Quiet!' snapped Sir Robert, and turned to Berenz, who was with them in the room placed at their disposal at the Senate House. 'Can I have a few words with Murdoch and his merry men, Berenz? In private.'

'Of course.' Berenz left the room, while Bruce, Ted and Mick looked lazily up from the easy chairs they were occupying, Bruce with one arm in a sling but making inroads on a huge open sandwich and a glass of beer. Mary was with Hilde Mureth, and had gone to the doctor's home, where Mureth would join them. A lugubrious and disappointed Percy who had obeyed instruc-

243

tions and let Smith, Victor and the others get out of the room at the Schohn without a fight, was trying to make a Scovian guard understand plain English.

Allaway, slumped back in his chair, pale-faced and tired about the eyes, was astonishingly like his sister. He fingered his long nose, then ran his thumb along his thin upper lip.

Holt said gruffly: 'I didn't know, I guessed. You and your sister hatched it, didn't you? The memorandum, nicely whetting the Cabinet's appetite. A Plan to take care of the interests of the neutrals, the one thing the world wanted. You had vague ideas . . .'

'I had practical propositions,' said Allaway wearily, 'but no one would act quickly. All propositions would have to be discussed and talked over, submitted first to one Government and then another. I could get no real action. I thought . . .' He hesitated, and passed a hand wearily across his brow. Holt glanced at Bruce, who nodded.

'You thought,' said Bruce, 'that a faked kidnapping and the loss of the Papers would jolt the authorities into action. You worked partly through Lucille, of course, and Lucille introduced you to Arnould. There was the necessary sinister visitor, seen by your servants, and there in the safe were the details of your Plan—no more than economic propositions often discussed but never presented with the full weight of Allied and American support. They were filed under the heading "Plan", or something like it.'

'How did you know?' Allaway asked, and his eyes showed more interest, something of his weariness went.

'Chiefly because your sister fainted when she found the safe cleared. She was afraid that if the contents were recovered it would be realised that you had nothing new. She fainted from sheer relief.'

'I didn't know this.'

'No need to worry, Henrietta will be all right,' Holt
244

said gruffly. 'Now, here's what happened.' He explained enough to satisfy Allaway, and then Bruce continued:

'Arnould knew that there was no Plan, after taking the papers from the safe, and he guessed Henrietta would know. So he kidnapped Henrietta.' Bruce was speaking slowly, almost dreamily, as though to himself. 'Many things fall into position when we know for certain that there was no remarkable panacea for neutrals. And Henrietta certainly would not consider talking when she was rescued; your reputation was at stake, and that has been Henrietta's one obsession. What did she think of your association with Lucille?'

The question came casually, his pause more than his words demanded an answer.

Allaway said wearily: 'She—disliked it, but since Lucille was married and Devereux wouldn't divorce her, it did not worry Henrietta.'

'Devereux was murdered at Lucille's flat,' said Bruce.

Allaway started, leaned forward, raised a hand that was shaking with a sudden, fierce emotion.

*'Are you sure?'*

'Quite sure.'

Allaway leaned back in his chair; he seemed free from tension for the first time, as though a spiritual peace had fallen on him.

'Thank God for that! Lucille . . .' Then, sharply: 'Where is Lucille?'

'Quite safe,' said Bruce, and he felt a deep, inward satisfaction.

Neither Lucille nor Allaway had murdered Devereux. There remained only two uncertainties: what part the Coles had played, and who had murdered Lucille's husband. Had it been Cole? Or was Cole Vaaron?

And, of course, the whys and wherefores of the murder, the explanation of the postcard photographs found

245

in so many unexpected places, were needed. But the major issues were settled.

So much turned on Lucille.

Lucille, who appeared to have no virtue, and would even tolerate von Rintzen, but Lucille who was obsessed by her love for Allaway. No one loved more passionately than the *cocotte*, that was accepted the world over. Arnould, knowing through Cole of the Allaway-Lucille association, approached Lucille to help him to obtain the Papers, and used as an inducement the one thing Lucille could not resist: the possibility of marriage with Allaway. Lucille cared nothing if the diplomat was disgraced, she wanted him free from all ties, particularly those which held him so close to his sister. Lucille, prepared to fight *against* Allaway's success so that she could get the man, not the diplomat.

Lucille introducing Arnould . . .

Henrietta and Allaway listening at first with contempt, and then—through Henrietta—seeing the possibility that a fake kidnapping and theft would enhance the prospects of the Plan being taken seriously and quickly by the Government.

Arnould's discovery that the Plan was no more than a defensive *bloc*, and nothing sensational. His—or perhaps Vaaron's—daring decision to kidnap Allaway and thus compel world attention on the Plan, and increase its value to any of the belligerent countries. And all the time Arnould could work behind his position with the Scovian Intelligence.

There were the wider repercussions, chiefly Mitzer's fear of the Plan and his effort to crush Scovia before it could be submitted. Arnould afraid to send Allaway to Berlin for fear the Nazis should discover that there was nothing new and vital. Arnould—and when he thought of Arnould he also thought of the still mysterious Vaaron—dealing first with von Rintzen then direct with Berlin.

246

Von Rintzen flinging all this in Arnould's face; Arnould demanding what money the Ambassador had available. Von Rintzen defiant until Arnould's men began to shoot; then Arnould's merciless attack to get the money—and that photograph.

Supposing that photograph was used as a code or a password; that Kurt had found one and Lucille had told the Ambassador of its importance. Arnould, knowing his time in Litrakka was limited, would go to any extremes to get it back.

'Well now,' said Holt briskly, 'we're going to return to London, Allaway, and this time you've a chance in a thousand to put a new Plan over. After this scare it will have attention fast enough, the Government can move fast if it wants to. Can you co-ordinate all your ideas by the time we reach London? Say in five hours?'

'Yes,' said Allaway.

'Make 'em seem damned convincing,' urged Holt. 'There's no need for the fake part to come out. Arnould will be shot, no need to fear him talking. Nor the others, for that matter. One thing—the man Cole . . .'

Allaway laughed.

'Cole was Lucille's brother-in-law. He married her sister.'

'How long has he been Vaaron?' asked Bruce.

Allaway stared, and then sat up abruptly.

'Vaaron? The man who was with Arnould? That's not Cole. There is a close resemblance, but . . .'

'It was the man I knew as Cole,' said Bruce sharply. 'Voice, face, expression, everything was the same. If you knew Cole well perhaps you know why he sold the Papers to Devereux in the first place.'

'*Cole* did? Nonsense, Devereux bought the papers from a clerk who was bribed by Arnould. There's no doubt about it.'

'There's a lot of doubt about it,' Bruce said softly. 'Are you sure Cole has been in England all the time?'

247

'He was when I had your radiogram, yes.'

'So there *are* two of them.' said Bruce, and his expression was strange as he looked at Allaway. 'With a facial resemblance so strong that acquaintances had no doubt about Vaaron being Cole. For sentimental reasons Cole and his wife occasionally spent a night or two at the White Swan. They'd been there so often that it also seemed normal. But if Cole is in Hampshire *now*, couldn't he have been at Frayle Manor when his wife and the other man were at the Swan? The other man being Vaaron. If Vaaron and Anne Cole met there regularly, it would explain a great deal. Each time Vaaron wanted to contact others, it was at the Swan, with a false identity at hand, the woman to substantiate it. It was there, as Cole, that he met the Devereuxs . . .'

'Who sold the Allaway Papers to Cole,' interrupted Holt sharply. 'According to Allaway, that is. *Your* evidence was that the Devereuxs bought the Papers from Cole, who had the money in place of them.'

'Right enough,' said Bruce, 'but remember Arnould and Vaaron, working in concert, were extremely careful. Smith searched the rooms only for evidence that *someone* was there to watch Arnould and Vaaron. After I'd let Smith go, that was enough of a hint to Vaaron. There was another exchange, the Devereuxs handed the cash back against the Papers, so that if the Papers *were* found only the Dees would be implicated, Vaaron and Arnould were quite clear.'

'Very involved,' remarked Holt.

'The Arnould-Vaaron business is, from start to finish,' retorted Bruce. 'But that can easily be sorted out afterwards, our chief problem is Vaaron. Before we get to that, remember that if I'm right the Swan is a regular rendezvous, Garsting, the manager, is probably involved. A model pub, in short, an ideal meeting-place for spies —official or otherwise. So the White Swan calls for in-

248

vestigation as well as Mr Cole, *and*,' added Bruce very softly, 'it's as likely a place as any for Vaaron to visit, particularly as he's having an *affaire* with Anne Cole.'

'Can you be sure of that?' demanded Holt.

Bruce grinned: 'I saw them sleeping together!'

.     .     .     .     .

Herr Gustav Morenson entered the lounge of the White Swan two days after Herr Vaaron had escaped from Reikmann's Folle. With him was Mick Fuller, who had not been to the Swan before and was quick to pronounce the beer passable. Herr Morenson was most particular about his room, and insisted on personal attention from the manager.

Garsting was aloof and faintly disdainful when the 'Swede' was ushered in. He listened, and shrugged.

'You have no need for anxiety about the rooms or linen, sir, I . . .'

'I am more concerned with meeting a friend,' said Bruce stiffly. His heart was pounding. A great deal hung on Garsting's reaction to the postcard photograph he took from his pocket. He held it so that Garsting could see the Devereuxs and the Coles, and in a moment Garsting's aloofness disappeared.

'I did wonder,' he said, and he adopted an air of affability that made Bruce want to smite him. 'They're coming today, I knew they'd be meeting someone.' He grinned. 'If I were Old Man Cole I'd wonder where my wife got to, wouldn't you?'

'It is not a matter I wish to discuss,' said Bruce frigidly, as became Herr Morenson.

'Please yourself,' said Garsting.

'Will they have their usual room?'

'Number 5,' said Garsting. 'They'll go straight up, and I won't be in, you'll have to introduce yourself.'

'Thank you, I will.' Bruce stood up, bowed, replaced

the photograph and went to Room 3, which he and Mick had been allotted. He saw Mick lounging back on the bed by the window, and remembered Mary curled up there in her pyjamas.

Mary was at Cliff Cottage with Percy.

'Any luck?' Mick asked.

'Garsting's in the game all right, but he's going out. As soon as he's gone you can decide to use Room 4, next to the "Coles". It's got a communicating door, we'll hear what there is to hear, and the talk should be illuminating. Meanwhile . . .' Bruce stepped to a small table on which there was a portable wireless, and switched on. He was in time for the four o'clock news, and he heard:

'Today's event of major importance in diplomatic activity in European and American capitals is the reactions so far available of the Allaway Plan for neutral countries. As listeners already know the Plan involves economic support for all neutral countries joining the *bloc* by this country, France, Italy, the United States, Turkey, and other countries. An essential factor in the Plan, it is stated by an authoritative source in Copenhagen, is that economic relationship with any country guilty of an act of aggression against any Power in the *bloc* shall automatically be broken off. German and Russian influences are endeavouring without success to counter the effect of this far-reaching arrangement, but reliable sources in this country and America agree that reactions are favourable. It is pointed out that such an agreement would prevent Germany and Russia obtaining vital imports from any part of the world should they commit further acts of aggression or endeavour to exert undue diplomatic pressure. A warm reception of the Plan is assured, says a British United Press message from Budapest, in all Balkan countries. The Oslo Powers have already accepted the Plan in

250

principle, and the United States is expected to announce a favourable decision . . .'

Bruce switched off.

'It's working,' he said slowly. 'For a while Russia will stay nominally neutral, it's little us and France against Mister Mitzer. Slip down and see whether Garsting's gone out yet, and arrange about the room.'

It was half past six when the "Coles" entered Room 5, unaware of the two men in the next room, who could hear every word. 'Cole' told the porter he would ring when he needed service. There was a pause before Anne Cole's voice came softly:

'Oh, my darling, it's good to see you. But you're worried.'

'Worried! Anne, I daren't risk coming here again. Everything that could go wrong.'

'I was afraid so when I heard Allaway was back.'

'He wouldn't be but for Morely, blast his eyes!' the man said harshly. 'There was a hundred thousand pounds in it for me, a hundred thousand, and . . .' He broke off. 'I suppose I'm lucky to be alive. Anyhow, I can't operate in England any longer, they'll be watching that precious husband of yours and it won't take them long to discover that you're here with me. So—it's good-bye for the time being. I have to become Vaaron again.'

The woman caught her breath.

'No sense in dragging you into it,' said Vaaron. 'We might claim that you've done no more than give me an alibi, but it will take a lot of proving. You were there when I shot Devereux, too, you might be implicated in that. Don't look at me that way! We've had some wonderful times.'

'*Did* you shoot Devereux?' asked Anne Cole quietly.

'You know I did.'

'You told me . . .'

'You'd hardly believe all I told you about that,' protested Vaaron. 'Listen, my dear. I could never stay in the same place for long, this espionage business is in my blood and always will be. It's fast, it's paying, and it suits my peculiar mind, trick-counter-trick all the time. If people get killed in the course of it, what does that matter? A lot more would have died if Allaway had reached Berlin, but that's not my side of it, there would be wars anyway. And murders. Devereux knew the truth about Allaway's Plan, and tried to squeeze me on the strength of it; he didn't try again.'

'You—killed him for *that*?'

'His life or mine, really,' said Cole *alias* Vaaron. 'And I've paid for it, Anne. I had a fine understanding with Arnould in Scovia, we worked it damned well. Everything of importance reached him there, that's how we learned so much, how we started on the Allaway job. Arnould put up the fake kidnapping idea, the sister helped, and even wrecked the room to make it look impressive!' The man laughed, and to Murdoch it seemed that he was talking because he craved an audience; he was falling into the fatal mistake which so often caught those men who had to keep a tight leash on their tongues. 'Well, it's over, England won't be safe for me after this. It isn't safe now, but I had to see you before I went for good. Anne—we've just one night. Just one.'

'Yes.' Bruce could imagine tragedy in the woman's fine green eyes. 'How often have you come here just to be with me?'

'Just to . . .' Vaaron broke off. 'Darling, I've come here every time I could, always to be with you. How long is it? God, seven years! Since two years before you were married. I can remember it now, you looked like a ghost when you saw me, and I looked like one afterwards when I saw his photograph. It was a God-sent opportunity. I had Garsting stationed here so that it was always quite safe.'

'Just'—she sounded faraway—'mixing business with pleasure.'

'Oh, don't put it like that! I'll never forget you . . .' He stopped, and then laughed as if with real humour. 'That photograph of you two and the Devereuxs, it gave me the finest passport I've ever had. No one discovered it, it was worth its weight in gold to Arnould and me. More than its weight! You see, darling, you're part *of* the game. If I've got to go away it's only for a while. I—Anne!'

'Oh, God!' she cried. 'I thought you loved . . .'

'Stop this!' interrupted Vaaron harshly. 'I've loved you as much as I'll ever love a woman.'

Bruce glanced at Mick, and nodded. Mick pushed the door open, and Bruce stepped through, an automatic in his hand. There was nothing more to learn, he could only save the woman from agonies of bitterness, perhaps despair.

Vaaron swung round, and his eyes widened to their uttermost. His lips worked for a moment, and suddenly he jumped. He struck the woman across the mouth, sending her reeling towards Murdoch. As she fell he snatched a gun from his pocket.

'You bitch, you set this trap for me . . .'

And two guns crashed out, a third—Mick's, from the door—followed fast upon them. A bullet buried itself in the carpet, not an inch from Anne Cole's head, another struck Vaaron's shoulder. He swayed, saw the two guns trained on him, and then sharply and without warning turned the gun on himself.

The woman screamed.

.     .     .     .     .

Afterwards, with Lucille's help, they were able to piece together Vaaron's history. He had worked for a dozen different countries in his time, but more often for himself.

He had, Lucille assured them, dominated Klein alias Arnould—and that was evidence enough of Vaaron's capability. He had always remained in the background, contacting lesser agents at the White Swan when in England, and using his peculiar likeness to Cole.

Vaaron *alias* Cole and Klein *alias* Arnould had come to the Swan, not wholly trusting Lucille nor her husband, who had agreed to act as go-between for the Allaway Papers. For the start of that great venture, Smith had been used to check on everyone concerned.

Von Rintzen *had* learned the purpose of the photograph: to get that back, and to get what money von Rintzen kept Arnould had savagely attacked the Ambassador.

Then he had learned that Holt was in Litrakka, word had been telephoned to the Embassy. Arnould had known himself finished in Scovia, saw all his plans smashed . . .

And went quite mad.

Lucille—whose story came from Berenz in Litrakka—had watched from the bedroom, until Klein had calmed down a little and gone to the Folle for the last act in the Allaway affair.

'Altogether a very comprehensive story,' said the Pink 'Un, a few days later. He was sitting back in an armchair at Cliff Cottage and stirring his tea. He sipped and grimaced. 'Who made this? Faugh, poison! Hope it wasn't you, Mary.'

'It was Percy, and he's proud of his tea.'

'Proud? Sack the man! Well . . .' Holt sipped with obvious enjoyment, staring owlishly at Bruce and Mary, who shared a couch opposite him. 'So Garsting languishes in jail, don't they say, and we've got the whole story from start to finish. Didn't think you would, Bruce; smart idea of yours that Vaaron would come back here. Only thing wrong—too much romance. I knew it when you faked a honeymoon. Lucille'—Holt

254

chuckled—'is getting out of this well. Berenz agreed to believe her story and since Allaway won't get any kicks in the pants, Lucille is going free. Arnould and that servant of his, Jem Dace and one or two others—all discreetly liquidated, good expression that. Everything's in apple-pie order, Mitzer's apology gracefully accepted. A breathing space for a while at least—and all through a Plan that wasn't.' He chuckled, and then scowled. 'Not nice, all the same. Don't blame Allaway as much as Henrietta, the evil genius. She'll recover, Weir says. Allaway will wait until the fuss and bother's blown over, and then he'll resign. Shock and whatnot. Man's quite determined to marry Lucille, but won't until he's free from official ties.'

'Or can't,' interposed Bruce drily.

The Pink 'Un chuckled.

'Worrying about those contracts? Should think before ⟨…⟩n, my boy, it's a habit that pays. Eh, Mary? ⟨…⟩s going to say something else—oh, yes, the Cole ⟨…⟩ sorry for the poor thing, as you said I would, ⟨…⟩, though, the lack of intelligence in some ⟨…⟩ and *believes* she was with a woman ⟨…⟩ he's told us all she knows—well, why ⟨…⟩?'

⟨…⟩e got a heart,' said Mary gently.

⟨…⟩ heart. Is *that* what it is? By the way, ⟨…⟩s they are and you two liking to work ⟨…⟩'t mind removing that no-marriage clause. ⟨…⟩ on you agreeing to work separately if neces-⟨…⟩' The Pink 'Un stared, frowned, plucked his mi⟨…⟩ and stood up, going to the window and look⟨…⟩ Soon Mary came behind him quietly, and put h⟨…⟩ about his waist.

'Th⟨…⟩, Pinky dear.'

The ⟨…⟩ Un's eyes gleamed.

'Dam⟨…⟩ young pups, both of you, I'll have more respect. ⟨…⟩d the tea's got cold, I was enjoying it. Get

255

that excellent fellow to make some more.'

'Tea be damned!' said Bruce Murdoch, looking ten years younger. 'Percy. Percy! Go to the nearest pub and get champagne, bottles of champagne, magnums of champagne, casks of champagne!'

Percy poked his head round the door, and beamed.

'All okey-doke, sir. Old feller's come to his senses at last, 'as he?' He lifted a hand to the Pink 'Un who found it impossible not to beam even on Percy's irreverence. And beaming, thought—as he had thought when he had stared and frowned after telling them of the new contract —that Bruce and Mary and Percy would be working again soon, and their life might be much shorter than they might reasonably expect.

But after all, thought the Pink 'Un more comfortably, even this war wouldn't last forever.